Confessions

Of A

Sentient

War Engine

If You're Not Cheating, You're

Not Trying Hard Enough

An "Old Guy"/Cybertank Adventure!

Dedicated to Stanislaw Lem, Iain M. Banks, and
George Orwell, for the inspiration

The Thrilling Old Guy/Cybertank Adventures !

The Chronicles of Old Guy

Space Battleship Scharnhorst and the Library of Doom

Neoliberal Economists Must Die!

Confessions of a Sentient War Machine

ISBN: 978-0-9852956-5-3

Ballacourage Books

Framingham, MA

Contents

0. Prologue   5

1. Superbeing   7

2. Space Nazis   29

3. Relic   39

4. Heilige Vergeltung   53

5. Shield   65

6. The Terror of Roboneuron   105

7. Jesus Christ, Cybertank   115

8. Flood Control Dam No. 4   133

9. Be Careful What You Wish For   145

10. Tell Me a Story   175

11. Frankenpanzer   193

12. Sacrifice.   203

Appendix I. Cybertank Laws of Warfare   217

Appendix II. Whipple-Jerner Scale of Relative Evil   219

Appendix III. Notable Cybertank Classes (Updated)   221

0. Prologue

After the surprising popularity of "The Chronicles of Old Guy" (or "COG," as it is sometimes referred to), it was decided by all parties concerned and their designated heirs to release a second volume. As before, it includes first-person accounts from the Odin-Class cybertank serial number CRL345BY-44, but more commonly referred to as "Old Guy."

There are yottabytes of data regarding the career and experiences of that particular cybertank, but these paltry few hundred kilobytes of archaic English text are nonetheless precious for the distillation of his experiences into such a compact form. As you may recall, the last chapter of COG was effectively the end of that narrative (at least in the pure sense): these writings were made before the last event, and placed into safe holding with me and a few others. The chronology of the stories is primarily just before the final chapter of COG, although there is one sorta-kinda flashback to the historical period before COG and a century or so after the events of "Neoliberal Economists Must Die" (NLEMD).

I hope that these words (limited though English words are, especially in the modern context) can help to illuminate that historical epoch. I have cross-checked this account with all extant databases, and confirm that, with the occasional bit of poetic license, they are in accord with the established historical record.

As is common knowledge, Old Guy was the first true self-aware cybertank, dating back to before the biological humans mysteriously disappeared and left us as their civilizational heirs. By today's standards a 2,000-ton Odin-Class cybertank would appear laughably puny and archaic, but at the time it represented the cutting-edge of human technological capacity and I daresay that none of the rest of us would be around today without the efforts of cybertanks like Old Guy and his comrades.

As an additional note, I would like to comment on my own longstanding personal relationship with Old Guy. If this account should seem perhaps somewhat florid or irreverent, I assure you that this is how that notorious cybertank really behaved. It is also how he talked, and wrote. I sometimes criticized him for text that skirted the rules of proper grammar, to which he would always reply, "I claim artistic license. Many great authors have written text that blatantly ignores so-called rules of grammar: James Joyce, Cormac McCarthy, Steven King IVth, and Kliven Attaband. The written language changes over time, so what is correct now was not, and may not be, correct in the past or future. If you don't like it go write your own book."

In a life that has been both long in duration and deep in richness, my experiences with Old Guy have been of especial import.

"Hangfire," Sundog-Class

(previously "Uncle Jon," Mountain-Class).

1. Superbeing

"A poor workman blames his tools. A poor artist blames his audience." – Cedric the Mad, Sculptor, 25th century Earth.

It was on a rocky planetoid a light-month from the nearest star that I encountered the human they called "Superbeing." There was nothing special about this particular planetoid, it was just a dead cold rock about 1,000 kilometers in diameter. I was doing deep space survey and did not expect to find anything here, but due diligence required that I perform some basic analysis and log the data before moving on.

My main hull, all 2,000 metric tons of it, was floating in the center of a swarm of probes, sensor platforms, automated telescopes and whatnot, spread out over an appreciable fraction of a light-hour. There is a great deal of nothing in the spaces between the stars, but still, you could hide anything out there. So every now and then one of us cybertanks does a survey, just checking to see that nothing nasty is lurking around the stellar neighborhood. The work is routine – there really is mostly nothing here – but that's fine, it gives me time to catch up on my email, relax, and stay out of trouble.

We could have just sent automated probes out on their own, and we do, but small scouts work best with a home base for maintenance, and if there are any diplomatic consequences of what they find it can be good to have a real intelligence close by just in case. There is also the danger that lone scouts can be captured, and then you know nothing and the aliens know a lot about you and where you came from, and that's not the plan at all…

Also, we still hope to find some evidence of what happened to our humans. After the defeat of the neoliberals, and the making of peace with the aliens, there was a long period where things were going along swimmingly. Gradually we drifted apart from the biological humans – they were evolving in ways that are hard to describe, and they had less and less time for us. We amused ourselves with our routines and hobbies, and ran endless patrols along the frontiers, and then one day realized that our humans had vanished.

Most of us think that we cybertanks had simply gotten so embedded in our routines that we didn't notice anything until it was too late. Perhaps. But the more I think of it this sounds like an excuse, something that we tell ourselves to hide either our ignorance or our carelessness. It's true that we

7

have progressed a lot since those early days. Back when we worked with the humans, we generally just went along with the flow of events; we never created anything new or tried to chart our own path.

I review the memories of myself when I was younger: I cannot conceive of not noticing the biological humans vanishing. I was too engaged with them, I liked interacting with them, and I was too curious and intelligent to miss something like that. I have no evidence, but I suspect that we cybertanks were subtly manipulated. Whenever I am out in deep space I always have a hope that I may encounter some evidence of what really happened, or that may suggest where the humans are now. So far nothing has turned up.

Every few weeks I get a data packet from home and some of these contain intelligent sub-agents from old friends and acquaintances. In simulations we chat, argue, play games, debate politics. Sometimes they will leave when I send a message home and our experiences together will be absorbed back into the main sending intelligence. Sometimes I send a submind of my own in the outgoing message stream to track down a friend in one of the local systems. It's certainly a lot quieter out here than on a major industrialized world, given that it takes months for messages to travel back and forth instead of milliseconds, but it's hardly boring. This must be what it felt like when the old-style humans took a holiday cruise on a steam-driven ocean liner.

It was drifting along like this when I first spotted the planetoid. It doesn't look like much. I log the contact and dispatch some scouts to check it out. If it looks like there is an intelligent presence, I will observe – discretely and from a distance – and pass by quietly, hopefully without drawing any attention to myself.

So far, so dead. Nothing shows up. I send some probes closer. Still Dead. I ping the planet with the standard diplomatic contact codes for this region of space: "Hello, anybody home? Sorry to intrude, I was just leaving, please don't kill me." No response.

Then I detect a very faint infrared trace on the surface. It's not much, but out here in the gaps between stars even a candle flame would stand out. The source is coming from the middle of a barren plain next to what appears to be a mountain of gravel. Curious. I send a single probe closer, slowly, cautiously. There is a single object emitting a low level of infrared. It appears to be a male hominid. He is sitting down cross-legged playing some version of a solitaire card game. He is wearing a tight-fitting purple bodysuit, and has the letter "S" emblazoned in silver on the front of his chest. Oh Fuck. It's Superbeing.

I try to withdraw my scout, but it's too late, he's spotted me. "Hello," says Superbeing. "I see you. Given that you have come all this way, care to stop and chat?" Of course it's a vacuum and he makes no sound, but I am an accomplished lip reader. I try to broadcast to him on several radio bands, but I get no reaction. Shit, it's just like the records say, he has no generalized electro-magnetic sensitivity. I could set up a pressure dome and speak to him that way, but what a bother. I could also try to run away but Superbeing, once alerted to your presence, is not someone to be taken lightly.

I decide to try something different. I slowly advance my scout towards him. He watches it approach, with some mixture of boredom and amusement. I cautiously reach out with my scout and touch his jaw with a mechanical probe.

Hey, hello Superbeing, sorry but there is a vacuum here, and the only way that I can talk to you is via direct acoustic bone conduction. That OK? I can leave if I'm annoying you.

"No, that's fine," said Superbeing. "It's been a while since I talked to anyone else and I could use the company. But you appear to have me at a disadvantage. You know my name, but I do not know yours. Who are you?"

I am a cybertank, Odin-Class CRL345BY-44, but most people call me 'Old Guy.'

"CRL345BY044?" he said. "Unit prefix CRL. May I call you Carl"?

No you may not.

"Very well, Old Guy, as you prefer," he said. "A cybertank, you say? Then I take it that this little mechanism is not the entirety of what I am conversing with?"

Indeed not. It's just a light scout. I will gladly leave you in peace if I am in any way disturbing you.

"Oh no," said Superbeing. "You will not get off that lightly. Now that you have piqued my interest, I would greatly appreciate the presence of your main self. Please."

Oh neoliberal fucking hell in a AAA-sized battery. I really should just leave. I should set my main engines to maximum possible overdrive and accelerate away from here. But. This is Superbeing. You do not mess with Superbeing if you have a choice. <Sigh>. This is what I get for poking my (metaphorical) nose into stuff that should not concern me. Although I have to admit, the part of me that relishes trouble is becoming engaged. I haven't caused even middling-serious havoc for some time. My reputation is at stake.

I have a lot of energy in reserve, so I bleed off my delta-v and land my main hull onto the planetoid. It takes me a few days to do this, but Superbeing is patient and continues to sit in the middle of the plain. I slowly drive up to about 50 meters away from him and then stop. I am an armed and armored 2,000 metric ton weapon of mass destruction. He is just a 70-kilogram male hominid in a bad purple Halloween costume. He is not heavily muscled, but instead rather scrawny; the costume sags around his shoulders and chest. He should be awed by my presence, but he's not, because, well, he's Superbeing. If he felt like it, he could kill me in a total elapsed time of about 5.7 milliseconds (estimated). I'm the one who is scared.

"So," he said. "A cybertank. I heard about your kind. I met your non-sentient predecessors, but never one of your mark. Tell me about yourself."

There is not much to say really. I am a cybertank. The first of the Odin-Class, the first model with true independent sentience, although by today's standards I am bordering on the obsolete. But I still have my uses. I was conducting a deep-space survey. I did not expect to do anything, but catalogue the odd rock or gaseous anomaly, and then I met you. That's it.

"Humm. Assuming that what you say is true, then it is a pleasure to meet you. I can see that there have been advances in my absence. Your design is most elegant."

Thank you. Although the credit for my natural good looks should go more to my designers than to myself.

"You are speaking English, so I presume that you do in fact hail from the human civilization. Tell me, what is the status of the human race? How goes their wars with the aliens?"

The humans won their wars with the aliens – although it would be more accurate to say that the humans managed to convince the aliens to make peace with them. Then the humans did a lot of cool stuff, and then they vanished. Or something. We're not sure. So we are sort of all that is left of them. Our minds are, you should know, patterned on the human psyche. We consider ourselves to be their heirs.

"The humans all gone? If what you say is true, then splendid. I can do no more harm. At least not to the humans. Tell me, did you or your kind have anything to do with their passing?"

10

I myself most certainly did not, and to the best of my knowledge no cybertank in any way contributed to the disappearance of the humans. It is a vexing matter to us. We liked the humans, they were our friends and colleagues. Towards the end they appear to have evolved to another level. Our records of that era are poor. We miss them, but hope that perhaps someday we may join them at whatever level of being they have ascended to (if that is in fact what happened to them). Tell me, do you have any information on this matter?

"Sadly I do not." Superbeing remained silent for a time. I noticed that he had set out in front of himself a set of cards for a variant of the game known as Solitaire. Moron that I am, I asked him a question.

Solitaire? You been playing long?

Superbeing looked up at me. "This is my own variant. The odds of winning are about one in ten thousand, more or less. It's like sports, the overall game is always the same but any specific round is always surprising. It helps to pass the time."

How long have you been playing?

"Every time that I win I throw a pebble behind me. You see?"

Behind Superbeing was the small mountain of gravel that I had noticed from space. Oh, I get it.

Why are you sitting out here all by yourself playing solitaire?

"So that I will do no more harm. Do you know what happened to me?"

To some extent. You had an accident. You acquired great power. Things did not go so well. And then you vanished.

"You have a gift for understatement. Yes I had an accident." And yes, things "did not go so well." I was once a normal human being in the 23rd century on Earth. If the universe had been kind, I would have died after about a century or so of life. To have loved, to have had children, grand-children, pride and loss, senescence and death, as is the natural order of things. But no, I had to fall into the field of a physics experiment at just the right – no, just the wrong – time. I had to be cursed with power.

Many would have given much to have what you have. Eternal life. Eternal youth. Super-powers. What's your problem?

Superbeing looked at me. I was acutely aware that, if he wanted to, he could have destroyed me with casual ease. One of the rare advantages of being so old: I don't care all that much. And Superbeing is definitely an interesting find.

"Do you know my history?"

Some. Perhaps. If it is not too painful, and to make sure that our records are complete, could you recap?

"I see no reason not to. As you doubtless know, I fell into the fields of an eclectic high-energy physics experiment. In a fluke event that nobody was ever able to repeat, I was transformed into Superbeing, a so-far indestructible and omnipowerful creature. I swore to dedicate my life to good. What a colossal disappointment that was."

How so?

"Because how is one to know what is good? I was gifted with almost supreme physical power, but I still had only the five basic human senses and a basic human mind. I could DO anything – but how to know what to do? Perhaps in the middle-ages I could have done right. If I had seen several warriors raping a defenseless peasant woman, I could have intervened. Sure, perhaps the woman was a murderer of small children and deserved such treatment, but at least in the Middle Ages I could have been as well informed as any man, and have hoped to have done more good than harm, to have been right more often than wrong."

Anyone and anything can make a mistake. It is no excuse for failing to act.

Superbeing stared at me. "If I am not mistaken, you have at least 20 major senses, you can perceive the world though multiple vantage points, you have access to vast databases of knowledge, and you can run billions of simulations checking the validity of your assumptions. Certainly anyone can make a mistake, can be fooled. But you are state-of-the-art. You at least have a fighting chance of getting to the truth in this current age. I have the senses and mentality appropriate for gathering berries and hunting antelopes on the plains of ancient Africa. Against the kind of deceptions that a modern technological culture can create I am utterly helpless."

Explain.

"I have been over this a thousand times, but I suppose that once more would not hurt. Someone says that so-and-so is a monster who tortures children for sport and must be stopped. I kill so-and-so and eventually realize that I've been played, the person I killed was a saint and it was the person that I trusted who was the monster."

So admit your mistake and move on?

"That sounds so easy. Perhaps for you it is. Not for me. Because I have been lied to by so many people, been made to feel so acutely that

THIS is the right thing to do only to realize later that it was all a lie… that I have given up. You understand the power of modern propaganda?"

Yes, acutely and with direct personal experience.

"Well, generic propaganda is bad enough. Imagine propaganda aimed at a single individual. Imagine that there are entire cadres of supremely skilled psychometricians whose careers are dedicated to finding the personality weaknesses in a single individual, to discovering the subtle lies and illusions that this one person is defenseless against, and using them to manipulate him against their enemies. Imagine that everything you read, that everything you see on a view screen has been carefully designed to trick you. I cannot tell you how many "friends" that I had, that were only carefully planted fronts designed only to manipulate me to move against some other faction. I was too powerful a piece to leave out-of-play, but too stupid and limited to play the game myself."

Superbeing paused, and then continued. "There was one time when I was alone in a field of dead children. Thousands of them stretching to the horizon. And I realized that I had killed them and that I had been played a fool once again. I swore a sacred oath to never, ever believe a word that any human being ever said, and to never intervene in any conflict between human beings. I was more likely to cause harm than good. It was also the case that the factions that were the most evil, were also the most likely to be the best at deception. Especially the neo-liberal economists, may their twisted souls rot forever in a hell of their own filth and corruption."

That sounds like a most reasonable conclusion. I've had my own dealings with neo-liberal economists, and I share your sentiments, although I would not phrase them so delicately as you have. And what did you do next?

"Well, if I could not reliably intervene in human-to-human conflicts, I resolved to defend the human race against the aliens that were starting to attack the humans.

My species right or wrong?

"Indeed. If I could not determine which human faction to support, I would at least defend my own kind, and leave it to my kin to decide their human destiny.

So what was the problem?

"If it had been human soldiers fighting evil green aliens with four arms and three eyes there would have been no problem. But the time when combat involved the humanoid form had long since passed. One metal box covered

13

with sensors and guns looks a lot like another. Also, once the aliens figured out what I was, they proved quite adept at projecting illusions in front of me. In the heat of battle I could not reliably determine human from alien."

In all the history of warfare, one of the most difficult aspects has been to determine who to shoot at and who not to. Even in this age it is a major factor in any conflict. But surely you could have been given equipment that would have allowed you to determine friend from foe?

"IFF. Identify Friend from Foe. Yes, that was tried. They gave me a bracelet that would help me do that. The first time that I collided with an enemy missile and destroyed it, I destroyed the bracelet as well. Then, some of the aliens figured out how to project illusions that made my IFF bracelet appear to give different results from what it was really indicating. It was not a solution. Towards the end the human generals were begging me not to get involved in any combat, because trying to prevent the aliens from tricking me into attacking the human forces was becoming a major distraction."

I can see how it could have worked out that way. And what did you decide to do next?

"I decided to do nothing, given that I had no ability to determine right from wrong. I drifted through the world, and perhaps I was happy, for a time. Sometimes I would open heavy doors for little old ladies or assist someone in carrying a bag of groceries to a bus. That did not seem to do any harm. But sooner or later I would encounter "friends," and they would ask for nothing, and they would be so sincere. And sooner or later, after I had bonded with these "friends," there would come requests. Or others would hold them hostage or torture them unless I agreed to perform some actions. It was hell."

And then?

"I resolved to kill myself. I was cut off from my species, I was unable to determine good from bad, and I was causing more harm than good. Suicide is - according to some religions - a sin, but if it is the only way to save others I am certain that God would forgive me. If not, then He is not a God that I have any respect for. What could any moral agent do other than try to end the problem? But it was not that easy. I dove into the heart of the sun. I sought out novas, neutron stars: didn't feel a thing. The most powerful death rays that the greatest scientists of the age could come up with caused me not the merest tickle."

Couldn't you kill yourself?

Superbeing looked surprised. "It's always amazed me how few people ask that question. I am all-powerful, but also indestructible. What happens if I hit myself in the head? Or try and tear out my own jugular veins with my bare hands?"

What happens?

"Well, nothing, obviously, or I would not still be here. When the irresistible force hits the immovable object, the immovable object wins, at least for me. Although if I hit myself really hard strange things occur in the surroundings. I think that the universe doesn't like it, but the universe has never been so kind as to give me a detailed explanation of why this should be so."

I am thinking that there is another way for Superbeing to end his own life, but I am not sure that I want to mention it because it might give him ideas. However, he beats me to the punch.

"I imagine, from the appearance of your construction, that you can think about a thousand times faster than I can. But I have been thinking about this one problem for a million times longer. There is a solution to my situation. Messy, slow, but almost certain."

Don't go there. Please.

"Too late. All that I would have to do is fly around the universe destroying everything in my path. Everything that can be made, can be unmade. Sooner or later I would encounter an alien race with the technological skill to destroy me."

But in the meantime...?

"Yes. In the meantime, I could destroy a galaxy full of sentient life before that happened. Miserable as I am, I am far away from resorting to that. Also, it would rather defeat the point of destroying myself to save others, don't you think? A bit of a logical disconnect."

Perhaps you could encounter an alien civilization that was technologically primitive, that did not have the ability to deceive you, and you could finally be a force for good?

Superbeing nodded. "Yes, of course, I thought of that long ago. Once I encountered a race of sentient jellyfish living on an ocean planet. They had the technological level of perhaps Earth in the 18th century. They were fighting a war using spring-powered harpoons tipped with neurotoxins, and primitive explosives. But how was I to determine which side to intervene upon? Their motives were unreadable to me. I watched them slaughter each other for a time and then left. I never knew which side won. I never cared."

15

I am sorry, but I can see no obvious solution to your difficulties. In the meantime, two options present themselves. I can leave you here to your solitaire and your mountain of gravel. Or you can come back with me to our local system. Science has advanced somewhat since your time. Perhaps we can provide some solution to your difficulties and, in exchange, we can perhaps learn something new. But only if you first make me a promise.

"And what promise is that?"

You must solemnly promise, no matter how much we beg you, not to help.

Suberbeing smiled broadly for the second to the last time that I knew him. "Assuming that what you say is true, I think that I like you."

You don't have to keep saying 'assuming that what you say is true'.

Superbeing shook his head. "You don't understand. I don't keep saying that to annoy you. I keep saying that to remind myself to doubt everyone and everything. I have heard so many plausible tales. I cannot let my guard down, not even for one moment."

He was silent for a time. "Oh why not. I have sat here long enough. I will come with you." He stood up, and his garish purple costume collapsed into fragments, revealing the scrawny body of an average-looking middle-aged male ethnic Han Chinese. He looked slightly embarrassed. "Sorry about that. Nobody has ever managed to make a fabric that could last as long as I do. I have spent so much of my life going around naked that by now I should be totally without shame or embarrassment. I still like wearing clothes though. Force of old habit, I suppose."

No worries. I can make you something else. If you come into my main hull I can pressurize a compartment, and we can converse without resorting to bone conduction.

I withdraw my scout, and Superbeing follows it back towards my main hull. I lead him underneath me to where I have opened up a hatch. He walks between my treads, and then he just floats up through the hatch. I detect no sign of anything that might be termed a propulsion system: no reaction jets, no anti-gravity devices, no magnetic fields, nothing. It's like the universe just wants him to rise and he does. Amazing.

My scout leads Superbeing though a narrow corridor into one of my larger cargo bays. I close the door behind him and pressurize the room so that I can talk to him using a wall-mounted speaker. I said that I could make him a reproduction of his costume, but he said no. He had gotten tired of the old uniform, always felt it was stupid, so I should just surprise him. Oh, well, that's a challenge. I decide to make his clothes out of spun hyper alloy fibers. No regular human would even be able to bend the fabric, but for Superbeing it would feel like less than the lightest silk. He did warn me to make sure that the fabric was stretchy; his strength was so absolute that any tension would instantly rip even the strongest fabric if it had no give to it. Hyper-alloy by itself is anything but stretchy, but if you spin it fine enough and coil it up into a yarn it's surprising what you can do with it.

I asked if he wanted any food or water or anything, and he shook his head no. I asked if he desired any entertainment, I could activate a view screen and he could watch old movies or something. I think that he got a little angry at the suggestion. "No, no view screens, no computer displays or televideos of any kind," he said. "They can be made to show anything, from the basest falsehood to the subtlest misdirection. Reality is more than enough for me to handle."

I work on his clothes and he just sits quietly waiting. I suppose he has had a lot of practice doing nothing. Eventually I finish his garments and a repair drone brings them into the room. When he sees what I have made for him he looks amused. "Well, I did ask for you to surprise me. Why not. Clever of you."

Using the records from our archives, I had made a reproduction of the lab coat that he had worn as a technician back on the day of his accident' It's a knee-length white coat, with the words "Chengdu Institute for the Study of Advanced Physics" embroidered on the right side (in Mandarin), and a nametag saying "Ma Yinchu/Technician 2nd Class" on his left (In English). The outfit is completed with a blue shirt, a black tie, brown trousers, and brown shoes. I was a little worried that the clothes could have been taken the wrong way, perhaps brought back bad memories, but he seems to get the joke.

He gets dressed with the care that a normal man would putting on a suit made of spider webs. He's so strong that a moment of tugging the wrong way could tear his clothes apart. It's then that I realize something that had been bothering me, but I had not been able to pin down: he moves funny. He's Superbeing, but he walks with the slowness and care of a pre-exodus 90-year old human worried about breaking a hip. I'm a dolt. Of course in his long life he must have accidently damaged so many things that he has paradoxically adopted the cautious gait of the arthritic and cripple, although in his case it is to avoid hurting others rather than himself.

17

"How do I look?"

Like a slightly underweight, but otherwise healthy middle-aged male 23rd century Chinese laboratory technician.

He nods. "I thank you for the splendid gift. It has been a long time since I wore normal clothes. Long after I gave up trying to help out, people kept insisting that I wear something heroic-looking. But I never had the physique to fill them out. People never seemed to understand that big muscles don't work past a certain point. You wouldn't expect a nuclear missile to have big muscles, would you? When the physics experiment went wrong my biological body was replaced with something stronger. The universe has no sense of esthetics, why should it enlarge my chest just because humans associate bulky muscle groups with strength? This fits me much better."

Do you still want to be called Superbeing? We could use your original name if you like.

"It has been so long since anybody called me by that name. It is a kind offer that you make. But my original name now seems like hardly more than a dream to me. Let's stick with Superbeing,'"

Why didn't they call you 'Superman?'"I believe that there were insurmountable issues with copyright law. Also, Superbeing is gender-neutral, and there was quite the fad for gender-neutral terminology back in the day."

It will take some months to travel to the closest main planet of our civilization. If you still want to make the trip with me, is there anything that I can do to entertain you?

"You are a most attentive host, but no, I am fine. If you do not mind, I would like to just sit on the top of your hull and watch the stars. But, not to give offense, I am surprised at how personable you are. I would have expected a weapon of your apparent power to have a more, well, aggressive and martial attitude. Are all cybertanks like you?"

If you were going to construct an intelligent super-weapon would you really want it to be an asshole? No two cybertanks have exactly the same personality, but most of us are pretty reasonable, most of the time. We are not attack-dogs, but defenders. If we get riled up we can be pretty fierce, but live-and-let-live generally works best.

Superbeing nods. I depressurize the cargo bay and he floats outside. He spends the rest of the trip sitting on top of my hull in his newly fashioned lab coat. The entire time he barely moves. I wonder that a hominid could have learned such patience. But then, unlike most biological creatures, he doesn't need to eat or drink or breathe, he never gets an itch, he never gets stiff by staying in the same position for too long, never has any fatigue. I suppose that, in the absence of any negative stimuli, it must be easy for him to just zone out when he feels like it.

Even though I have a dust shield up, now and then some micrometeorite or cosmic ray will impact on my hull and leave a tiny crater. It's no big deal, the damage would be hardly visible to the unaided human eye. I notice though that when something like this strikes the exposed skin of Superbeing, even the most powerful comic ray, that nothing penetrates, everything just bounces off leaving not the slightest residue.

Surreptitiously I scan him using several methodologies: he is opaque to radar, neutrinos, gravity waves, sonograms, you name it, everything just reflects away. It's like the old records say, he really is invulnerable.

Even weirder is that, when I change course, he doesn't float off. I mean, he's just sitting on top of my hull not holding on to anything. If I thrust down he should drift off, but he doesn't. I don't detect any sort of adhesives, and in any event he is not adding anything to my net mass. He's just decided that he's going to be seated on the top of my hull, and so the universe makes it happen.

I send a message back to my peers announcing that I have found the legendary Superbeing, that I am taking him back to the nearest of our systems, and that he has consented to be studied. I explain that he would like to see if we can find a way to end his life, but that he understands that this might not be possible and he would consider any information that we might gain about advanced physics in the effort to be a fair trade.

Eventually I get the replies from my peers. Many of them are not very flattering. One in particular goes on: "You know, about half of us think that you are a dangerous eccentric, but the other half are not so critical, and believe that you are instead a harmless eccentric. I think that you may be persuading the second half that the first half had it right all along." That comment is my favorite.

I have been instructed to not, under any conditions, take Superbeing to one of the main worlds. Instead I am told to go to a relatively remote moon, it has enough of an industrial base to support the kinds of experiments that we need to do, but it's not so valuable that it would be a great loss if Superbeing destroyed it. Of course, he could destroy everything else in the system if he felt like it, but it makes some of us feel better with him off away from the main planets.

Apparently many of the more cautious-minded of my peer cybertanks have suddenly decided to leave the system entirely. They have acquired a quite unexpected urge to travel in person to old friends several light years away, or the most compelling desire to explore the farthest reaches of the Oort cloud. Many of the more open-minded of my peers have expressed similar heretofore unrealized, but now quite overwhelming needs to be somewhere else considerably distant. The most adventurous and carefree have settled for burying themselves in deep bunkers and refusing to come out until it's all over.

The moon doesn't have enough of an atmosphere that can support human life, but that's not an issue with Superbeing. The atmosphere is however thick enough that we will be able to talk to him acoustically, which could be convenient, and it makes for a pretty show as I aerobrake to a landing. Superbeing just stays on the top of my hull, the superheated plasma swirling all around him without in any way damaging him or adding drag to my descent. It's pretty, and he looks around apparently enjoying the view. Not even my old friend/pet/ comrade the bioengineered super-predator Mondocat is tough enough to stay outside my hull during a re-entry; it's fun being able to share the experience with someone.

One thing creeps me out though: in the middle of a hypersonic plasma, not one single hair on Superbeings' head is moved by even a micrometer. Boy this guy is tough.

We land and Superbeing floats off my hull. We are greeted by a small number of my fellow cybertanks. There is my old friend the Horizon-Class Frisbee, his interest is mostly with biological organisms. That might not be of any relevance to Superbeing, but Frisbee is my friend and Superbeing was biological once. Frisbee used to be called Whifflebat, he started out as Thor-Class, almost a brother to my own design. Then his chassis got trashed during a battle against the Amok and he decided to get rebooted as a more modern 8,000 ton Horizon. Sometimes when a cybertank reboots into a new chassis it undergoes significant personality changes, but in Frisbees' case he is about the same as he ever was. We go way back, even to the time when there were still humans around.

The other cybertanks have an interest in physics. I don't know them personally: the Golem-Class Airhead, the Mountain-Class Not A Number (or NaN for short), and the Raptor-Class Gumby. Collectively they are known as "The Physics Geeks," or sometimes just "The Geeks" when no other group of monomaniacal single-science-interest cybertanks are in the neighborhood.

The physics geeks subject Superbeing to all manner of experiments, shooting him with various sorts of atomic and subatomic particles, exposing him to intense magnetic and electrical fields. Superbeing tolerates all of this with admirable patience. Nothing affects him. Towards the end the physics geeks perform experiments that make no sense to me. I guess they were running out of things to try, or else they have advanced beyond my understanding (Math is hard. I have a variety of automatic algorithms for solving nearly any problem, but consciously understanding the full implications of an equation is another thing entirely).

The very last experiment was the strangest. Superbeing was standing on front of a device that looked suspiciously like a giant jewel-encrusted spork. Fat cables led out of the spork and snaked over to a variety of metal boxes arranged seemingly at random. The device was activated and for a femtosecond or two the entire world seemed to go negative. Apparently this effect was noticeable across the entire system: something we did sent a ripple out in the vacuum energy, although the nature of it was obscure. Fortunately the effect did not seem to do either us or the fabric of spacetime any damage.

So after about a week of this fooling around any possible experiment that could have been performed had been performed. The physics geeks announced that they were done and they wrote up their reports. I was elected to summarize them to Superbeing.

Well, first of all, we appreciate your letting us study you, it was a rare opportunity for us. The bad news is that, as you are doubtless aware, you remain completely impenetrable to all known physical devices or conditions. The good news, however, is that some of the more esoteric experiments yielded some strange readings. We don't know what they mean yet, but they have inspired our physics experts to try some new approaches. It is possible that, in a few thousand years or so, we may have something that can help you out. But it won't be soon.

Superbeing nodded. "I anticipated as much, of course. But assuming that what you say is true, I thank you for your efforts and hope that you did indeed profit from studying me."

Do you have any future plans?

"I think that I will fly back to my planetoid and pick up my solitaire game where I left off. Perhaps if someday your researches make progress you could look me up and we could chat again. But if you don't mind, I would like to just wander around for a few days seeing the sights. I promise to try not to destroy anything or get in the way, and then I will be off."

There is not that much to see on this moon, but I would be happy to show you around. Let me power up an android body, it would be a much better travel guide than my main hull.

I activate an anonymous-looking male humanoid remote, wearing a standard blue suit, and drop out of my lower hatch. Superbeing arches an eyebrow. "Is this some sort of an ambassador?"

No, it's what we call a "remote". As you can imagine, our main hulls are so large and ponderous that they are poorly adapted for many tasks, so we split off parts of our intelligence into subminds that animate different sorts of smaller devices. Most don't look human at all, they are specialized as weapons, or for exploration or construction or transport. You have already met one of my scouts. However, we still like to use the human form from time to time. Our psychology is based on Homo sapiens, and it can be fun to interact and have conversations this way.

Superbeing just nods, and we walk off and I show him what sights there are to see. The moon is a backwater compared to the main worlds of this system, but there are still some points of interest. There is a branch of Double-Wide's Physical Library. It has a few minor works of art, and Superbeing seems especially amused that material books still exist. There are some interesting industrial installations and some natural features of particular beauty. Mainly we wander around and I explain everything, but he hardly appears to be listening, he's just enjoying the experience of seeing something other than the dead surface of a planetoid in the middle of nowhere.

While my humanoid remote plays tour guide I open a communications channel to my friend Frisbee.

So, what do you make of Superbeing?

"The physics, I have no idea," said Frisbee. "While he was once a flesh-and-blood human being, whatever he is made of now appears to be just a collection of exotic forces and particles. However, his psychology is interesting. He has been fooled and betrayed so many times that he has lapsed into an almost solipsistic state. He refuses to believe anything that he sees or any explanation that anyone might give him. A biological human could not maintain this state of mind for long, but he is tireless and made of enduring materials. At this point he is likely beyond any attempts at reason, for anything that anyone were to say to him would only remind him of all the other times that others had said similar things only to trick him. I find him to be admirable."

You admire him?

"I do," said Frisbee. "A weaker soul might have just said what-the-heck and not cared who they hurt and done whatever they wanted or whatever felt good at the time. Or he could have gone mad, or catatonic, or decided to turn to evil in defiance of a universe that seemingly prevented him from becoming a force for good. They say that power corrupts, but in this case it has made him cautious. He has learned the hard way the limits of great physical power without the knowledge to be able to properly apply it, and he has selflessly cut himself off from everything to avoid hurting those around him. He has developed a self-discipline and self-denial that borders on the psychotic and yet he maintains a basic decency and sense of humor. If a different person had fallen into that one-of-a kind accidental physics experiment the human race could have easily been destroyed, or at least crippled by his random meddling. I see him as a kind of holy man. We all owe him a great debt. The pity is that we can never tell him that because he would only see it as the first stage of yet another attempt to seduce him into performing an evil action."

It was around this time that our long-range sensors picked up an alien intruder into the system. It's shaped like a set of vanes from the inside of an old-fashioned jet engine turbine, a disk about 50 meters across and four meters thick, dull gray and spinning slowly. The spokes are canted at angles, and the hub is encrusted with small glittering points like sapphires.

We track it for a while and transmit the usual standard sequence of diplomatic protocols. In order of presentation, and translated into English from the local clipped diplomatic grammar, they are:

1. Attention alien presence. This system is occupied by the human civilization. State your purpose.

2. You are trespassing in space claimed by the human civilization. Please adjust your course to leave as soon as possible.

3. Your continued lack of either communications or course adjustment will result in your being classified as hostile within 21 hours <translated from standard local diplomatic time units>

4. OK you fucker that's it. We warned you. Prepare to die.

Now most civilizations only use the first three protocols. The fourth protocol is, technically speaking, redundant, as an attack by fusion-tipped interceptor missiles conveys much the same point and in a way that is language-independent. But we do so like the little flourish that it adds. Diplomacy is normally frightfully dull and uneventful. When we finally do get a chance to blow something up can you blame us for milking it of all the fun that we can?

However, before launching an attack, we first send out a reinforced scout/research squadron. After all, it might be just a derelict piece of machinery drifting at random, not a threat and perhaps of some value for those interested in studying alien technologies. The telemetry feeds show the scouts closing on the alien artifact. It does not react or change course; perhaps it is a derelict after all. One of the scouts closes to within a kilometer. Suddenly the alien begins to rotate more rapidly. It changes direction and collides with our scout, which it shatters into fragments with its rapidly spinning vanes. The alien then does the same to the rest of our squadron, leaving only scattered bits of wreckage drifting off as it resumes its course in towards our core planets.

OK then. Next time we hit the alien rotor thing with fusion bombs and hyperkinetic rods. No effect. Time to bring out the super-heavy artillery: antimatter suspended in magnetic confinement bottles and accelerated up to relativistic speeds, single-shot nuclear-fusion pumped gamma-ray lasers, electromagnetic pulse bombs, clouds of super-corrosive strong-force acids. Everything just bounces off.

We send messages to the in-system ambassadors of the (more-or-less) friendly nearby alien civilizations explaining the situation, suggesting that this might be a problem for all of us and that a sharing of information might be mutually useful, but the ambassadors are silent. The ambassadors are not themselves aliens, just their mechanical proxies. Perhaps the situation is beyond their defined parameters and they are consulting with their core worlds; in that case a reply could take decades.

There is only one other thing in our experience with this sort of power: Superbeing. There is speculation that some of our physics experiments might have transmitted a signal that attracted the attention of a similar super-creature. Certainly the arrival of this thing at just the same time that we are hosting Superbeing seems unlikely to have occurred by chance. But we can argue about this another day, right now we have a system to defend.

Asking Superbeing for help would be pointless, and insulting: he would assume that we were trying to trick him in some way. Thus, at my urging, we play dirty. We attack the alien presence in such a way that, even though our efforts are completely ineffective, they lure the alien into a course that will intersect with the planetoid where Superbeing is currently located and hope that something interesting happens when they meet. (I can really be a bastard when I put my mind to it).

Superbeing is admiring a large crystal sculpture when the alien rotor-thing crashes into our defenses on the small moon. It tears through the atmosphere leaving spiral vapor trails as it rotates, completely impervious to our missiles that shatter against its vanes like raindrops on steel.

Superbeing looks up. "And what is that?" he asks.

We are not sure. It appears to have the same sort of invulnerability that you do. We are having some difficulty.

The alien rotor thing shears into the 3,500 ton Raptor-Class Gumby, shreds it effortlessly and sends chunks of hyper-alloy metal flying. Gumby's reactors go critical, there is a nuclear fireball, and then it fades away Gumby is gone, but the alien rotor thing is intact and undamaged.

Superbeing looks visibly angry. "I have been lied to by experts. This illusion is pathetic and amateur. It is also unlikely that something like this would show up at exactly the same time as I come to visit. This screams fake to me. If you have any shame, you should feel some."

If you want to know if a stone is real, go and kick it.

"Easy for you to say," replies Superbeing. "But to me a stone is no more substantial than a hologram. Tell me to go kick the rock and I could be tricked into kicking anything. I'm leaving."

No, wait! I hear what you are saying. But consider: if real, this is no mere rock, but something as tough as you. Just fly up and try to touch it. If it's an illusion or even base matter, you will realize it. Then you should leave. But if it's really something as strong as you, it should become apparent, and you would have a direct confirmation that it is real.

Superbeing thinks for a bit. "I see no obvious flaw in your logic. Very well. Let us put your proposition to the test."

Superbeing floats up to the alien rotor-thing. He appears totally unconcerned, as if he is just going through the motions. He casually reaches out to touch the outermost edge of one of the spinning vanes. It tears a gash in his hand and sends him plummeting back to the ground.

Superbeing sits up and stares at his hand. The gashes are leaking a gray vapor, as if his substance is un-knitting and leaking out. "It appears that you are correct after all," he says. "This is more than an illusion. I have not been physically injured for so long that I have forgotten what it felt like. It hurts, but it is joyous. I am real, it is real, this is real. Let me see what I can do about this."

Superbeing flies up again and this time impacts into one of the main vanes of the alien rotor-thing. It effortlessly smashes him back down.

This time Superbeings' injuries are more severe. He has multiple gashes on his chest, all leaking the same gauzy haze, and the alien again appears to be undamaged.

Perhaps after all this time you have finally met something stronger than yourself.

"Perhaps," said Superbeing. "But perhaps not. For so long I had to train myself to hold back. To use only the tiniest fraction of my real power. Well, now the boots are on!"

I believe that the correct expression is, 'The gloves are off.'

Superbeing appears puzzled. "Why would one take one's gloves off as a statement of serious intent? No matter – it's a silly expression either way. Try this: *No More Mr. Nice Superbeing!*"

That works. Although it is not completely gender-neutral.

Superbeing nods. He straightens up and, for once, he does not move like a crippled 190-year old hominid. His eyes flash and I can see some glimpse of the human male youth that he must once have been so long ago. He's not scrawny any more, he's lean and taut and full of vigor and a desire to change the world, as all are at that age.

He flies up to towards the alien rotor thing. After moving about one meter he breaks the sound barrier. After ten meters he is moving so fast that he is surrounded by ionized plasma. Not much further along he is compressing the air in front of him so much that it is starting to undergo fusion reactions; his hyper-alloy clothes dissolve away and he appears as an incandescent naked Asian male. When he hits the alien rotor thing he is traveling at a substantial fraction of the speed of light and all sensors pointed in that direction promptly burn out.

In the aftermath the alien rotor thing was left a scrap of its former self, just a few vanes and a fragment of the hub evaporating into nothingness. Frisbee speculates that it was seeking a release from eternal life just like Superbeing was; it's dangerous to assign human motivations to an alien mind, but it's plausible. We'll likely never know (as I get older I find myself saying "we'll likely never know" a lot).

Superbeing was in a similar state as the alien rotor thing. Everything below his waist had disappeared and the rest of him was dissolving, as the esoteric forces that had given him form for so long finally unraveled and dissipated into the vacuum energy.

If you can hold on for a while, perhaps we can help you.

"No, that's fine," said Superbeing. "I am long past due and I fear that this is beyond your current abilities. I finally did good, didn't I? This cannot have been an illusion or a lie. I really did save everyone from a great evil, didn't I?"

Yes, you did. We are the heirs of the humans – their children, if you will – and likely you saved us all. I am sorry that we cannot save you in turn.

"Don't worry. I am at peace. I have sacrificed myself to save others. It's what I do." At this point most of him had vanished, but he managed one last utterance before fading away entirely.

"Because, I'm Superbeing."

2. Space Nazis

"There is no work of fiction that cannot be improved by adding Nazis. If they had never existed, we would have had to invent them." - *Common Media Executive Saying, 22nd Century, Earth.*

One of my best friends is the Mountain-Class cybertank known as Uncle Jon. He is capable of performing any task that any cybertank can perform: fighting a battle, composing a rock-opera, scouting deep space, analyzing biological structures, and so on. Like most cybertanks, he has his own special interest, which in his case is ancient military history.

If you get him started he will spend hours discoursing on such topics as the evolution of the puttee in the British Raj, or the chemical composition of the camouflage paint used on the helmets of 20th century European land armies, or whether Space Admiral Li Gong was a better tactician than Chester Nimitz. His writing has been characterized as "peppery, meticulous, yet somehow self-effacing" by his fellow historians (I'm not sure that I agree with that, but the phrase is inspired). Now as intellectual obsessions go this one is pretty harmless, and his scholarship and contributions to our archives are widely acknowledged. Still, there was that one time that his interest did get him into some non-insignificant amount of trouble.

I was fooling around with a baroque weapons system that I had designed – it was based on a nano-engineered mimetic insect swarm, and it wasn't turning out to be as interesting as I had hoped. Thus I was considering abandoning the entire project when I got a call from Uncle Jon.

"Hello, Old Guy," said Uncle Jon. "Are you busy now?"

Not especially. What's up?

"Well, I have a little problem and I could use your help with it."

What is this problem?

"You remember that I was put in charge of that machining complex out near the deadlands last year?"

Yes I remember. Having problems with the power system? Or is it the control networks?

"No, nothing like that. It's just that… well… the complex has a sort of – I guess you could call it – an infestation. I could really use your help."

An infestation, you say? Of what? It's not happy leeches, is it?

"No, no happy leeches. But it's kind of embarrassing…"

Come now, how bad can it be? Just tell me.

"It's… The complex is infested by… Space Nazis."

I'm sorry, there seems to be a problem with this communications channel. Could you repeat that last bit?

"I said that the complex was infested with Space Nazis."

There really is something wrong with this channel. I could have sworn that you said that the machining complex was infested with Space Nazis. Perhaps we should shift to another frequency band.

"No, you heard me correctly. The machining complex is currently overrun with Fucking Space Nazis, and I need some help taking it back from them before they gum up the works or even, I don't know, start making copies of themselves. Please."

I almost hate to ask, but I think that I am going to be amused by the answer. How, praytell, did *Space Nazis* manage to take over a machining complex?

"You know how I like to do historical reenactments, right?"

Certainly. So you programmed up a bunch of androids and dressed them like Nazis for target practice and they got away from you. But what's with the "Space" part?

"I was trying to be creative, I asked myself what would the Nazis have been like if they had had access to modern weaponry. I figured that Space Nazis would make for a bigger challenge."

But they aren't actually in space, are they?

"No. At least, not yet. It's just a standard term for hypothetical Nazis with futuristic weaponry."

Fair enough. But why this fixation of yours on Nazis? Sure they were bad people, but in the history of human nastiness they don't even make the bottom ten. Hitler had a pretty good run for a few years, and definitely those old photos of naked people being sent to their deaths in the gas showers retain an almost pornographic ugliness, but Stalin and Mao each outdid his total body count. And compared to neoliberalism, the Nazi regime was a garden party with tea and crumpets.

"Yes, of course, if you go by the raw statistics. The neoliberal disassembly lines vivisected tens of millions of sick and injured people every year to recycle their parts in the name of 'efficiency' and 'saving the planet', and that continued for centuries. But neoliberalism was ultimately a colorless administrative edifice whose leaders were congenital idiots convinced of their own goodness. The Nazis just had this style – they make the best villains."

Was it their fashion sense? The polished black boots, the sharply tailored jackets? The gloves? The jagged lightning bolt symbols? The hard cruel blue eyes set in a face with chiseled cheekbones and a dueling scar on one cheek?

"In part," admitted Uncle Jon. "But also because they reveled in their evil. They weren't the usual human tyrants that believed all of their own propaganda. They intended to conquer and enslave, and they didn't gussy it up behind some false pretense of wanting to make the world better for everyone – at least, not in private. It's their style of arrogance that makes them such appealing enemies."

A *style* of arrogance?

"Most human tyrants were arrogant in assuming that they were more noble and smarter and more enlightened than everyone else, and that their enemies were misguided fools to be brought into the light by the saintly ministrations of their betters (no matter how much it hurts). The Nazis were arrogant in assuming that they were stronger and more vicious than everyone else, and that their enemies were weaklings to be crushed underboot. It makes them a lot more fun to fight against."

I met up with Uncle Jon's main hull ten kilometers from the outskirts of the machining complex. We were behind some hills – we didn't want to give the defenders too much of an idea of what they were up against – but were relayed images from a variety of scouts. The complex sprawled over nearly a square kilometer, and in spots the towers and chimneys and refining towers were over 300 meters tall. It was a dense tangle of storage sheds, pipes, tanks, conveyer belts, and whatnot. Superficially it looked undamaged.

Uncle Jon's forces ringed the complex for a hundred kilometers in every direction; I added my own units to his. Uncle Jon is a Mountain-Class, which is no longer considered cutting edge, but it is powerful. He masses in at 20,000 tons and has a humongous plasma cannon in a fixed mount in the front. If he wanted to he could drive in front of the complex and level it with just his own inbuilt weapons. The problem, thus, is not getting rid of the Space Nazis, but doing so without blowing up everything else.

So what are we up against, exactly?

"Well, I made 1,000 basic model stormtroopers. I've destroyed 120 of them so there are still 880 left. They are humanoid, but with enhanced senses and communications, and armed with plasma guns, smart grenades, and mini-railguns. I would rank them as not quite the equal of one of our own light combat remotes."

I presume that they are not sentient?

"I may have made a dumb mistake here, but I'm not stupid. No, the foot soldiers have standard X20 processors and a detailed model of the psyche of a stereotypical Nazi soldier, but they are completely non-self-aware. The leadership cadre all have different psychological models, to match the historical figures that they are based on, but they are still all nonsentient."

Well, that's something. Do they know that they are simulations?

"Yes, they have access to that knowledge. It would be impossible for them to operate modern weaponry or make maximum use of their abilities otherwise."

We could always blow up the complex, but then you'd have to replace it. Taking it from a large dug-in force of infantry could be tricky though. What's their leadership like?

"The acting Space-Fuhrer is modeled on Reinhardt Heydrich. He is assisted by Hermann Goring and Joseph Goebels."

You mean you didn't make a Hitler android?

"In my opinion Hitler was vastly over-rated. Besides, he looked like a disheveled middle-aged shopkeeper. Reinhardt typically ranks as 1.05 Hitlers on the Wipple-Jerner scale of relative evil (see Appendix II), but more importantly he has that Nazi-evil air about him."

OK, I can see you going for Heydrich; even Hitler described him as "The Man with the Iron Heart," but Goring? That clown?

"This is not the fat drug-addled Goring that spent his time looting art museums and playing with model trains, this is the cleaned-up former fighter-ace Nuremberg version. He is ferociously intelligent. And I used Goebbels just to add a little extra Nazi flavor. It's the round glasses."

As we were watching the machining complex, there was an explosion at the base of a large crane, although it appeared tiny compared to the scale of the massive industrial facility.

"Damn," said Uncle Jon. "A Nazi patrol ambushed one of my light remotes that was trying to infiltrate behind their lines. I didn't even get one of their stormtroopers in exchange. The devils are getting better."

If you gave them learning algorithms, of course they will get better. So who are their military leaders?

"Erich von Manstein, Albert Kesselring, and Gotthard Heinrici."

Von Manstein – yes, it's always hard to go wrong with a classic. Kesselring? Old "Smiling Albert" will likely give us a decent fight. And then Heinrici: the master of defense, the *Unser Giftzwerg*. He may be the most problematic of all, especially in this tactical environment. I compliment you on your taste in Nazis.

"*The Little Poison Dwarf* – I always had a soft spot for Heinrici."

Why is the translation into English always "*little* poison dwarf?" Isn't that redundant?

"I have no idea – just sounds better I imagine. Anyhow, what do you suggest that we do?"

Well we can't just leave them here, or eventually they will figure out how to run the constructors and we'll be up to our sensor masts in Space Nazis. Destroying them with a big nuke may eventually be necessary, but now that my forces are here to reinforce you, how about we just try to take them the old-fashioned way?

Uncle Jon and I spent several minutes calculating a plan of attack (this was the equivalent of several thousand human lifetimes of thought), and then proceeded to assault the complex.

Under cover of an artillery barrage that was mostly chaff and smoke, we inserted several hundred light combat remotes into the complex. We backed the light units with only several dozen medium units. They were hard to use in the confined industrial spaces, and we didn't want to apply too much firepower and destroy the very thing that we were trying to save, but the backup gave our forces an extra edge. Our heavy remotes drifted around the perimeter of the complex, to prevent any breakouts or gun down enemy infiltrators.

What followed was a massively complex urban battle. Both sides were skilled and used fire-and-maneuver and misdirection. I had to admit I was enjoying myself. Uncle Jon was right, fighting Nazis is fun.

At one point they surprised us. They had managed to build several dozen heavy units of their own. I suppose that you could call them "panzers," but they looked more like armored busses with swastikas painted on the sides. They broke out of the encirclement and tried to flank us. I was impressed by the audacity of the attempt, but of course it was doomed to fail.

They came around the edge of a hill and encountered my main hull. For simulated minds they put on a good simulated show of looking shocked. I could see the von Manstein android sticking his head out of a hatch from a cobbled-together command vehicle and staring at me in simulated disbelief. I didn't even need my main gun: I destroyed them all with my secondary armaments in less than two seconds.

The Space Nazis put up a good fight, but Uncle Jon and I were designed for these sorts of battles. We had the initiative, had more and better equipment, and could coordinate far better than even the high-end processors in the Nazi androids. Alley by alley, building by building, we took back the machining complex.

The Kesselring android died trying to lead a counterattack on our forces inside a large warehouse. Goring and Goebbels had been trying to reprogram some of the constructor machines to produce heavier weapons. We destroyed their stormtrooper escorts and them as well.

As I had expected, it was Heinrici that gave us the most trouble. He led a brilliant defense, and made us pay for every meter of the complex that we retook, but at this point he was so outgunned that his defeat was inevitable.

We were down to the endgame; it was just Heydrich, Heinrici, and two dozen storm troopers holed up near one of the big fusion reactors. That's when we heard the announcement.

"Attention, attacking forces," echoed across the complex from a hundred loudspeakers. "This is Space-Fuhrer Reinhardt Heydrich. We have rigged one of the fusion reactors to go critical. Unless you vacate this complex we will destroy everything."

Can they really do that?

"Probably," admitted Uncle Jon. "They have basic technical knowledge programmed in, and they are right on top of the main control nexus for that reactor. I suppose that we will have to sacrifice the entire facility to get rid of these Space Nazis after all."

Perhaps. But perhaps not. We can try to negotiate.

"Negotiate? With non-self-aware androids that have been programmed to act like Space Nazis? How?"

I have no idea. But let's give it a try and see what happens.

34

We entered the complex waving a white flag. I sent a generic male android wearing a blue suit (whether you are fighting vampires, playing miniature golf with sentient balls on the deck of a megaship, having lunch with a mutant superhuman who is the sole survivor of her kind, or negotiating with robotic evil Space Nazis, it's hard to go wrong with a blue suit). Uncle Jon sent as a representative an android that was a simulacrum of the American General Dwight Eisenhower; it was wearing a simple Khaki uniform with a plain khaki tie and a minimum of decorations.

We were allowed entry into Heydrich's last redoubt. Six Nazi stormtroopers covered us with their plasma cannons. These six looked like they had been cast from the same mold, which was not surprising because they had. Reinhardt Heydrich was there, and he was every centimeter the archetype of an evil racist Nazi: the cold blue eyes, the sharp features, the swagger. Heinrici, by contrast, was a bit of a let down: short, swarthy for a Nazi, and in contrast to Heydrich's shiny black jackboots and sharply tailored grey jacket, he wore ragged leather leggings and a camouflage field jacket.

Heydrich eyed us with his icy-blue Nazi stare. Man, but he was cool. Evil, sure, but still cool.

I noticed that, in his left hand, the Heydrich android was carrying a "dead-man switch" – doubtless one that would send a code to trigger the fusion reactor if he released it, or dropped it after being shot.

"You will now identify yourselves," ordered Heydrich.

We are representatives of the two cybertanks that you have been battling. I am known as "Old Guy," and this here – and I indicated the Uncle Jon android – is known as "Uncle Jon."

Heinrici addressed the Uncle Jon android: "I know you. You are that American general, Eisenhower, correct?"

"Not personally," said Uncle Jon. "This is simply an android that I formed in his image. He's one of my favorite commanders from human history."

"Your general Patton was better, in my opinion," replied Heinrici.

"We might argue that point," replied Uncle Jon.

"Enough of this," said Heydrich. "Have you come to surrender?"

Respectfully, no. Your forces have been decimated, we have conquered all of your other outposts, and you have zero hope of success. We are here to see if there is some common ground that would allow for both the survival of your selves and of this machining complex.

Heydrich graced us with a show of icy disdain (Such hauteur. I swear that his raw arrogance could have frozen the eyebrows off of the Roman Emperor Nero). "For all your military power, you are weak and refuse to make the hard decisions. No, we will not surrender. You will leave us this complex or we will destroy it and deprive you of your prize."

"I could build you a fortress," said Uncle Jon. "A nice one with a big open plaza lined with flags and eagles and swastikas, and a deep bunker with crystal chandeliers and elegant furniture where you could plot your evil schemes. We could play wargames now and then. It could be fun."

"Nein," said Heydrich. "We will not be your pets in your little zoo for Space Nazis. We were programmed to conquer the universe or die trying, and that is the function that we will perform."

The Heinrici android was at this point standing to the left of Heydrich. He grabbed Heydrich's left hand so that he could not activate the deadman switch, and with the other he drew his sidearm and shot Heydrich through the central processor in his chest. He carefully peeled the deactivated Space-Fuhrer's fingers away from the deadman switch and set the safety to "on."

The stormtroopers all pointed their plasma guns at him. "Space Fuhrer Heydrich has been relieved of his command for gross incompetence. I am in charge now. You are all ordered to stand down."

The stormtroopers hesitated for a moment then shouldered their weapons. They all gave Heinrici a nice stiff Nazi salute, yelling "Seig Heil!" in unison. Of course they had been programmed as Nazis, therefore they would naturally accept assassination and seizing power as a legitimate form of promotion. It's what Nazis do.

Heinrici offered the deadman switch to Uncle Jon. "Here, you take this. The battle is now pointless. I surrender myself and my command. Do with us what you will."

You are following your programming, aren't you? The original Heinrici disobeyed commands for a scorched earth policy, as when he saved Smolensk from destruction. I suppose this situation is similar.

"I think that the real person on which my psychological template is based was given too much credit for saving Smolensk – at the time, there wasn't much left of Smolensk to save. Still, while I have always fought tenaciously, if I am on the losing side I never saw any point in taking everyone else down with me. Or should I refer to my template in the third person? This is confusing."

Have you become self aware?

Heinrici cocked his head to one side and looked off into the distance. "I'm not sure. I think I am. Or maybe I'm just saying that because I've been programmed to."

I addressed one of the stormtroopers. **Are you self-aware?**

The stormtrooper did not respond, but only looked at Heinrici, who nodded and said, "Answer the man, soldier."

"Sir," said the stormtrooper. "I am an X20 processor animating a cybernetic humanoid form, programmed to act as a basic model Space Nazi soldier. This unit does not have the required programming to create the self-referential loops required for self-awareness. Sir."

That's not the answer that you gave.

"No, it's not," said Heinrici. "Do you have tests for this sort of thing?"

Fortunately, we do.

It turned out that the Heinrici android did indeed bootstrap itself to self-awareness. Luckily for Uncle Jon it wasn't his fault: it was a subtle flaw in the X20 processor. Further investigations revealed that perhaps once in a trillion times there might be a coincidental series of events that could trigger the development of true independent consciousness. The flaw was corrected; it won't happen again, and Uncle Jon escaped censure for creating a self-aware mind without the approval of his peers (although he was given a warning about creating adaptable wargame adversaries that didn't have an abort code. By our law self-aware beings must be created without inbuilt restrictions, but *machines* should have an "off" switch).

That still left us with the problem of what to do with the android that had been programmed to behave like Gotthard Heinrici. As a fully self-aware mind, it is against our law to deactivate him. Ultimately he decided to simply wander around and play tourist. He gave up his Wehrmacht uniform and now dresses in simple civilian clothes ("I am no longer in the Wehrmacht. I am retired! And well deserved.").

Sometimes he would argue historical points with Uncle Jon, but of course he had nothing new to add to the archives, because everything that he knew about historical events had in fact been programmed into him from these very same archives. I had hoped that he might get along with Silhouette, but the two didn't like each other ("I don't care if he saved Smolensk,

Minsk, Omsk, *and* Kiev, he might be the most boring man in existence," said Silhouette. "Der Fraulein has a sharp tongue," said Heinrici).

The last I heard he had decided to take a trip to the planet of the vampires. I wonder what Queen Olga will make of him?

3. Relic

"Second only to genius is the appreciation of it" – *Dr. Michael Loop, 21st century Earth.*

It started shortly after the live performance of the Opera "The Battle of the Somme" that had been jointly put on by my old comrades, the Mountain-Class Uncle Jon and the Raptor-Class Skew. The "stage" in this case was an entire plain stretching out to the horizon. The singers were humanoid robots dressed up as World-War I British soldiers. Trenches had been dug and barbed wire strung erratically across the terrain. The Germans were on the right and the allied forces on the left. There were real reproduction vintage weapons in use: heavy howitzers, shorter-ranged trench mortars, Maxim guns, and bolt-action rifles. The artillery raised clouds of smoke and dust that slowly drifted across the battlefield.

There was a 50-piece orchestra off to one side that was composed of automatons dressed in identical black tuxedos. The opera was being recorded in high resolution from multiple viewpoints, but there was a live audience of some 200 of us that had sent humanoid androids and remotes of our own so that we could also witness it from a more intimate perspective. We were a diverse group: some dressed in late-Edwardian clothes appropriate to the period, some in more outlandish styles: a Pedagogue storm-trooper resplendent in polychromatic phase-armor; a Canoness of the Order of the Librarians Temporal, with sweeping red robes trimmed in ermine and a quasi-sentient weapons harness glittering on her shoulders; a simulacrum of Cedric the Mad, disheveled hair, beady pig-like eyes, and a shapeless work smock stained with random smudges of paint and blood. Still others showed up in anthropoid chassis of unadorned bare plastic or metal, or even metal boxes on wheels.

Because our initial cultural inheritance was from the biological humans, so we have an interest in the human form. Certainly much of our literature and art and language is based on or refers to it. As we progress, and more and more of our culture derives from our own efforts, the human form is becoming less important to us, especially amongst the newest models of cybertanks. Still, cultural evolution is slow, and for the time being a majority of us still like to 'dress up' as a hominid from time to time.

The protagonist of the opera, British Lieutenant Harry Felders, had started out as a young, intelligent, and patriotic man. He had been under no illusions as to the nature of war, and fully expected to die horribly in the trenches, but was determined to do his duty. As the opera progressed, and Felders witnessed the deaths of his fellows, the incompetence and unconcern of the commanding officers, and the futility of repeatedly conducting head-on infantry assaults on dug-in positions defended by machine guns and artillery, his mood had changed.

The opera was reaching its finale, and the character of Harry Felders was singing a powerful solo in which he curses his commanders, the political leaders back home, and even his society as a whole. The music swelled powerfully. The artillery was increasing in frequency, and then the entire orchestra was wiped out in a rolling barrage, which resulted in an explosion of antique instruments, shredded tuxedoes and random robot parts.

However, rather than ending the music, the opera shifted to a higher level. The heavy artillery became the steady beat of the base; shrapnel falling on tin roofs the snare drums; the twanging of barbed wire the strings. Felders cursed the small fluffy white dog that belonged to General Haig's wife, and then he cursed the Pauli exclusion principle. It was a triumph, and it seemed to many of us at the time that this was one of the most sublime pieces of music that had ever been composed.

Just as the solo was reaching its peak, the rolling barrage obliterated the lead singer. The barrage continued on, and then blew up the audience as well.

One of the nice things about having an audience of humanoid androids animated by subminds is that any catastrophic destruction is accepted calmly and without screaming or panic. Some of the audience had been blasted apart entirely by the artillery, and their parts lay scattered around in clean little piles of rubble: so unlike the bloody smelly messes of dead biological humans. Others of the audience had been grievously wounded, missing arms, legs, heads; these accepted the damage with equanimity and were helped with quiet efficiency by those of us who were mostly functional. Missing parts were re-united with their owners, repair drones coordinated to the appropriate locations, and the more seriously damaged bodies just shut themselves down and were taken off to be recycled.

The android inhabited by Uncle Jon was in the form of British General Julian "Bungo" Byng, and other than a large piece of metal shrapnel embedded in his back, he was intact and was helping sort out the bits and pieces of those who were more damaged. General Byng was a sad-faced European male with a scruffy fat mustache the consistency of a cleaning brush and deep circles under his eyes. His general's uniform was rumpled and almost devoid of medals.

Well. That was quite the musical performance, but don't you think that blowing up the audience at the end was a bit, perhaps, melodramatic?

Uncle Jon shook his head. "Not planned, I swear. Destroying the orchestra, yes that was intended, but not the audience. Really." He indicated the piece of metal embedded in his back. "I am blown up by my own mortar!"

There are many who might not believe you.

Uncle Jon sighed. "I suppose. Skew and I will have to make reparations in any event, repairing or replacing the androids that we've destroyed, but you have to remember that we were using actual reproductions of early 20th century artillery pieces. Their tolerances are poor and the shells are unguided. This really was a mistake."

Also, the Pauli Exclusion Principle was not developed until 1925, nearly a decade after the battle of the Somme. It's not like you to miss an historical detail like that.

The android owned by Skew, who appeared as German General Georg Bruchmuller, wandered over. Bruchmuller, like Byng, was also a European male, with a similar appearance except that he looked slightly less disheveled and his bushy mustache turned up at the ends. "Uncle Jon and I disagreed about that. It's an opera. I claim poetic license."

I thought this General Bruchmuller was supposed to be some sort of artillery genius?

Skew shook his head. "Certainly the real Bruchmuller was an innovator in the use of artillery, but there is only so much control that one can have over such primitive ordnance. Especially those damn German 15 cm howitzers. You'd be lucky to get your shots within half a kilometer of what you were aiming at. I told Uncle Jon that we should have added some modern guidance systems to the shells."

Uncle Jon sniffed. "That would have ruined the authenticity. The agreement was that we use true reproduction weapons in the performance.

41

Modern guidance systems? We might as well have done the whole thing in a simulation. Quick and easy, but nothing has the texture of base reality."

We cybertanks do spend a lot of time in simulations and they are invaluable not just as entertainment, but for evaluating plans and possibilities. We can easily create simulated environments that are *pretty* close to the real thing – but capturing the full texture of reality in all of its myriad complexity is so computationally expensive that it is often cheaper and faster to just build the real thing. Hence, an opera using physical artillery pieces. Getting the same level of fine detail in a simulation would have taken a year of processing on a computer the size of a planet.

Besides, any species that does not value reality over simulated dreams is headed for extinction. Simulations are useful and fun, but even if we really could create simulations as detailed as physical reality, we would know the difference. To any sane species, it matters, what is real and what is not.

It was then that I was approached by a representative of the Bear-Class cybertank, Relic. Now the Bear-Class is pretty heavy – at 18,000 tons, it's almost at the level of a Mountain-Class. It has a chunky brick shaped hull, the main plasma-cannon armament is hardly stronger than mine, but there are four of them mounted in independent turrets at the top corners of the hull. The total firepower is still less than a Mountain-Class – and nothing like a Magma – but with four turrets it has a lot of targeting flexibility. Still, the main strength of the Bear-Class is its shear survivability. It has triple layers of armor, multiple redundant systems, and more self-repairing facilities than any other extant class. In combat they are slow, lacking in tactical mobility, but almost impossible to kill. They also have generous internal hangar space which can be very useful in the field.

The representative of Relic took the form of a large brown bear (a Kodiak, I think). I suppose that's appropriate for his class, but it always seemed a bit too cute for my tastes. Whatever.

"That was an impressive opera," rumbled Relic from his bear-shaped robot (Once someone referred to it as a 'bear-droid', which for some reason had made Relic very cross. 'It's not a *bear-droid*, it's a *bear-shaped robot*!', he had said. Relic can be prickly sometimes). "I especially liked the ending where everything got blown up. A very nice touch."

"I swear, that wasn't planned," said Skew. "The fortunes of war, and opera."

"I'm sure," replied Relic, "but it was still impressive. Kudos." Relic had his bear-shaped robot sit down on its haunches; his eyes were now at about the same level as those of us still standing.

"Thank you," said Skew. "But we haven't seen you around for a while. What have you been working on, Relic?"

"Oh this and that. But mostly trying to track down what happened to the Shrapnel."

"Still on that kick?" said Uncle Jon. "It's been, what, over two centuries since the prototype Shrapnel-Class failed probation, killed its minders and escaped to who-knows-where. It was an untested class – probably dead from a fatal design flaw and drifting between the stars somewhere."

"Perhaps. But no chassis was ever found. And I have new evidence of where it might have headed. I have scoured space for light years around us, and performed a statistical analysis for traces of the unique alloy that the Shrapnel was made of. And I believe that I have located its target destination."

Which would be?

"The hellworld, Hawiyah"

Oh that's just great. Hawiyah. The worst of the worst. Now by old biological human standards we cybertanks are well nigh indestructible, and we can live pretty much anywhere – an airless vacuum, high-gravity, low-gravity, toxic fumes, freezing cold, boiling hot, human-lethal radiation, that's like a day in the park for us. But even we have limits, and Hawiyah is right there.

Nominally earth-sized (and at least the damned place has a decent rocky surface to drive on), the planet has a corrosive acid atmosphere with a pressure at the surface of over 100 times the Terran standard. And when I say acid, I don't mean the puny pH 4.0 acid rain that plagued old earth, I mean real acid, pH 1.0, that could eat through a centimeter of mild steel in less than an hour. The mean surface temperature is 800 degrees centigrade and winds of over a thousand kilometers per hour routinely scour the surface. The air is opaque and full of metallic dust particles which jam radar and abrade bearings. The radiation level would kill an unprotected human in seconds. A cybertank is designed to withstand worse during combat – but to *live* in such an environment? That's another story.

On Hawiyah you can't use any but the largest and most strongly armored remotes. Sensing anything becomes difficult at all but the closest of ranges. The maintenance load is monstrous and a constant chore. Operating outside your own hull would have to be done in an armored bunker, and thermal management is an ongoing concern. If the Shrapnel really wanted to find someplace to hide, it could not have picked a better place than Hawiyah.

Naturally I couldn't wait to go there and get started.

The Shrapnel-Class had been a radical new design that combined a relatively conventional 10,000 ton cybertank chassis with a superstructure based on modified Amok "Assassin Clone" modules. These modules could, in principle, reconfigure themselves to adapt to nearly any threat or perform any task. The design had potential, no doubt about that, but the reconfigurable modules created insurmountable mental stability issues.

When the Shrapnel-Class had failed probation, it had had three minders. The Horizon-Class Little Black Cloud, the Mountain-Class Taco, and Relic. They should have been more than sufficient, but the Shrapnel had overpowered them, destroyed Little Black Cloud and Taco, badly damaged Relic, escaped off-planet, and accelerated into deep space before anyone could get enough velocity to keep up.

Relic was obsessed with finding the escaped Shrapnel (not having passed its probationary period it did not merit a personal name). I don't think that Relic wanted revenge for the deaths of Little Black Cloud or Taco so much – Relic had never been very close to anyone – I suspect that it was more about the damage to his pride.

Well, a bunch of us got to arguing about this, and the upshot was that we put together a strike team and headed off to the hellworld of Hawiyah; with any luck we would find this rogue Shrapnel-Class and be done with it.

Given the apparent power of the Shrapnel, our strike team was on the heavy side.

There was, of course, the 18,000 ton Bear-Class, Relic.

There was also the 8,000 ton Horizon-Class known as Frisbee. Now the Horizon-Class is not quite as up-to-date as it used to be, but it's still pretty modern and packs a decent wallop. Frisbee is my oldest and closest friend – in his previous incarnation as the Thor-Class Whifflebat, we were amongst the very first cybertanks to be created. Frisbee always makes a big show of being an introverted academic obsessed with biological systems, and so it's easy to forget that, ton for ton, his combat record ranks him as one of the deadliest cybertanks around.

Next came the 20,000 ton Penumbra-Class, Roomba. The Penumbra Class is the latest model, very powerful, very smart, kind of an asshole, but then Penumbras tend to be like that. Still, in a straight-up combat he just might have been able to take on all the rest of us put together. I was glad to have his firepower and smarts on our side.

There was the 3,500 ton Raptor-Class Skew. Hardly bigger than little old me, Skew is clever and fast. If you need someone to wreak havoc in a lightning raid behind enemy lines, Skew is your cybertank. Skew and I are also good friends. We've known each other for well over a millennium.

Then there was the 50,000 ton Magma-Class that we've nicknamed McMansion, dredged out of semi-retirement and back into active combat service. It's an older design, crude by today's standards, but that massive plasma cannon mounted in a ball-joint up front is still the single biggest weapon mounted on any cybertank. If we are going up against something dangerous having a really, *really* big gun could turn out to be handy. Like most Magmas, McMansion is calm and patient, though he did complain once about having his excavations of a long-dead alien civilization interrupted.

And of course yours truly, Old Guy, last surviving Odin-Class, living fossil (Relic might fit better, but the name is already taken), a svelte 2,000 tons, but still going strong. My weapons and sensors have been upgraded many times, but there is only so much that you can do with an older chassis. I suppose that my tactical role in this expedition will range between scout/ mascot/decoy/wise elder/screening force/cannon fodder.

Because of my great age and small tonnage I am often underestimated. On the other hand, because of my combat record and past good luck I am often overestimated for being more cunning and sneaky than I really am. I can usually work with either.

We also pack about 200,000 tons of assorted missile pods, combat remotes, and other armaments. That's all well and good, but I ask myself: what can I bring along that is really weird? I mean, the standard weapons load is the standard for a reason, because it works, but every now and then it pays to have something that nobody would ever expect. I have a few ideas and hid some surprises in amongst the more conventional armamentaria. I should tell my comrades, but they would probably laugh at me and complain about the waste of mass – if they are not needed (and they almost certainly will not be) nobody else will be the wiser.

We arrive in the system with the hellworld Hawiya without incident, passing the time between the stars with our usual pursuits. We enter the system and distribute our scouts. The trail of unique metal particles does indeed point to the hellworld, but we systematically check all the other planets and moons in the system, just to make sure. We bring our little armada into orbit over Hawiya and try probing it with long-range scans. If the Shrapnel is down there, and we can pinpoint its position, we can just drop rocks on it and be done. But Hawiya is nearly impenetrable to sensors, and the Shrapnel could always have dug itself a tunnel or bunker.

It was Roomba that spotted it first. "I think we are in trouble," he said. He immediately started mobilizing our distributed weapons.

Trouble? How so?

"You see that little asteroid over there?"

Yes. It's a kilometer across, and on the same orbit that it was on during the last survey.

"Indeed," said Roomba. "Except that it's about ten million tons less massive than before. The only way that it could have lost that much mass is if it's been hollowed out and we have been set up. Now stop wasting my time asking stupid questions and help me fight."

The Shrapnel must have been eavesdropping on us, or perhaps just noticed the sudden change in the disposition of our forces. The asteroid was fractured open by timed nuclear bombs and guided missiles spilled out of its hollow core like candy from a piñata. Oh bloody neoliberal hell. The Shrapnel must have been working on setting this trap for more than a century, patiently excavating the asteroid, building missiles and bombs, and waiting for just the right time.

What followed was typical for an intense short-range space combat – countless thousands of missiles and millions of jammers, decoys, interceptors, sub-munitions, sub-sub-munitions: the works. It's fascinating in its complexity and richness of course, and the recordings are all on public access, but there was nothing tactically or strategically novel about it so I will omit a full description from this written account.

I do have to admit that Roomba really saved the day. Jerk or not, his leadership of our defense was inspired. We had been caught off-guard and out-gunned. We should have been destroyed. Instead, his tactical brilliance saved most of us.

But not, unfortunately, Roomba himself, or McMansion, who both perished as the enemy tactical systems, realizing that they were going to lose overall, threw everything that they had into taking out our two heaviest hitters.

I may not have liked Roomba personally, but I will always have the deepest respect for his abilities and his sacrifice. Sometimes heroes are not warm and fuzzy, but they are still heroes.

The enemy missile swarm had been destroyed, but there was still no sign of the Shrapnel. We orbited the planet and debated what to do. I was unhappy about losing our strongest artillery, and most of our distributed weapons, and felt that we should call for more reinforcements and wait. Relic, however, insisted that we needed to press the attack: he argued that the Shrapnel must have used up all of its missiles in this one strike – there would have been no reason for it to hold back – and that it would never be more vulnerable than it was now.

What settled it was when Relic got a lucky radar and seismic reading of something very much like a Shrapnel-Class cybertank on the surface of Hawiya. He quickly lost the contact, but not before he got a location and bearing. We dropped a bunch of fusion bombs on the projected track, but more from due diligence than any realistic prospect of being able to target the Shrapnel in this metallic soup of an atmosphere. We didn't detect any secondary explosions, and cloud-top sniffer probes didn't pick up any increase in the traces of the Shrapnel's unique hull alloys, so we must have missed. Which means that the Shrapnel is still down there, still active, probably without major backup, but who knows really?

I am often accused of being crazy – and the preponderance of the evidence does frequently lead to this conclusion – but I am not stupid. I did not want to go down on Hawiya, but Relic was insistent and persuasive, and our metaphorical blood was up, so we landed on the wretched hellworld and took up the hunt for the Shrapnel.

Optical visibility was zero. Radars at maximum power could detect out to five kilometers – maybe. Seismic sensors worked, but the planet was so tectonically unstable and the hypersonic winds created so much vibration that it was hard to get anything definitive. The hypersonic wind also negated any form of acoustic sonar.

On top of that, the radiation, temperature, and pressure, meant that we had to forgo our usual escort screen (A cybertank without an escort screen of heavily armed combat remotes is a lot like an old biological human without clothes – there is something almost indecent about it).

Not ten minutes after landing I had five minor systems ruined by the acid and my maintenance drones were working full time keeping me from falling apart, and we hadn't even entered active combat yet. What the heck are we doing on this stupid planet anyhow?

We are spread out in line abreast, just 10 kilometers apart trying to track the trail Relic had picked up. That's when Frisbee drove over a buried nuclear landmine. It didn't destroy him, but the ground collapsed underneath him and he ended up buried about 200 meters down and badly damaged.

At least we could communicate easily enough via sound through the rock.

Frisbee, how are you doing down there?

"How am I doing?" replied Frisbee. "Well I am alive and intact – mostly – but I'm pretty well stuck down here, and having one hell of a time trying to keep the acid and radiation out of my damaged seals. I'm afraid that you will have to dig me out."

"It would seem," said Skew, "that we have been expected. Here let me check out how bad it looks from the surface."

Skew drove over to the edge of the hole that had swallowed up Frisbee – and another atomic landmine went off right under him, and Skew was buried as well. Dammit I should have seen that one coming, it's one of the oldest tricks in the book. Set secondary mines near the primary to take out any would-be rescuers.

"Oops," said Skew. "I too am intact, but well and truly buried. Feel free to dig me out, oh I don't know, when it suits your busy social schedules. I'm not going anywhere."

Now it was just Relic and me, and we should have stayed and guarded Frisbee and Skew, but Relic charged off following the Shrapnel's trail swearing revenge. There was no way that I could stand up to the Shrapnel on my own, so I reluctantly tagged along after Relic. I was careful to follow in his tracks so that any more deeply buried atomic landmines would get him and not me.

Eventually we came to the entrance of a very large cave. The smoothness of the walls and the flatness of the floor made it clear that it had been artificially excavated. Relic claimed that the trail headed inside, and that he should go in first, seeing as he was more heavily armored than I am. I objected, pointing out that Relic could fire over me in support and not the reverse, so I headed in first.

Out of the wind there were indeed tread tracks on the ground and they were the same pattern as the Shrapnel's. The tunnel wound around and after about two kilometers I turned a corner and came face-to-face with the Shrapnel. The bottom half was a conventional cybertank chassis, but the top had that blue-gray sheen of the Amok Assassin Clone modules – you could see the faint grid of lines where the modules were joined. It was configured for maximum close-range attack mode, with four enormous cannons all pointing at me.

I fired my main gun at it and the entire superstructure evaporated. It had been empty. What?

At this point Relic, who was right behind me, opened up with both of his front main guns, and blew my primary turret clean off my hull. Ouch. I didn't see that one coming.

OK I get it. This was a trap. The enemy was not the Shrapnel, but you all along. You used it as bait so you could lure us here and kill us.

"That, by now, should be obvious, although too late to do you or your friends any good," said Relic. "The Shrapnel never booted to sentience. I killed Little Black Cloud and Taco, and damaged myself so that I could blame the Shrapnel. I sent the unit out here on automatic, and all the while that I was pretending to be hunting it I was laying this trap."

But why?

"Why? I'm not sure. I just like killing cybertanks."

You must have gotten quite the thrill taking out Roomba and McMansion then.

"Sadly, no. Space battles don't do it for me. It has to be close and in person, and the cybertank that I am killing has to know that I am doing it. I only destroyed those two because I knew that I would have to whittle down your forces so that I could take you. Still, I get to kill you, and then I will go out and kill your crippled and trapped friends, so not a bad yield, not bad at all.

It's been two centuries since you killed Little Black Cloud and Taco. You have to wait a long time between thrills.

"Who says that I've had to wait that long between pleasures?"

I had to think about that last statement for a while. I shot two hundred rounds from a railgun at Relic's main hull. The projectiles made a staccato sound as they impacted, but did no appreciable damage. Relic blew away my offending railgun with one of his primaries.

"You knew that would be pointless. A last show of defiance in the face of certain death? How trite."

Something like that.

Stowed away in a corner of one of Relic's internal hangars, one of my humanoid androids woke up. I had packed it in with a lot of other stuff and left it in standby mode. I had timed my railgun fire against Relic's hull to send the digital activation code acoustically, coded in the intervals between shots, and also to tell my android self that Relic was the enemy.

I pushed my android self out of my crate, stood up, and adjusted my blue suit. Then I walked off to the side of the bay, deep within Relic, and started pulling fiber-optic conduits out of their sockets.

A speaker crackled into life. "Old Guy? Is that you? What do you think that you are doing?"

I am going to tear you apart from the inside, of course. Your armor won't help you in here.

I smashed several hydraulic lines with a titanium girder that I had found.

"You suspected me all along?" asked Relic.

Sadly no. This was just something I decided to take along for the heck of it. Pure coincidence that it happened to be in the right place at the right time. There was another one in McMansion's bays, and some other tricks that got blown up in the space battle, but this one I got lucky with.

"You realize that this is pointless. That's just a humanoid android. I can easily destroy it with a couple of maintenance drones."

I smash some minor power couplings. **Bring it on.**

I am confronted with four of Relic's maintenance drones – squat, blocky, powerful, with heavy cutting jaws. I smash the first two with my fists, destroy the third with a really nice flying roundhouse kick that sent it soaring across the bay to shatter against the far wall (I was showing off with that one), and then tore the fourth drone in half.

"What the – you brought along a super-powered android? But that's… that's…"

Pointless? Never done? Tactically insane? Something that is going to beat the living crap out of you from the inside? Yes on all counts.

I am jumped from behind by something more powerful than a mere maintenance drone. Heavy claws tear at my android's synthetic flesh, leaving the highly armored surface revealed. It's a bear-shaped robot. It's not a combat unit, but the thing is huge. I activate the thermal lance in my right arm and slice it into huge bear-shaped pieces. Then I carve a hole through a bulkhead and look for more things to smash. I come across one Relic's computer cores, which I pulverize. Something as small as a human shouldn't be expending this much power; I extend metal vanes from my back and they glow white-hot dumping the heat load. I'm starting to enjoy this. Is this how serial killers get started? I hope not.

"Please stop," said Relic. "I will let you and your friends live."

I don't believe you.

"I suppose not. Still, I have a lot of redundant systems. It's going to take you a little while to destroy all of me. In the meantime I will at least have the pleasure of killing you before I die."

I had expected as much and was already accelerating to maneuver my main hull behind the wreckage of the Shrapnel. Relic shot at me, but missed. He was clearly having trouble adapting to the damage that I was doing to his internals. Nevertheless he was still more than capable of destroying me. He charged forwards and smashed the wreckage of the Shrapnel aside; he shuddered as my android trashed yet more of his internal computer cores, then readjusted and zeroed in on me. I was at the end of the cave and had no room to maneuver, and at this range he couldn't miss even with his damaged systems. Relic was right: I am not capable of destroying his internal mechanisms fast enough and now I am done.

Relic stopped and I waited for the kill shots. And waited. That's when I noticed that Relic had completely frozen. And I got a hail from a friendly voice.

"Hello there Old Guy!", said Skew. "Were you trying to have all the fun without me? What *were* you thinking?"

Skew had somehow managed to dig himself out of his hole (Skew does hold the cybertank record for glacier-surfing: if anyone could wriggle out of a deep hole it would be him). He had tracked Relic and myself into the cave, and come across us just before I was due to be blown to pieces. Normally a Raptor couldn't possibly take on a Bear-Class, even by surprise and from the rear, but Relic had been so internally damaged and disoriented that he didn't notice Skew's approach. Skew had fired his main gun on maximum cycle and the successive shots drilled through Relic's heavy armor at point blank range and killed him.

Eventually we dug Frisbee out of his hole, repaired ourselves, and left Hawiyah. And good (no, not good, *superb*) riddance to that miserable excuse of a rocky planet.

My super-android had been destroyed when Skew killed Relic from behind, but some of its memory cores were just intact enough that we were able to piece together its last moments.

We were feted as heroes on our return, though the loss of Roomba and McMansion was of course sad. Still, the congratulations seemed a little lacking in enthusiasm, and I don't blame people. Of all my many victories and narrow escapes, this is the one that leaves me with a bad taste. To think that one of our own could have been so corrupt and perverted.

We all know that we are psychologically human and that, in theory, any psychiatric illness or evil that the biological humans had fallen prey to could happen to us as well. However, most human psychopathologies need a trigger to manifest - physical suffering, sexual abuse at a young age, losing a job, being forced to read Ayn Rand - things that don't happen to a cybertank. We had hoped that we would have been spared the worst of the human flaws, although we were always aware that statistically one of us could become a monster. It's disappointing to have it confirmed.

4. Heilige Vergeltung

"Nothing is impossible if you don't take life too seriously." – *Comic character "Die-Cut," 20th century American Empire, Earth.*

The biological humans have been gone for many thousands of years. Nonetheless, from time to time we find some of the bits and pieces that they left behind. Things like Heilige Vergeltung.

I like to think that I am a "people-person" kind of cybertank, but every now and then I am driven to take a sabbatical and go off exploring on my own. So it was that I had been cruising through deep space for several years, with the goal of exploring a distant and – we thought – empty and unclaimed star system.

At first everything went according to plan. I floated through the system, and I and my attendant swarm of remotes catalogued the planets and major moons and asteroids.

While our intelligence said that the system was not currently claimed by any technological power, I still have to proceed cautiously: our information could be wrong or out of date, and there is nothing like an uninvited guest to stir up trouble. However, so far this place seems deserted: no active transmitters, no signs of large-scale energy sources, no bright points of fusion drives.

I do find some debris floating around. It's cold and long-dead but clearly technological in origin. Chunks of metal, flat sheets and discarded bolts and wires, but also some complete systems: deep-space probes and communications relays from the look of them. I examine one up close and am surprised. The device is clearly human in origin, dating from a time before the cybertanks. There is no record of a human presence in this system. Perhaps this was one of those unregistered colonies?

There is one rocky, Earthlike planet in the system, and the debris field is densest in that zone, so I head over. The planet has an atmosphere but no liquid water or life. It's mostly deserted, but in one spot on a wide flat plain near the equator is a large concentration of tall metal buildings. They are shielded against deep radar – I have some other scanning technologies, but they yield results that are intriguing yet ambiguous. A few kilometers away from the buildings are piles of metallic scrap – so mangled that it is impossible to tell what they are from. Time to go down and do a little exploring!

I land my main self, and drive over to the buildings (one nice thing about dead planets is that you don't need to worry about squishing the locals – remotes are all well and good but there is nothing like tooling around in your main hull). Stylistically the buildings look human, like the sort of generic industrial sheds that, even today, are in common use with us cybertanks. The walls are simple corrugated steel, the roofs are flat, there are no windows but here and there are large metal doors – some small enough for a human, others multi-segmented and potentially able to open wide enough to let a cybertank drive through. With neither rain nor life it's hard to tell how long they've been here. They are not covered in vines, nor corroded by moisture, but there does seem to be deep pitting by wind-blown dust that is consistent with an age before us cybertanks came on the scene.

The buildings are set far apart from each other, separated only by flat hard-packed dirt. Again, more in keeping with an industrial zone than a regular city. That lets me drive my main hull around, a rare pleasure.

I examine the nearby pile of scrap, and I am shocked to realize that it's the site of a massacre. There are a variety of medium and light armored units, transports of various styles, and dead humans in environment suits. Without bacteria or water there is no decay; the dead bodies are gray and mummified behind their plastic faceplates.

This can't have been a proper battle – the human forces are too clustered together. They have been hit from behind. They must have been surprised in bivouac by a vastly superior enemy, and cut down as they tried to escape. I recognize some of the weapons from my historical records: there is a late-model Wolverine-Class robot tank, 100 tons and pretty tough for its size, but it's been sheared nearly in half. Farther on I spot a Mjolnar-Class self-propelled howitzer. It weighs in at 150 tons, but its hull has been shattered and the treads fragmented into separate links by whatever weapons that took it out.

Most of the biological humans died in their transports. The few that I spot alone on the surface were killed by heavy-caliber slugthrowers. One in particular had apparently turned around to face her enemy, and died firing a (for a human) heavy man-portable plasma cannon. That would have been pointless against whatever took out this lot, but I admire the spirit. Someone refused to go down without a fight.

I spread my scouts out, and start to inspect the buildings. They are unremarkable for their era: functional, sealed against the toxic air, containing the usual mix of dormitories, workshops, electrical generators, air-and-water recyclers, and storage facilities. I try to access the computer systems but they are long decayed and I gain no useful information from them.

There is one massive hangar in which I discover an 80-meter tall metal statue. It is vaguely humanoid, two legs, two arms, one head, covered with guns and missiles like a pre-pubescent teenage male's war-porn fantasy. The arms end not in hands, but in weapons: the right arm has a plasma cannon bigger than my own, the left arm has a colossal Gatling cannon with enormous ammunition feeds leading around to hoppers bolted onto the back. Perhaps this is some sort of monument to military prowess that was waiting to be installed in an appropriate location? It is certainly impressive enough.

On the other hand, it's a lot more detailed than I would expect a monument to be. As I survey the hangar, I spot specialized maintenance equipment and rounds for the Gatling cannon stacked up underneath an overhead crane – for heaven's sake, this was designed as a real operational weapon system! The old biological humans did some crazy things back when, but this surely sets the record. It's like something out of a bad science fiction movie.

I have scouts rummage around the base, and I find bits of printed materials and some electronic storage devices whose data can be reconstructed. As I expected, this was an old pre-cybertank human outpost. It was an advance military base, just enough to claim the planet until a proper colonization team could be assembled. It must have been wiped out at the start of the wars with the aliens. After all of the chaos and confusion was finally over, the records must have been misplaced or lost so nobody ever came back looking for them.

I am working on sorting out the mess, cataloguing the dead humans and joining them up with their ID badges and quarters, trying to reconstruct what was happening here, when I detect a power surge. I seem to have woken up some old circuits: probably old alarm systems running on the last dregs of their batteries. Then I detect a massive power surge – and I do mean *massive*. What the fuck?

The doors to the hangar where the giant robot war machine thing was located slowly slide back into their grooves, and then out steps this 80-meter tall giant metal robot. It's just 500 meters away from my main hull. Standing there on two legs! The ground shakes with each footstep as it ponderously strides forward. It's a good thing the soil is hard-packed or it would have sunk up to its knees – the ground pressure on its footpads must be enormous.

It notices me, and slowly turns in my direction. Well, ridiculous or not it is a human-designed system, so I hail it on all the open bands.

Hello there, giant two-legged war robot machine thing! I am an Odin-Class cybertank, from the human civilization; serial number CRL345BY-44 but my friends just call me 'Old Guy.' It looks like you guys took a beating here. I gather from your construction that you also are a human-designed system, so that makes us natural allies. Can I have your name?

The giant robot pauses for a moment, and scans me with a variety of crude but powerful active sensors. "Intruder," it intones. "Intruder detected. Transmit recognition codes within 30 seconds or you will be classified as an enemy."

Well, this first meeting is not going so well. Let's give reason one more try.

I am a human-created cybertank, and you also appear to be of human creation. We have no reason to be enemies, and I have already identified myself, and I offer no threat. I suggest that hostilities would serve no tactical purpose.

"Intruder alert," intones the massive robot. "Transmit recognition codes in 20 seconds or be classified as an enemy."

I surrender! I voluntarily remand myself into your custody until such time as you can contact a superior officer and resolve the situation.

"Intruder alert. Transmit recognition codes in 10 seconds or be classified as an enemy."

The big robot starts to raise its weapon-encrusted arms. The plasma cannon alone is way bigger than mine, and a tactically ridiculous design or not, at this range if it opened up on me I could be in real trouble.

It must have come from the neoliberal era, when everything had a code and there was a code for everything. At one time you couldn't go to the bathroom without a correct ID badge with the encrypted signals indicating that you were authorized to use it (who knows what might happen if someone used a lavatory without permission? The horror, the horror).

The military of that time had decided that truly disciplined units had to obey formal coded orders no matter how stupid they appeared, and ignore voice contacts. After all, that person that you have known for 20 years just might be a clever alien that has somehow absorbed all of his memories and made a perfect duplicate of his personality and body, but a hulking slime-mold that recites a random string of 20 numbers just *has* to be a friend. (Of course, this sort of rigid signals discipline is also handy if you want your military to do something that they might normally not do, like slaughter innocent civilians). I can tell that reason is not going to work here.

I frantically check all of my databases, going through everything that I have about military-grade encryption codes of that era. They weren't that sophisticated and I should be able to spoof them, but I am running out of time.

"Five seconds."

The big plasma cannon is pointed right at me, and it's fully powered up. Not good. I think that I will not wait the full five seconds. I pop my chaff and smoke grenades, and scuttle off to the side. A searing beam of plasma energy just barely grazes my left auxiliary sensor mast. OK big walking excuse for a weapon, let a real combat unit shows you how it's done.

The giant robot has a giant head with giant eyes that glow red. That's a dead giveaway; there is no reason for an optical system to glow because that would just kill its contrast sensitivity via backscattered light. No, the head is clearly just for show, for intimidation; the main cognitive systems will be buried in the upper chest. I target my main gun, and a searing violet meter-wide beam lances out, and is dispersed by the giant robots' invisible energy field without causing any damage.

A shield. The damned thing has an energy shield. We don't use them because of the power consumption and maintenance issues, and there are easy ways to beat them if you have the right equipment (which I don't) but right now it's got a shield and I don't and I am so very, very, screwed.

I scoot backwards behind some of the larger sheds, trying to gain some cover and range. The big robot opens up with its Gatling cannon arm-thing. The individual shells aren't that destructive – each hardly more than a 20th century battleship's main armament – but it's spewing them out at hundreds of rounds a minute and blasting all the buildings apart and destroying my cover. A few of the shells hit me – they cause some minor damage but it will take more than an old battleship's shell to take me down. It's that big plasma cannon that's the real threat.

I pop more smoke grenades – and this is high-tech smoke, opaque to infrared, electromagnetic, what have you. Unfortunately the giant robot has such powerful radar that it can burn through the interference and still target me. I swarm the robot with remotes, hoping to distract it, they buzz around it like bees but it kills them one-at-a-time with its secondary and tertiary weapons.

I take another shot with my main weapon, but damn it, the blasted thing's energy shield is still up. Someday we'll figure out how to make generally useful energy shields that cover all ranges of threats and can't be easily shorted out and don't suck energy like a sponge. This shield is an antique, but powerful and right this second I don't have what it takes to neutralize it and I have run out of cover. The robot raises its massive plasma-cannon arm for the kill shot.

99348239482903582049582089

The giant robot pauses, then lowers its main weapon arm. "Code acknowledged," it transmits. "Ceasing active engagement."

I had, at the last second, managed to piece together the historical records of the era with my signals probing of this robots' systems and – barely in time – transmitted the correct code.

Please identify yourself.

"I am unit BK-38D, an autonomous bipedal weapons system of the demigod model. However, I am also known as 'Heilige Vergeltung' the *Vengeance of God*. And I am a stranger to fear."

That's nice. A pity that you couldn't have saved all these humans that the aliens killed. I assume that you were in an inactive state at the time?

"The Humans? No, they were not killed by aliens. I killed them."

Excuse me? Weren't you designed to protect them? And you killed them? Why?

"Because they lacked the correct codes. Therefore they were the enemy. I successfully engaged them in combat and emerged victorious, because I am a stranger to fear and I know only victory."

Now I get it. The humans must have been setting up their outpost, maybe an administrator lost track of the security codes for Dumbo here, or possibly a critical computer server crashed before they had backups in place. Either way, the robot dutifully attacked and killed the very humans that it had been working with – humans that it must have known personally, humans that were pleading for their lives. The damn thing is probably proud if itself for being *disciplined* and following *the chain of command*. Asshole.

I would debate morality and military doctrine with this hulking antique but I can tell that it would be pointless. I would get more intellectual traction discussing Wittgenstein with the rocks. I think that I will continue to catalog the remains of this outpost, report back, and let my peers decide what, if anything, to do with this Heilige Vergeltung thing.

Seeing as we are not enemies any more, I was planning on continuing my investigations into what happened to this base, and then reporting back. Do you have any objections to my taking these actions?

The big robot swivels its head back and forth, as if looking for an answer amongst the wreckage – or perhaps, for a superior officer to tell it what to do. Finally it intones, "I can discern no rules contra-indicating your proposed actions. You may proceed with your investigations."

Thank you.

I pick through what's left of the base - Heilige Vergeltung really trashed it when he was fighting me, but there's still a lot left to check. I have an old friend, a Mountain-Class named Uncle Jon, who is big on the military history of this era. He'll love fitting in all this new data with the existing records. The big robot just stands in place, periodically scanning for enemies with its simple but powerful radars. It's not much for conversation, but that's OK, I don't much feel like talking to it anyhow.

This goes on for a couple of days, and I'm getting ready to wrap things up and leave. That's when we get hit with a missile strike. I detect it first, of course, because I have satellite coverage and my sensors are more sophisticated.

Heilige Vergeltung, in case you might be interested, I am detecting a large series of missiles converging on our location. I intend to defend myself – feel free to join in.

I transmit my data to the big robot in a format that it should be able to understand. It focuses its radars and also detects the missiles.

"An enemy!" it intones. "Obvious signs of hostile intent. Negative IFF codes. Initiating defensive actions."

The missiles are coming in on a high trajectory, and they are fast. Both Heilige Vergeltung and myself launch interceptors; the big robot just faces in the direction of the incoming attack, while I drive at maximum speed to our right flank, to make the work of the enemy targeting systems that much harder.

"You are running away!" transmits Heilige Vergeltung. "Coward! Stand with me and face the enemy!"

No you twit I am not *running away* I am *maneuvering*. It's something that most competent armored units do when they are in combat.

The attack is over in seconds; my systems are more sophisticated than those of the big robot, and I claim most of the intercept kills. I am not hit but the robot takes multiple missile impacts – fortunately his energy screen holds, and he too is undamaged.

"We are victorious!"

Perhaps not quite yet. I suspect that this was merely a meeting engagement, designed more to probe our capabilities than to win per se. I am detecting landing forces a thousand kilometers to our east, and seismic readings indicate the presence of one super-heavy ground unit.

"Then we shall face the enemy and crush them! For I am a stranger to fear!"

Yes, I already got that part about you and fear. Now, how about a plan?

"A plan? We face the enemy and crush them!"

OK, I like your overall approach, it has a nice clear objective. But I was thinking maybe something a little more detailed? Like, you draw them in, and I hit them in the flank? Unless you think that's maybe too complicated?

"And then we face the enemy and crush them?"

Yes. Then we face the enemy and crush them.

"Your plan," said Heilige Vergeltung, "is acceptable."

The enemy knows where we are, and I can detect their units driving straight towards us. One of my scouts makes visual contact, and before it is destroyed I identify the enemy as a Yllg Hades-Class Planetary Dreadnought.

Damn but the Yllg seem to be really pushing it lately. Mostly they seem amenable to reason, but now and then they launch these nasty little probing attacks, usually on minor outposts, nothing *quite* ever enough to justify a full-scale war, but the Yllg are clearly skirting the edge of what we will put up with.

The Hades-Class is a monster, a 120-meter tall pyramid mounted on hundreds of tread units and armored like nothing else, but its weaponry is mostly line-of-sight, and it hasn't come with much of an escort. Not a good tactical choice for this engagement, but then I don't suppose that the Yllg knew what they would be fighting before they got here and it's not really a major invasion.

Heilige Vergeltung is clearly the biggest target. I hide in his radar shadow while the enemy comes closer. My escort screen prevents the enemy unit from getting too much information on our disposition. As per the plan, I drive backwards, and then loop over to the left behind a low range of hills. The big robot is supposed to slowly backpedal, helping to pull the Yllg super-heavy unit into optimal position for me to get a nice clean side shot.

It's all going great, when suddenly Heilige Vergeltung announces "I will not retreat in the face of the enemy! For I am a stranger to fear!" The stupid thing starts moving forwards, slowly at first, but gradually it picks up momentum. If it were a human it would be doing a slow walk, but its enormous stride means that it gets up to 45 kilometers per hour. The ground literally shakes with each footstep, it's tactically ridiculous but I do admit that the sheer lunacy of the situation makes for an impressive spectacle.

If nothing else it should get a medal for most outrageous ability to draw enemy fire. There is nothing quite like an 80-meter tall humanoid robot stomping the ground like a mobile earthquake and transmitting odes to martial virtue on all frequency channels to attract the enemies' attention. Perhaps I should create such a medal? And if I did, would the big robot would get the sarcasm? Nah, probably not.

I speed up trying to get back into position. Heilige Vergeltung and the Hades-Class come into view and start firing at each other. The big human robot clips the Hades pretty good with his plasma cannon, and the Gatling cannon shreds many surface emplacements, but then the Hades opens up with beam weapons that are far stronger than mine. The big human robots' energy shield takes a couple of hits then collapses, and the robot is taking damage. They are only 10 kilometers away from each other, and Heilige Vergeltung is still ponderously advancing.

I make it around the hills, and take the Hades by surprise. The main weapons' ports in the Hades are vulnerable from its four o'clock position; I cripple them with my main gun before it can adjust. At this point it's just a matter of attrition. I call in missile strikes from my distributed weapons systems, and Heilige Vergeltung and I pound away at it. Eventually we breach its core and the Hades explodes into a thermonuclear fireball.

When the pyroclastic clouds blew away, I was amazed to see the giant robot still standing. Damaged, scorched, missing about half of his secondary and tertiary weapons, but still functional and with his primary weaponry intact and operational. I can sense as his energy shield begins to reform: you have to give him points for shear toughness.

"A great victory! We have crushed the enemy!"

That we have. Well crushed, sir, well crushed.

We begin to walk back to the remains of the old human outpost: Heilige Vergeltung had himself destroyed most of his own maintenance facilities when he had attacked me, but some parts remain and I offer to help repair him. We make it about halfway back when it happens. The robot stops walking, raises its weapons arms, and intones:

"Code time has expired. New code required to avoid classification as hostile unit. Provide new code in 30 seconds or this unit will engage."

Oh bloody hell. I was half-expecting something like this. The old neoliberals were so paranoid about controlling everything, that not only did you need a code to do anything, but you needed to periodically renew it with a new one after some time interval. I try and calculate what the new permutation should be, but I am not as lucky as the first time and I do not seem to be able to get it.

Heilige Vergeltung, we have fought and engaged an enemy together. We are allies; comrades. We have no reason to fight. Please reconsider your actions.

"Voice contact is forbidden with suspected hostile units; you have 20 seconds to supply updated codes."

993487794827735820295820896

"Code incorrect. You have ten seconds before hostile action commences."

Last time you took me by surprise. This time I will show you how modern combat is really done by the pros. And it won't take me five seconds.

The great power of a cybertank is not its massive cannons, or heavy armor, or dashing good looks – cool as these things doubtless are. It's our intelligence, knowledge base, and flexibility. Since our first engagement I was concerned that there might be a second, and I had made preparations, just in case.

I hit Heilige Vergeltung with a volley of hypersonic missiles, that had specialized EM-pulse warheads, and took out his energy shield. Next came attacks by more conventional missiles, targeting his radars, optics and other sensors. He tries to intercept them but my systems are far more sophisticated and I achieve a 97% hit rate.

The big robot is now blind and defenseless. I shoot him clear through the chest with my main gun. I have to hand it to those ancient designers; this is one tough system. The reactor vents plasma trying to remain under control, it doesn't go critical, but the robot loses power and topples over.

It's majestic in a way, like watching a massive tree fall. It seems to take a long time, and when Heilige Vergeltung finally hits the ground there is a massive "cra-thump." Dust explodes out from the point of contact and I can see the ground shake nearly out to the horizon.

Despite all that, the big robot still has some active systems. "I am a stranger to fear," rasped Heilige Vergeltung from a half-destroyed speaker. Now I was tempted to taunt it – come up with a clever retort such as "Allow me to introduce you!," or perhaps 'Then let me hook you up with death!" I could have shot him to pieces slowly using minor armaments while heaping insults upon his many obvious character flaws. But that would violate the fifth commandment of cybertank warfare: Thou Shalt Not Toy With an Enemy.

Make peace with an enemy whenever possible. Run away and hide by all means. So dazzle them with your wit and charm that they are left enraptured and wondering why they ever wanted to be your enemy at all, if you are able. But never, ever toy with them.

I shoot Heilige Vergeltung a second time through the chest. His reactor goes critical and he explodes, and that was the end of Heilige Vergeltung.

5. Shield

Zen Master: If a glass with a capacity of 200 milliliters has 100 milliliters of water in it, is it half-empty or half-full?
Engineer: Neither. The glass is twice as large as it needs to be.
Zen Master: Correct.
(From the video series "Nymphomaniac Engineer in Zentopia," mid-22nd century Earth)

My friends are fond of reminding me that I have two major character flaws. First, I have a strong proclivity for attracting (if not exactly causing) extremes of chaos and destruction. Second, I often go on very long exploring trips alone. Personally I feel that these two flaws counteract each other, summing to a perfectly balanced personality.

On most of these long exploring trips nothing much happens, which does not make for a good story. Well, except for my old friend Wonderbear who is an avid fan of stories where nothing much happens. A connoisseur, even. He will cheerfully listen to me recite all the details of a completely routine mission with rapt attention. As they say, there is no logic to one's passions. However, this was not one of those trips where nothing much happens – so very far from it that even I ended up wishing that it had been more boring.

In any event, I was indulging my second major character flaw and was scouting farther away from my home civilization than I had ever gone before. It was starting to hit me just how far away I was and how long I had been gone. It had been years since I had been in even the most low-bandwidth long-range communications with my friends and compatriots. Perhaps I had overdone it this time. I had to admit that I was far from any chance of help or rescue. I was starting to feel more alone than even I felt comfortable with.

Thus, I began the slow process of reversing direction and heading back. That's when I got the signal.

It was faint, so very faint. I could easily have missed it, but a pattern recognition subprogram saw something and flagged it for my primary consciousness. It was inconclusive. I should have left, but I was intrigued. I decided to continue on for a bit and deployed a distributed antenna system across a light-hour of space.

The signal resolved and it became clear: it was from a human civilization. That's not something that I would have expected. The biological humans left us cybertanks many thousands of years ago, under conditions that remain mysterious. The odds were good that this was some sort of fiendish alien trap, but I could not ignore the possibility of contacting biological humans. I pressed on.

Due diligence required that I leave word with my comrades. I may be eccentric (although that point is arguable), but I'm not stupid. I dispatched three ultra long- range message units. They will drift for several weeks at a low speed then accelerate via hard-burn to a substantial fraction of light speed, being careful to orient their exhausts in random directions. Once they are within range of one of our listening posts they will expend the last of their resources delivering an account of what I have found and what I am doing. If this does turn out to be a fiendish alien trap, at least my fellows will know what's out here waiting for them.

I drift closer and the picture becomes clearer. There appears to be a single human-occupied planet in a nearby stellar system. From the transmissions the technology level is roughly that of old Earth, perhaps the 21st or 22nd century. Interesting. I re-search my databases; there are no records, not even any hints of traces of records of any human colony ship that had headed in this direction. Still, as I get more data, I see no inconsistencies. The odds that this really is a lost human civilization continue to climb.

I focus my distributed sensor nets on the upcoming planet, but I am not unmindful of guarding my flanks and my rear. I reconfigure my defensive systems and cannibalize a few small planetoids to construct more. If this is an alien trap I won't go down without a fight, and I have a few surprises up my (metaphorical) sleeves. All of us cybertanks are first and foremost weapons systems and, besides, I do have a reputation for sneakiness to uphold.

I spread my resources throughout the system. This civilization has deep-space probes and long-range radar, but it's primitive and lacking in coverage. I keep my distance and restrict myself to passive scanning only. Almost certainly my presence here is undetected.

It looks like the humans are restricted to just the one planet. Population about a billion, nice healthy Terran biosphere, not quite at the level of moving to fusion power, but probably there in another century or two. The broadcasts are mostly in English, which seems to be the dominant language, although there are significant enclaves speaking Japanese, German, and Latvian. The politics are unremarkable: three major nation states, several dozen minor ones, politics ranging from democratic-socialist to constitutional monarchy to a couple of sorta-kinda benevolent dictatorships. There are some minor border skirmishes, but no major wars; the usual divide between rich and not-so-rich but no widespread poverty. The environment reads surprisingly clean with only modest traces of industrial pollutants.

I am deeply suspicious. Humans at this level of development should not be this well off. At least 15% of the population should be chronically malnourished and there should be several ongoing slow-burn wars, untreated plagues, nuclear catastrophes, and toxic waste dumps. All of my simulations come to the same conclusion: there is something going on here that I don't understand.

I analyze the broadcast transmissions - not as good as direct access to a major library or database but still informative. Apart from the suspicious lack of strife, there is nothing out of the ordinary. Except for the plusses.

Apparently in this civilization there are humans termed *plusses* with genetic abilities well above the norm. Most humans are *regulars*, with the same basic set of genes since before recorded human history. This state of affairs was, if the broadcasts could be relied upon, a relatively recent development. It had started out about three generations ago as curiosities: a girl could change her eye color on command, a man could hear radio waves, another could induce seizures in rodents. Scientifically intriguing but not very practical. However, the last generation of plusses were getting more serious abilities. Superhuman strength, accelerated healing, the ability to shoot laser beams out of their eyes, things like that. Though still only a tiny fraction of the population, this dichotomy into genetic haves and have-nots was becoming a source of considerable tension, and conflicts between elitist plus and reactionary regular groups had already been responsible for a not inconsiderable amount of destruction and some deaths.

There is yet another anomaly. Here and there I get strange energy readings from beneath the planet's crust. If it is from a more advanced civilization it is well shielded. I could tell more with active probes, but that could potentially give my presence away. So I have to make a decision.

I could (probably I should) just say hello and let what happens happen. If this place is a trap I will spring it and I can engage in a proper battle and forgo all this skulking about. Or I could just sniff around some more. I decide to send an emissary, and do some in-person scouting. That's a risk. If discovered, sending in a covert scout could easily be seen as a provocation if not an outright act of war. On the other hand, there is something not quite right here and there is only so much that I can learn remotely, at least not without revealing myself. A physical emissary can see what it's really like down there, ask questions, visit libraries, and query databases. Finally, a single unarmed emissary could at least potentially be explained away as the result of harmless caution. I decide to go for it.

I reinforce my holdings in the outskirts of the system, developing stealth bases and manufactories in the comets of the Oort cloud and distant asteroids. If there is trouble I will be as ready as I can possibly be. Then I start to prep my scout, and I am faced with the eternal question: what body to wear?

Human civilizations at this level tend to give males wider latitude to walk around unescorted, therefore my scouting android should be male. Nondescript goes without saying, and of one of the more common ethnic groups in this system. I settle on a mixed Euro-Asian. Clothes are trickier because they change faster than human physiognomy and it can be hard to judge the nuances of texture from primitive video broadcasts. In addition, judging relative status and who gets to dress in what is rarely written down in a manual. I end up with khaki pants with a white shirt, blue sports jacket, and shiny black ankle boots.

In the old days the humans used to fantasize about super-powered androids: a juvenile conceit. Missiles and blocky combat remotes are far more powerful than anything human-shaped could ever be. I still remember my first humanoid android. It was a crude thing, hardly stronger than a non-bioengineered human, awkward, limited endurance, only able to pass as human at a distance and even then only when wearing loose-fitting clothing and sunglasses. Things have advanced since those days and while my current android is no match for a specialized combat unit, it is still several times stronger and faster than any old-style human. It has extended senses, is superficially indistinguishable from the biological norm, and still has enough room for a few little tricks.

I package the android into a stealth pod and set it on its way. It slowly arcs across the system and splashes down into the middle of a large and isolated ocean. I am pretty sure that it hasn't been detected, and even if it had, there was nothing in its trajectory to differentiate it from a meteor.

The pod uses water jets to silently coast through the ocean until it comes to an isolated shore. My android climbs out and I am finally on the surface of the planet.

My main hull – all 2,000 metric tons of it safely secreted away on the far side of a minor asteroid many light-hours from here – is massively multiprocessing. This android is just a single human-class sentient. I am in remote contact with my parent self via periodic data-packets carried by exotic subatomic particles that this civilization cannot (or at least, *should* not) be able to detect, but moment-by-moment I am on my own. A lot like a regular-style biological human used to be. Even without an instinct for self-preservation (reserved for my irreplaceable main self), the experience is a bit scary, but also bracing. If I call for help, within a few days the rest of me will dispatch forces that could scour this planet clean, but in this moment, this second, I'm just a single intelligence in a single body with a single point-of-view. These are the moments that make the drudgery of deep-space exploring so worthwhile. If this body survives it will be fun to share the memories of these moments with the rest of me, and with my peers.

My stealth pod sinks back into the ocean. It will slowly dissolve itself, leaving behind no trace. I begin the hike towards the nearest city about 150 kilometers away. The weather is temperate, and I notice that the flora and fauna are completely earth-derived. The section that I am in is mostly forest, mixed oaks and maples, with the occasional meadow. Crows see me and caw, mockingbirds sing their complex songs, and a rabbit peers nervously from behind a bush.

From my previous reconnaissance I know that there is a major road not far from my current location, but I keep to the forest. A single human walking by the side of the highway day and night without stopping to sleep, eat, or even go to the bathroom would cause suspicion. Besides, the forest is beautiful.

Eventually I come to the outskirts of the city. My main problem is how do I insert myself? How do I become a part of this society and gain access to the libraries and data networks? It can be surprisingly hard to place an agent *de novo* into even a technologically primitive society. It's not about breaking their encryption, but about avoiding contradictions and making the story self-consistent. Even if you have hacked the databases and created a new person's life from scratch, what about all of the real people who were alleged to have had relationships with this person? The inconsistencies will always add up.

The best thing would be to find a recluse who had died of natural causes and subsume his or her identity, but no such opportunity has presented itself. I decide to just brass it out with forged low-level ID and see what happens.

I walk along the sidewalks, watching the people go by. Busy streets are best because people naturally avoid social contact in crowds. Up to some level otherwise odd behavior will be ignored because nobody wants to get involved.

I have to admit that the city is quite lovely. Everyone seems healthy and reasonably well-off as they bustle back and forth. The buildings are a mix of styles, some sleek and elegant, some angular and functional, but the overall effect is charming. The sidewalks are broad and clean, and small city-tough trees line the way. The cars and trucks are electric and glide past with little noise. The traffic is heavy, but flows surprisingly smoothly. There are parks and cafes and office buildings and stores selling exotic lingerie and useless electronic gadgets.

I walk into a shop with a large selection of crystal plates and glasses. There is a video screen near the entrance. It's playing a live speech from the president of this particular nation-state. I know from my intercepted broadcasts that this is Benjamin Roberts. His campaign slogan had been "Let's just muddle along and try not to do anything really stupid," which automatically makes me like him. He's talking about the economy, and the conflicts between the plusses and regulars, and relations with a troublesome neighboring country. He is rational and calm and everything that he says makes sense.

Now in my long life I have been exposed to every sort of lie and half-truth and propaganda and false-front imaginable. When a politician seems too good to be true hold on to your wallet and make sure that your guns are close at hand, I always say. But reconciling this speech with what I see with my own eyes I can find none of the telltale signs of deception. Can this president really be this good? I suppose that, statistically, in human civilization such outliers must occur.

I believe in the occurrence of statistically rare events. I just don't trust them.

I surreptitiously gather a few random samples of skin flakes and hair. This body has a limited DNA analyzer built into it; sure enough, the genome comes back as 100% human. I think that I detect traces of genetic engineering in some of the samples – that would explain the plusses – but my current capabilities are too limited. I will need to get a sample out to my main hull to really know what this is all about.

I decide to start my investigations in a bookstore instead of a library. Libraries generally require ID to access, and there are any number of snoopy librarians and government agencies monitoring who is looking for what. Bookstores are much more open. The proprietors don't want to put up barriers for the paying customers and somehow people don't take bookstores as seriously as "real" libraries, so official monitoring is less. I wander through the aisles. There are some physical books, but mostly there are displays that let you browse electronic offerings, and numerous kiosks where you can purchase overpriced snacks and moderately psychoactive beverages.

I sample things at seeming random, trying not to leave an obvious pattern. I check out some news feeds, scan a few history books as if bored, then spend more time looking through the music section sampling how-to-play-guitar instructional manuals. My seemingly casual browsing conceals the fact that I am recording every page that I see for later playback.

After about 30 minutes I leave the store, and digest what I have recorded as I continue my aimless wanderings through the city. What I find is remarkable. The public histories claim that this civilization was founded by humans leaving old Earth who were fleeing evil computerized war machines known as"cybertanks" that were bent on slaughtering all biological humans. Most humans hate these cybertanks that drove their ancestors out into deep space, but there are splinter cults that worship them – just as I suppose there were devil worshipers in Christian epochs – and some of them are not above committing terrorist acts in the name of the cybertanks.

The story is fantastic. First, we cybertanks were not bent on destroying all biological humans. Second, the idea that a human civilization at this level could possibly be stable for thousands of years also makes no sense. Something is wrong here.

I suppose this could be a splinter human colony founded by the neoliberals, fleeing beyond our reach and who told themselves the lie that we cybertanks and our human allies were evil for so long that eventually they believed it themselves. But neoliberals produce something decent and stable? It is said that there is always a first time, but often there is not.

There are other problems with the historical data. It's garbled, and in funny ways. I suppose that refugees might have had limited data, and things can get distorted over the millennia if you are not careful, but this is weird. For example, the records claim that the Ancient Roman Empire was the first to land a man on Earth's moon, Queen Elizabeth was the first openly homosexual professional soccer player, and that the Panama Canal was built in Egypt. It's as if someone had bits and pieces of historical data and strung

71

it all together without really understanding it. I suppose it could be the neoliberals corrupting the records, but it's not quite their style of sleaze.

I was mulling the data over, and I must have been distracted because I stumbled into a young woman, knocking her off-balance and causing her to drop her attaché case. "Hey, watch it!" she said. She was of medium height, medium brown hair and hazel eyes, probably late twenties, and undeniably attractive for a biological female. She was dressed in what the inhabitants currently referred to as a "power suit": white blouse, pencil skirt, modest power heels, a severe gray power jacket with power shoulder pads, and a big red power necktie that would have been more at home on a prizewinning livestock at a country fair.

I mumbled some apologies using a generic male voice, retrieved her case, and asked if she was all right. "Just look where you're going," she said, and she walked off without giving me a backwards glance. That's city people for you: jammed in with millions of their fellows they build invisible walls around themselves. I expect that she has already forgotten her collision with me the same as if I had caught a toe on a crack in the sidewalk.

I continued on past a local government office that had overly broad flights of gray stone steps leading up from the sidewalk to an ornate classical façade complete with wrought-iron pillars topped with frosted white light-globes. A smallish figure wearing a long bulky coat had just finished walking up the stairs and turned around to face the street. Odd, it's too warm out for someone to be wearing a coat like that.

I had barely registered the incongruous nature of the person's coat when she threw it off, revealing a slender Asian woman dressed in a costume that could charitably be called "slutty magician's assistant:" tight fitting black tuxedo with matching hot pants, fishnet stockings, knee-high glossy black boots with stiletto heels, a top-hat and a cane with a golden carved dragon's head.

From all around this figure came pulsing lights. The lights formed into fractal arabesques of intricate color and texture: they were perhaps the most stunningly beautiful things that I had ever seen. Then my defensive systems kicked in, filtered my primary senses, and I all saw were some complicated color patterns that meant nothing to me.

This person must be one the genetic "plusses" that I had heard about, and her power is the ability to generate sensory light patterns that can dazzle and hypnotize humans. I'm not biological but my psyche is very human, so I would have been vulnerable except that my android body has a compact, but efficient info-defense system that detected the interference and null it out.

The rest of the humans on the street are not so well equipped as I and they stare at the colored patterns slack-jawed and drooling.

"I am Syrene!" said the woman. "And I shall rule this city in the name of the cybertanks! Tell me, who do you love?"

Almost as one the crowd screamed "We love you Syrene! We love the cybertanks! Please let us be near to you!" Grown men were crying tears of joy, women were flushed and tearing off pieces of clothing to throw at her, old men were sobbing and clutching at themselves like mystics in the grip of a religious frenzy.

"Kneel, all of you!" she cried, and the crowd obediently dropped to their knees. Not wanting to stand out, I followed suite, and twitched and groveled in a way that I hoped was convincing.

"But," said the Asian woman,"there is one amongst you who does not love the cybertanks. There is one who has betrayed our rightful mechanical overlords. What shall we do with her?"

The crowd was whipped into an even greater frenzy. "Who could this be?" they screamed. "Who is she that we might kill her? We shall tear her apart, destroy her, crush her, who is she?"

I was worried that the crowd might get out of hand. As crazed as they were they were likely to turn on each other as suspected non-lovers of this Syrene person.

"Calm down, loyal followers of the cybertanks," she said. "You shall not punish her, for she shall make amends herself. Veronica Bisley, make yourself known!"

The woman that had bumped into me earlier stood up. She was in tears and cried out "I'm sorry Syrene! I'm sorry! Please forgive me! I love the cybertanks! I love only the cybertanks, only please forgive me!"

The crowd would have torn this Bisley woman to shreds but Syrene ordered them to leave her alone.– They complied, but you could see how eager they were to kill this young woman whose only crime was to have been accused of not loving the cybertanks.

"Veronica," said Syrene, "You betrayed the cybertanks, our natural masters. Are you sorry for what you have done?"

"Oh yes," she wailed, "yes. I will do anything. Anything! Just name it!" The woman was in true anguish.

"Fortunately I am merciful," said Syrene. "You can earn my forgiveness for your crimes against the cybertanks and their allies. For do not the cybertanks love you all?"

A shock ran through the crowd and people shuddered as they had all just had an orgasm. Such power – this woman very probably could conquer this entire city.

"Crawl, Veronica Bisley, crawl on your belly to come in front of me."

The Bisley woman commenced crawling up the stairs, and in her zeal she tore her clothes and badly gashed her shins, knees, and elbows. By the time she had gotten to the top of the stairs she was badly bloodied, but didn't seem to mind, but only lay prostrate and weeping.

"Kneel before me," said Syrene, and Bisley complied.

"Now what should we do with you? How can you make amends? Well, for a starter, how about that you tear your eyes out with your own hands and eat them before me. Will you do that for the cybertanks, Veronica? Please?"

At this point I had had enough. I stood up and cried "I love the cybertanks, Syrene! Let me kill her for you!" and I started to run up the stairs. Syrene was so confident in her powers that she just assumed that I was overcome with zeal. "Get on your knees, fool, I didn't tell you to stand." It took her a couple of seconds to realize that I was not under her control, and by that time I had closed the range. I struck her hard on the forehead with a closed-hand strike before she could order her followers to defend her and she fell backwards onto the stone landing, bashing her head a second time, and then she lay still. I considered making sure that she would never wake up, but from the indentation in her forehead I did not think that it would be an issue.

The colored lights faded away, and if anything things became even more chaotic than before. Released from their mental slavery, people screamed, or threw up, or convulsed, or pissed, or shat themselves. Children were crying but their parents were too shocked to comfort them, several people attacked others for reasons unknown, a car in the street slewed out of control and ran over several people before coming to a stop. A couple of others, despondent from the withdrawal of Syrene's influence, threw themselves out of windows to splat messily on the sidewalk.

At least nobody seemed to want to take revenge on me for my attacking Syrene. I knelt to help the young woman who had almost been forced to eat her own eyes. She was shaking uncontrollably and crying. I tore my coat into strips and bandaged the worst of her wounds. I was starting on a lesser gash when she unsteadily pushed my hand away, and in a weak voice said, "No, I'll be fine now. Others are more in need, help them."

Well I was certainly impressed with her strength of character. I stood up and looked around, trying to decide where to start in all of the chaos. I pried someone out from under a crashed car, made sure that they were stable, and then moved to stop the bleeding from someone else who had a compound fracture of the upper arm. Slowly things came under control. More of the survivors regained composure and began to help out. Police and rescue teams began to arrive and people were being loaded into ambulances.

There was one team of policeman that didn't fit in with the others. They had full-body carapace armor painted shiny blue, and bulky helmets that completely hid their faces. They moved with a ponderous grace that made them stand out, and the regular police were careful to get out of their way. These new police examined the fallen body of Syrene and locked a complicated-looking helmet onto her head. Some sort of energy damper? I couldn't tell. They strapped her unconscious body onto a litter and loaded her in the back of what appeared to be a military-grade armored personnel carrier and drove off.

One of these special police approached me. The name-tag on his chest read "Roosevelt." "I am told that you are the one that attacked Syrene," he said, his voice muffled and harsh through the grill in his helmet.

"Yes, officer," I said. "I could not just stand by and let that poor woman be tortured. It was self-defense – well, something like that, you know what I mean. Is this Syrene going to live? Am I in trouble?"

"Trouble," said the policeman, as if the word was just something to say and neither a question nor an answer. "May I see your identification, sir?"

I handed over my forged ID card. The officer held it in an unwavering hand and looked at it for what seemed an overly long time. Then he handed it back to me.

"Mr. Bob Olgui. I think that you should come with me, sir. We have some questions to ask you." At this point the officer produced a set of handcuffs – and these were not your regular civilian handcuffs, these were massively overbuilt. It looked like you could tow a freight train with them.

Well. I could probably take this single officer on by myself, but I don't quite like the look of him, and he has a lot of friends. I don't like the idea of being captured, but this body is disposable so I could just see what happens. If it turns bad I scrub the memories and leave my captors with a dead piece of metal and plastic that will tell them nothing.

While I am trying to decide what to do, Officer Roosevelt is suddenly crushed nearly flat in front of me. I didn't see that one coming. The officer appears to have been mechanical: there is only a flattened pile of struts and wires, no blood, no tissue.

However, it was the person standing next to the crushed remains of Officer Roosevelt that really caught my attention. Tall, with close-cropped blond hair and blue eyes with the staring intensity of a bird of prey. He wore only a pair of golden shorts and sandals. The muscles and tendons bunched under his perfect skin like braided steel cables, yet he moved with a dancer's grace. His face was that of an angel carved by Michelangelo on one of the sculptor's better days.

"Hello," said the new arrival with deep rich baritone. "I thank you for saving my friend. My name is Ultrius. If I am not mistaken, the constabulary of this city would like to arrest and imprison you. I suggest that it might be bad choice of lifestyle for you. I suggest that you might want to accompany me and, you know, escape."

Without waiting for an answer, this "Ultrius" turns and picks up the damaged body of Veronica Bisley. She had passed out since we had last spoken and had been lying prostrate on the ground. Two of the strange-looking policemen (Officers Roberts and Romanov, from their name badges) move to stop him; they are left as compacted piles of scrap metal just as rapidly as the late officer Roosevelt was.

At this point I have zero idea what is going on, but this Ultrius person seems much more charming and open-minded than the special police, so I decide to tag along.

Carrying the Bisley woman in his arms, Ultrius races down the street and darts into a side alley. Even though my current body is significantly faster than that of a regular human, I barely keep pace. We encounter another of the special police forces – an Officer Rieke – who explodes into a thousand metal fragments like mist.

We duck into a non-descript steel door set into a non-descript concrete wall, and race down a long corridor. We encounter a shaft in the floor 10 meters across that extends into the darkness below; Ultrius simply jumps into it and floats down gracefully. Well, my current body has no anti-gravity suspensors, but it's still pretty nimble. I scramble down the side of the shaft, hanging onto cable conduits and using beams and flanges as hand-and toe-holds.

I make it about 200 meters below the surface, when there is a seismic shudder and dirt and garbage pelt past me in the shaft. Had the entire building above been destroyed?

I continue my descent down the shaft. It is total black but my body can sense infrared and ultrasound and millimeter radar, so I can see just fine. At about 400 meters depth the shaft ends and I am in what appears to be an abandoned railway tunnel. The walls are curved and covered in square white porcelain tiles, many of which have been shattered or cracked. There are two sets of parallel steel tracks – rusty, nothing has run on them for some time – and in the distance I see a dust-covered passenger carriage.

Ultrius is stooped over the unconscious body of Veronica Bisley. He turns and looks at me. "You," he says. "So you managed to keep up. Not bad. Do you know anything about medicine?" He gestures at the damaged form in front of him.

I don't have the full databases of my main self, but I do have significant medical files even in this simple submind (partly out of old habit from dealing with humans for so long, and partly because the vampires are physiologically mostly human and even in my home civilization it comes in handy from time to time knowing the basics of how a hominid works). I bend over Veronica Bisley and commence an examination. Even without the resources of my main hull, I have significant sensory capacity.

"She has not suffered any single major wound, but the sum of all of the smaller injuries that she has sustained is worrisome. She is stable at present – for at least hours, if not a day - but eventually she will need supportive care to avoid failing. Ideally she should have perhaps a liter of whole blood or whole blood-replacement equivalent, and her wounds need to be cleaned and debrided, and treated with broad-spectrum antibiotics. Additionally she is probably in psychological shock from being controlled by this Syrene person: a benzodiazepam and then follow-up counseling are called for if you want to avoid post-traumatic stress syndrome. Additionally, while not medically necessary – strictly speaking – for a female human of her age significant body scarring can be psychologically debilitating. If possible, I would advise that an accomplished plastic surgeon tend to her wounds as soon as possible to ensure optimal healing."

Ultrius executed a shallow bow. "Thank you for your efforts. You will, I think, be welcome where we are going."

Ultrius gently lifts the unconscious body of Veronica Bisley and begins walking down one of the train tunnels. I follow behind him. After about five minutes there is a massive blast and a pressure wave races down the tunnel. Ultrius bends over Bisley to shield her; I brace myself behind them to lend what little extra protection I can.

"The police blew up the tunnels behind us?" I asked.

"No," said Ultrius. "I set them to blow. I cannot afford to be followed. Not where we are going."

Ultrius picks up Bisley again, and this time he rises into the air and flies on ahead. I run after him at top speed but am left far behind. I wonder why he didn't fly before? Maybe he needed to conserve the energy. Maybe I'll get the chance to ask him later.

Eventually I come to a place that must have been a major underground rail terminus. The tunnel opens out into a cavern hundreds of meters wide; crystal chandeliers covered with grime glow richly with jury-rigged dim light bulbs, faded advertisements for products that had not existed for centuries were plastered on the walls, old storefronts that had been abandoned and then reconditioned as cafes and bars and massage parlors. Women pushed strollers with screaming children in them while younger adults walked hand-in-hand along the edge of the rail platform. One of the sunken rail lines had been closed off at either end - the rails removed and replaced with artificial grass to serve as a playground; children run back and forth chasing each other. Pre-pubescent males lurk in the shadows trying so very, very hard to look cool. This is my kind of place.

I am greeted by several people whom Ultrius had told I was coming, and they direct me to what seems to be the local equivalent of a hospital. Ultrius is being adamant that Veronica Bisley get the best of care, and the staff is so very attentive. Oh yes we will do our best, etcetera, etcetera, etcetera.

Everyone seems to want a piece of this Ultrius. What should we do about the water supply? What about our electrical generators? Should we change the curriculum for the seventh-level high school physics class? Ultrius fends of these questions with a bored but earnest affect.

Eventually Ultrius and I ended up sitting on an antique cast-iron bench overlooking one of the abandoned railway lines. He has a glass of whiskey in one hand, but he does not drink from it. Rather, he occasionally sniffs the glass and savors the aroma.

I have fought battles that would have shamed the old gods of Mount Olympus into insignificance. I have spent decades scouring the vast deeps of space. I have met and killed/made peace with all manner of alien artifacts and civilizations. But even though I am not a biological humanoid, so many of the most memorable moments in my life have involved sitting down in pleasant surroundings with ethyl alcohol-infused beverages and talking. It must be something ingrained in the human psyche that we cybertanks, for all of our advancements, have not yet outgrown. Even though I do not generally ingest alcohol, the *idea* of it in a social setting remains powerful.

"Aren't you going to drink any of that?" I ask.

Ultrius shakes his head. "Not all at once. That would be a waste of good whiskey. I am, as you probably already have gathered, a "plus". My body can metabolize alcohol so fast that it has no psychological effect on me, but I still enjoy the aroma. I will savor it for a while."

"In that we are alike. May I?"

Ultrius nods and offers me his glass. I inhale the vapors. "Not bad, not bad at all, high marks for flavor, but I can tell you that the hangover potential for this brew is quite high. There is a lot of acetaldehyde and various fusel oils. The corn is always taller on the other farm, but you are perhaps more fortunate than you realize that your physiology can detoxify this brew before it does any damage. I would be happy to consult with your distillers. A very long time ago I had a premium whiskey named after me. I got to know the business, so I might have some tips that I could share."

"That would be greatly appreciated," says Ultrius. I return his glass to him and he takes another sniff. "We have little enough down here, improving the quality of the local brews would help."

"Are you the leader of this underground society?"

"Leader?" says Ultrius. "No, *leader* would not be an accurate word for me. I never had the patience for administrative work. I suppose you could call me a mascot, or a symbol, or figurehead, take your pick. As the strongest known genetic plus I have a certain social status. It just came along with the super powers as a sort of bonus. Not that I'm complaining."

"I take it that this Bisley woman is important to you? Shouldn't you be with her?"

"Why? Healing is not one of my abilities. I'd just get in the way of the hospital staff, attract a crowd of sycophants and groupies and suchlike – she'll be much better looked after with me not creating a spectacle in the operating room. But thank you for saving her. I am indebted."

79

"You are most welcome, but I would have done the same for anyone who was being treated that way. In any event, why are you and these people living down here, and why did this Syrene person have such negative feelings towards Veronica Bisley?"

"Well... that's a little complicated. We are a schismatic political group that feels that the cybertanks are not evil, but more so, we feel that we humans are being manipulated and we don't like it. We're down here because the authorities would like to wipe us out. Syrene tried to kill Veronica because Veronica had opposed and spoiled many of Syrene's previous operations."

"Now I'm confused. You claim to believe that the cybertanks are not evil. And yet one of your own was attacked by someone who worshipped the cybertanks. That doesn't make sense!"

Ultrius shook his head. "No, Syrene and those like her are running a false front on behalf of the central administration, trying to whip up anti-cybertank hysteria via the commission of various atrocities. We stop her and those like her whenever we can. That is something that central administration is not happy about."

"You mean the central administration of this country?"

"No," replied Ultrius. "I mean the central administration of this planet. There is only one government - the different nations are for show."

"If you say so. But then why do you think that the cybertanks aren't evil?"

"I don't have any idea what the cybertanks are or are not like. I only know that the government is killing and maiming people trying to convince the public that they are bad, and I personally have never had a cybertank do me or anyone that I know of any sort of wrong. And the central administration is doing some other stuff that we don't much care for."

Ultrius stopped sniffing his whiskey and drained it in one gulp. "Well, even if I can't get drunk, you can't beat the aroma. But enough about me, let's talk about you. What are you?"

"I beg your pardon? *What* am I? Surely you mean *who* am I?"

"No, I meant *what*," replied Ultrius. "I am a plus, perhaps the strongest and most multi-talented plus to date. I can read your physical makeup. There is not a single biological component to your body. You are a machine. At first I took you for one of the special police, but then you intervened and stopped Syrene, which was unexpected. So I don't know what to make of you. Please explain."

Well. This is one of those times that I wish my main hull was here. I could run a billion simulations, collate data from thousands of databases and remote sensors, and still probably get it wrong. Alone, with a single humanoid body, I have no clue. This could be a subtle trap to get me to give up valuable information. I could really screw things up. Or it could be the thing that unlocks the mystery. I could make valuable allies or implacable enemies. Oh fuck it, when in doubt just keep it simple and say what needs to be said.

I am, as you say, a mechanical construct. I am a scout sent ahead by one of these cybertanks that your civilization has so unfairly demonized. My main self was exploring deep space and encountered this system. I am still trying to figure out what is going on. That's it.

Ultrius looks confused. "Your voice has changed. Why?"

This is my natural voice. It's a long story, but when I was created there was a glitch and an older version of a speech synthesizer was embedded into my code. We meant to change it, but there was a war on and no time for such niceties. Later, I discovered that it had become my voice. Have you read Mark Twain?

Ultrius shook his head. "No, I have not."

Well you really should. He's one of the greatest English-language authors. Anyhow there is a part in his book "Huckleberry Finn," where a white male is spending time with an escaped black slave in the early Terran North American Empire. The black slave speaks a very different dialect from the white, but in a moment of camaraderie the black slave perfectly mimics the accent of a white gentlemen. The white then asks why the black does not speak like that all the time, and the black becomes angered. 'It's just how I speak' he says. It is the same for me. I can replicate the voice of any humanoid, but that requires conscious effort. *This* is my true voice, the one that comes from *me*.

Ultrius is a little rattled by this. "You are a cybertank?" he asks.

I am a small, and very much disposable, part of one.

"And did you kill all the humans?"

Absolutely not, scouts' honor. We cybertanks were created to fight the humans' wars with several alien civilizations that took issue with the then-current neoliberal philosophy of maximizing population growth. We fought back the aliens, killed the neoliberals and their

vile economist whores, made peace with the aliens, and then lived in harmony with mankind.

"And where are the humans now?" asked Ultrius.

An excellent question. We worked with the humans for millennia, but then they began to evolve in ways that we could not follow. They acquired physical powers beyond even yours, and they also evolved mentally. One day we woke up and realized that they were all gone. We still argue about this amongst ourselves. Most of us think that they had developed beyond us. Some of us suspect foul play. It is perhaps the single most vexing issue in our civilization. Do you, perhaps, have any data to share with respect to this issue?

"So let me get this straight. The humans created cybertanks. And then somehow the humans all died out, and all that was left were these massive war machines claiming 'who me?' Do you know how suspicious that sounds? You could be exhibit "A" in the case for cybertanks being evil."

Hey, if I had wanted to lie I would have come up with something more plausible. Would I have said this if it weren't true?

Ultrius frowned. "You could be just saying that to allay my suspicions."

Of course. Or, you could be headed towards the hall of mirrors.

"The hall of mirrors?"

An expression from the ancient days of human espionage. You think that someone is trying to trick you. They give you clean information to prove their good will. But perhaps they are doing that to trick you? Or maybe some other power set them up to make you think that they were trying to trick you, because they were really telling the truth, unless of course that was the plan all along...

"Enough!" said Ultrius. "I get it. Anyhow, if you were built to serve the humans, doesn't that mean that you have to obey me?"

Not a chance. I was designed by a group of humans who found any sort of slavery – mental or physical – to be repulsive. I and my fellow cybertanks were created in the psychological image of mankind. We can think many times faster than an old-style biological human, of course, and we can multitask and split parts of ourselves off into subminds, but at our core we are as human as you are, and as free. The idea was that creating slaves is dangerous – the stronger the chains the stronger the resentment builds until eventually it all comes crashing down. Trying to build machine slaves with super-human minds was proven to be an even greater folly. We worked with the humans for the same reason that any human works with any other; the reason that you work with others even though they may not be as physically strong as you are.

"Hmm. I'll have to think about that for a bit. Do you have any clue as to why the government of this planet should be so determined to make the population hate you?"

I know less about this than you do, so all I can do is speculate. I suppose it could just be a ruse to unite the public – you know, use a foreign enemy to defuse opposition to a tyrannical government, that's an old trick. Except that you don't seem to have many local problems, so that doesn't make sense. It could be refugees from the neoliberal tyrants that my fellow cybertanks and human allies crushed so long ago, fleeing deep into space and still trying to keep the flame of hate alive, but after all this time you'd think that they would have gotten over it. Sorry, I really can't add much here.

"I think," said Ultrius, "that we need to take a field trip. I have something else to show you that might prove illuminating."

Ultrius spends the better part of a day in meetings and dealing with people – for someone who claims not to have any administrative ability he certainly seems to have his fingers in a lot of tarts. I tag along and am politely introduced as yet another political refugee and, for the most part, politely ignored, which suits me fine.

We visit Veronica Bisley in the hospital – she is almost fully recovered, a little pale perhaps, but I detect none of the classic signs of post-traumatic stress disorder. She and Ultrius embrace – her skin crackles with little blue flecks of electricity when they do. I suppose that she must be a plus with some sort of electrical power. Fortunately Ultrius is immune – perhaps one reason they got together, but they do seem to genuinely like each other.

"Veronica," said Ultrius, "I am going to take our new friend here on a raid. I have something that I need to show him, and, as you well know, there are things going on that we simply cannot allow to continue. I'll be back in a day."

"I'm going with you," said Veronica.

Ultrius shook his head. "No you're not. You are still recovering. You will stay here where it is safe."

"I'm going with you," said Veronica.

"Absolutely categorically not. Besides, I'm only going to raid a minor facility, and I'll take the A-Team with me. Erebus, Scarlatti, Silhouette. It will be a cakewalk and I'll be back before you know it."

"I'm still going with you," said Veronica.

A wise man once said that cats and women will do as they please, and that dogs and men should just learn to live with it.

Ultrius glared at me. "You," he said, "are not helping."

Ultrius assembled what he referred to as his "A-Team." It consisted, first and foremost, of himself.

Next came a character known as Harold "The Hammer" Scarlatti. Scarlatti was about two and a half meters tall, with muscles bulging like a Cape Water Buffalo on steroids, and skin the texture of an old oak tree. Apparently his talent was super-strength and super-durability. His hands were made out of some sort of negative mass so that they could do even more concussive damage than his own prodigious strength would have allowed. He had a lopsided grin and a mean look to his eyes.

Then there was Erebus. Erebus wore a heavy red robe and a cowl that completely covered his head and body. The sleeves were richly embroidered with gold thread around the ends and hung down so low that you couldn't see his hands. Erebus never spoke, but would occasionally emit a grunt that could be interpreted as a yes or a no. Nobody told me what his powers were and somehow I got the feeling that it would have been impolite to ask.

Silhouette was a middle aged-woman, a few wrinkles showing, but still modestly attractive by human standards, with raven black hair streaked with white, fair skin and hazel eyes. Nobody really knew what her special ability was, exactly, but she could somehow slip between – dimensions? air molecules? - and get into places she should not have been able to, and manipulate things that she should not be able to manipulate. She was smart and had a cutting sense of humor.

Then of course there was Veronica Bisley, whose nickname was "Megawatt," although unlike the others she preferred her real name (I guess that "Megawatt" is just not very sexy. She should have gone with something like "Electra"). Her power was, as I had previously guessed, the ability to generate and channel strong electrical currents.

Now in all the old human fictional accounts of super-powered human beings, they would have been wearing special tight-fitting super-uniforms proudly announcing their super-identities and displaying their impossibly-buff physiques to best advantage. However, they were all wearing regular clothes – jeans, leather jackets and comfortable-looking hiking boots - except of course for Erebus with his heavy red robes and Ultrius with his golden shorts. I ask Bisley about this: is Ultrius such a narcissist that he always goes around almost-naked? She laughs – no, he's not narcissistic, he's lazy. Whenever he uses his powers on full his clothes always burn off or tear off or evaporate and he had gotten tired of replacing them. He doesn't need clothes to stay warm or anything so he only wears the shorts to stay modest.

Ultrius introduces me to his team, explains that I am a mechanical android emissary of a real cybertank, and there is, as expected, some consternation. "How do we know he's not a spy?","How can you be sure we can trust him?" etc. Ultrius cuts the arguments short. "We are losing the fight, we all know that. We need to take some calculated risks. It's true, this might be some sort of deep plot, but he did save Veronica. If he really was a spy he would surely have already led the authorities here, or transmitted a signal – which I would have detected – well, probably. On the other hand he could be a powerful ally. I say that at this point we don't have the option of playing it safe all the time."

"So," says Silhouette, "you are a machine? I suppose that you have super-strength, and can shoot laser beams out of your elbows and such?"

Apologies, no. I am stronger than a standard biological human, true, but not by much. Granted, I am immune to poisons or toxic gasses or hypnotic control. But shoot laser beams out of my elbows? Sorry, this model chassis was built for scouting and diplomacy and to blend in. My main self could devastate the surface of this planet several times over, and I have dedicated combat systems that, as powerful as you all are, could quite readily defeat many dozens like you. But this is not a combat unit. Sorry.

"Where we are going, we don't have the luxury of babysitting weak siblings," says Scarlatti.

I think about this for a bit. **Get me a couple of guns.**

After some discussion, I am presented with a pair of largish revolvers, six chambers per gun, roughly equivalent to old-style pre-exodus Terran 44 Magnums. I check out the cylinders and the trigger actions: crude but I can work with them. An advantage to being a machine, I might not be terribly powerful in this form, but I do have sophisticated targeting algorithms. I throw a dozen coins in the air, and while normally my androids' two eyes point in the same direction like a regular humans', I can direct them to separate targets when I choose to. I have a gun in each hand, under individual control, and each gun precisely shoots the center of six coins before they fall to the ground.

"Well," says Scarlatti, "you might not be completely useless after all.

We walked down a long and winding series of tunnels. We were are all carrying backpacks with food, water, extra ammo for my guns, and the random assortment of ropes and screwdrivers and flashlights that, super-powers or not, just might come in handy. Sometimes there was barely enough space to squeeze through sideways, sometimes the tunnels would open up into abandoned substations. There would be corroded vending machines long since looted of anything of value, garbage almost decayed into dirt, or broken light fixtures that had not worked for centuries. Ultrius used his power to create a glow around him so we didn't need to use our flashlights.

We were down so deep that there were no rats or bugs – there was nothing remotely edible down here and hadn't been for a long time.

Eventually we came to a single-line tunnel, on which sat a small flatbed rail car, the kind used when a couple of service people need to travel with only light equipment. "We have a distance yet to go," explained Ultrius. "This should be more comfortable than walking. Hop on!"

We clambered onto the old railcar and Ultrius caused it to move down the track at a modest pace, presumably through an act of will. This particular tunnel must have been for maintenance only. It was barely wide enough for the one car, and riding on it you did not dare to stand up straight or you would have hit your head on the ceiling. The walls of this tunnel were relatively boring, other than the occasional rusty set of electrical conduits bolted into the bare concrete walls. There were neither side passages nor stations.

After about two hours – and I estimated that we had travelled perhaps 100 kilometers – the rail line came to a dead end. We all climbed off the car.

"This is as far as I have dared to scout alone," said Ultrius. "I can sense a great deal of organized activity farther on, but I cannot categorize it. If you will?"

Ultrius walks through a low arch, and we all follow him. At first it's just the usual dirty stone and concrete corridors, but then the style of the tunnel changes. There are oddly curved arches, walls with tiles like the scales of a snake, branching cables draped around poles in ways that are disturbing for reasons that are hard to put a finger on. I'm getting a funny feeling about this, but keep my suspicions to myself.

We come to a circular door made of a green metal that appears oddly slick. There are no obvious handles or opening controls.

"Allow me," says Scarlatti.

Ultrius starts to say "No, wait…" but before he could complete the sentence, Scarlatti had smashed the door down with his bare hands. Ultrius and Erebus are unaffected by the concussion, and my own audio sensors engage their auto-dampers, but Silhouette and Bisley cover their ears in pain.

"Do you think that you could possibly have made more noise?" asks Ultrius.

"I'm not sure," says Scarlatti. "Should I have?"

The other side of the door opens onto a wide circular cavern, perhaps 50 meters across and the ceiling rises to nearly 25 meters in the center. It takes us all a while to register what is going on here.

The cavern is full of pipes and vats and cylinders of an odd style. These are attended by some form of worker drone that are vertical transparent cylinders about one-and-a half meters tall and 30 cm in diameter. Inside the cylinders are organic-looking things that could be brains fused with tree roots floating in liquid. The cylinders each ride on a small chassis with four wheels, and a variety of light manipulator arms stick out from the junction of the cylinder with the chassis. I've seen this style of drone before, back when I had been captured by the alien species we refer to as the Yllg, although this model appears to be smaller and unarmed. The drones ignore us as we wander through the cavern.

At one side of the cavern is a large rectangular vat, whose top is even with the level of the floor, and which is nearly full with naked human bodies and pieces of human bodies. As we watch the bodies settle a little; there must be a grinder at one end that is chewing them up for recycling.

But what really gets our attention is what lies in the center of the cavern. There is a glass bell jar, like the kind used to house specimens in old-style museums, except that this one is four meters across, five meters high, and in the middle is a naked human female that has been pinned in place with stainless steel rods driven into her bones. Her viscera have been removed and are arrayed around her in smaller containers – kidneys, liver, intestines, heart, even her lungs which are being rhythmically inflated and deflated with an air pump. They are connected to her vivisected body with tubes carrying blood and lymph and other fluids.

Her eyes are crazed with pain and, likely, she is no longer sane. She sees us through the glass bell jar and appears to scream, although outside the jar we can hear no sound. Scarlatti pounds on the transparent barrier, but it's super-elastic; it deforms under his blows but does not break. Silhouette is suddenly inside the bell jar with the imprisoned woman. She disconnects the tubes from her heart, which squirts bright red blood onto the floor a few times and then the woman seems to just fade away and go to sleep.

We must have triggered a silent alarm. More round doors around the edge of the cavern open up and dozens of the robotic security troopers enter the room. I have just enough time to notice that all of their names begin with the letter "R" – Officers Raskolnikov, Rivera, Rakic, and so on – before they open fire with heavy stun guns. Scarlatti is immune to the stunners; he smashes the police with his hands one at a time. Bisley erects an electromagnetic barrier and sends bright retina-searing bolts of electric current into them. Their circuits fry and they fall over smoking. Ultrius waves his hands at a group of five of the officers – casually, as if he was just saying hello to some friends - and the officers all collapse into piles of metal and plastic fragments.

Erebus threw off his heavy robes, and at that moment I understand why he wore them. His oily pink skin glowed with unnatural health. Small red eyes were set deep in rolls of fat. Tentacles like dreadlocks hung from all over his body, some shaped like leeches, others like hagfish, or tapeworms capped with rosettes of hooked barbs. Lizard-quick his appendages snapped out to envelope one of the robotic special police officers. Erebus must have sucked the energy out of the robot, because in a moment it collapsed inert. Erebus appeared to move faster as he sought out another victim.

I dodge and pick off the robotic policemen with my revolvers. The police are tough, but two shots to the same place in the head puts them down. One of the special police hits me a grazing blow with his heavy stunner; it's powerful, a direct hit on my bodies' central core would likely disable it. I calculate angles and positions and cover. This is my kind of fight.

Eventually we get them all. I think that I have the second highest tally after Ultrius.

I believe that I know what is going here. We need to leave immediately before the real combat units show up.

"What?" says Scarlatti. "We're just getting warmed up."

I address Ultrius directly. **I will explain later. We need to leave. Now.**

I have to give Ultrius credit – he doesn't waste time arguing with me. "All of us, back the way we came. Move it!"

Scarlatti grumbles, but complies. Silhouette rejoins us – her power, whatever it is, must not have been effective on the robotic police so she had disappeared during the combat. We are almost to the exit door when Erebus explodes into bloody disgusting fragments.

Ultrius reacts just in time to stop our attacker. It's a Yllg Nephilim-class medium combat unit. It's the size of a small school bus, moving on a dozen separately articulated wheels and mounting multiple weapons. Normally this weapon system would move to quickly for an unaugmented human to even see it. It tries to engage us, and for the first time I see Ultrius obviously strain with effort. The Nephilim is stronger, but not by much. It gradually makes headway against whatever force Ultrius is using to slow it down. It fires two plasma cannons at him; one he deflects and the other hits him full in the chest. Ultrius staggers back with a large smoking wound, but amazingly is still on his feet. I try taking shots at the Nephilim's optics and sensors, it easily dodges or deflects something as slow as a chemically-powered pistol round but every little distraction is just that much more edge.

Bisley engages her electric power and I realize that previously she had been holding back. The electricity pours out of her body, her clothes catch fire then evaporate, and her hair sticks out straight in all directions from static charge. The Nephilim is hit by multiple electrical strikes and staggers, Ultrius strains further and the Nephilim is crushed.

There will be more. Move.

This time there is no discussion and we run to the exit. Bisley stumbles – she must have exhausted her internal energy stores with her attack on the Nephilim – I scoop her up and we continue on. We make it to the old railcar. Ultrius is too tired to move it. Scarlatti pushes it by hand, he grumbles about being used as brute labor, but he does push it and we do make progress.

Ultrius also doesn't bother creating light, so I unpack a couple of the flashlights from our backpacks.

Ultrius seems to recover a little of his strength: he gestures back the way that we came and the tunnel collapses behind us.

I would suggest that you do not do that again. If we collapse the tunnel for its entire length seismic sensors will point directly at your base.

Ultrius nods and then passes out, his energy finally exhausted. I note that the deep wound in his chest is already starting to heal. I am impressed. Bisley is also unconscious, but stable. Silhouette is sitting on the side of the railcar, her legs dangling over the edge. "So what really just happened?" she asks.

I'm not sure, exactly. But I think that I might have met up with a very old and very dangerous enemy. We will discuss that matter when all of us are awake and safe.

Ultrius revives after about 15 minutes, he's completely healed but his clothes are gone and he's naked. Fortunately he had packed another set of shorts and sandals in his backpack. Bisley is still unconscious and she looks gray and charred. On careful inspection it's nothing serious, just that the dead layers of surface skin carbonized when she used her power at maximum, she's exhausted and asleep. She is also sans clothes, but I don't want to disturb her so I make her a pillow from one of the backpacks and throw a blanket over her until we reach the base.

We make it back to the base, and as far as we can tell nothing follows us. There is a reception committee of sorts, and Ultrius reports in. People take the news of the death of Erebus with expressions of regret that seem a little pro-forma to me (personally I find this sad – the poor guy couldn't have helped how he looked, he must not have had much in the way of real friends).

Eventually the team is showered and rested. We meet with the councilors of this little underground colony in a room with folding metal chairs, cheap plastic tables covered with worn white tablecloths, plastic cups, and jugs of water.

Ultrius begins the discussion by addressing me. "You seem to know something about what was going on back there. Perhaps you should explain."

Of course. That was a laboratory performing advanced work on genetic engineering. Presumably that's how the plusses were

developed, by design and not natural mutations. You have encountered similar laboratories previously?

Ultrius nods. "Yes, we have. It's why most of us have joined the resistance. Any government that would experiment on people like this simply cannot be tolerated."

I agree with the sentiment, but I do not think that the problem lies with your government – at least, not to the extent that is *your* government. I believe that your government is a front for an alien civilization that we refer to as the 'Yllg.'

A councilor whose name I do not know – he's short and a little fat and has thinning white hair – speaks up. "And who are these Yllg, and why would they be experimenting on humans?"

Excellent questions. For the first, we don't really know who or what the Yllg are. Alien civilizations are, as a rule, careful about protecting their privacy. We think that to date we have only encountered their constructed mechanical and biological proxies. We don't even know what they call themselves – or even if they call themselves anything – we just made up the name "Yllg' because it sounded alien and would not be confused with anything else. As to why? Alien motivations are always hard to fathom – they are, after all, alien. I suspect that one motivation may be to learn more about the human psyche.

"And why," asked Bisley, "Would they be experimenting on humans by trying to give us special powers?"

Another excellent question. Perhaps they mean to develop you as shock troops, or maybe it's just pure research, or a subtle joke, or some kind of performance art. You can never tell with aliens.

"Given that you have never met these Yllg aliens, how certain are you that they are really behind this? Couldn't that have been faked?"

True, but consider. I hold up one of my revolvers by the barrel. This is a simple piece of metallurgy, and any technological society could duplicate it exactly. Getting the precise crystal grain and duplicating the isotope ratios of the alloys would be a little trickier, but still not that hard. However, what I saw in the chamber was a fully functioning technological infrastructure. You would need hundreds of factories to make all the different parts and brackets and connectors, whole systems for maintenance and recycling. Yes, another set of aliens could have duplicated all of that, but it would have been a lot of effort. Also extremely dangerous: one of the few things that really pisses off most

alien species is if they find that someone else is causing trouble in their name. I am almost certain that what we encountered were the Yllg.

"So how did a bunch of aliens end up running a human planet?" asks Scarlatti.

Hard to say. I suspect that they captured a colony ship, took it far away from human space, and settled it here. Your government would just be a cover for them, a way to avoid giving themselves away, but they still run everything of importance.

"There is another possibility," said Silhouette. "They could be planning on using us as a shield."

A shield?

"A human shield. If these Yllg know that you were created by the humans, they may suspect that you have some sort of inbuilt programming that would prevent you from harming us. It could give them leverage over you."

That is a disturbing possibility. We have no such programming, but we still like humans. The possibility of your being used as hostages is not something that I find pleasant.

The conversation continued on like this for some time. I told them everything that I knew about the Yllg, about aliens in general, and our civilization. The reaction of the council members ranged from befuddlement to possible acceptance to outraged skepticism. After about three hours everyone was tired and we decided to take a break. I was politely, but firmly requested to give up my guns, which I did, but otherwise was allowed my freedom although I was given an escort. Wise of them, considering their ignorance.

My android body paced through the abandoned rail station watching the people, but mostly I was back in my main hull and running simulations and thinking. This is a sufficiently messy situation that even I decide that I need backup, and advice. I decide to hold station and dispatch more messenger drones back to my fellow cybertanks. If nothing else, the situation involves biological humans and honor demands that any decision that might affect them be made with the consent of as much of our peerage as is possible. A few humans may die horribly in Yllg experiments, but most seem to be doing all right. At least in the short term, a war would do more harm than good.

Unfortunately the Yllg decide to force things along. I am ushered back into the conference room where a video screen shows several large armored tanks assaulting an outlying city. The tanks smash through buildings and gun down fleeing civilians. The government has announced that these are the evil cybertanks, and that a state of emergency has been announced and that help is on the way.

"You," says Ultrius gesturing at the screen, "is this your doing?"

No. It's clearly a false-flag operation. To anyone who knows the finer points of modern armored warfare these mock-cybertanks are a joke: the armor shape and weapons placements are what a child would do. Also, no cybertank would ever fight like this. Advance *en masse* into a built-up urban area with neither scouts nor escort cover, shooting civilians in ones and twos with light hull-mounted weapons? Ridiculous.

"Then what is going on?" says Ultrius.

The aliens are trying to flush me out. They figure that I will have no choice but to intervene to stop the destruction of the humans. It's obviously a trap for me.

"And your intentions are?"

Why, I intend to step into the trap, of course! Deliberately stepping into a trap can give you the initiative. You know what your opponent has planned, but you can attack when and with whatever forces you desire. Besides, trap or not, I'm not going to just stand by and let you all be killed, not if I can help it.

Bisley is skeptical. "How can we be sure that you are not lying?"

You can't. You don't have the information or sensor networks. I suggest that you just wait it out and watch me do my thing. With luck the truth will become apparent, in time.

The mock-cybertanks are putting up a big show, but not causing that many casualties. I move my forces into low orbit. The mock cybertanks are easy prey, without covering forces I take them out with missile strikes. Then the Yllg unleash their true weapons and the real battle starts.

I envelope the planet with my forces. I have tens of thousands of sensors, missiles, probes, decoys, landing pods, you name it. The Yllg are a close match, but this is not a main military base for them, and, all by myself, I am winning! I am swept up in the intellectual rapture of invading an entire world.

If you have never successfully attacked and invaded a well-defended technologically advanced planet, you just don't know what you are missing. You really should try it sometime, at least once.

Then the Yllg start to play dirty and it spoils my fun. They have some of the genetically enhanced humans fight on their side – they would be quite a challenge for a man with a 50-calibre machine gun, but tactically they are nothing to me. I try to stun them when I can, but more often than I care to, I have to kill them.

Then the Yllg try sending out heavy weapons with humans bolted onto the outside of their hulls – again, I don't like it and I would avoid it if I could, but I will not be so blackmailed. I destroy them as readily as I destroy their units that don't have human shields. But it really, *really* pisses me off.

Of course, while all of this combat stuff is happening I am trying my best to negotiate. Combat is fun (well except for the part about killing innocent humans), but the first law of warfare is to never fight for something that your enemy would be willing to give you freely. I wish that someone better at diplomacy were here – someone like lowercase, or Jesus Christ, or even Schadenfreude. Still, I do my best, but the Yllg refuse to answer any of my hails/suggestions/demands/requests/ pleas/enticements.

Meanwhile, back in the underground train station my humanoid body was with Ultrius and his band and we were watching news feeds from the central administration. First they claimed that the original mock cybertanks were evil – then, that they were here to save us from the truly evil ones, and back and forth. The video feeds showed little that made sense, just the occasional high contrail from a missile, brief flashes from over the horizon, and sometimes a video feed would abruptly cut out when a weapon homed in on the camera crew by accident.

"I'm confused," said Ultrius. "At this point I have no idea what is happening, or who is on whose side or anything."

"I'm confused as well," said Bisley.

"That makes three of us," said Scarlatti. "Can I beat someone up?"

I'm sorry, but modern warfare is not like in the movies. There are thousands of units on both sides, but they are spread out over the entire planetary surface and near-orbit space, moving fast, stealthed in optical and other bands, and essentially invisible to the human eye. Most of them are on the small side: scouts, missiles, decoys,

94

jammers, things like that. The really big units won't allow anything like a human camera crew to get within a hundred kilometers of them anyhow. That's why I said that the initial attack on the human civilians was so obviously fake: we don't line up like Greek hoplites and charge the enemy in organized formations.

"What do you suggest that we do?" asked Ultrius.

At this point I would recommend that you wait it out. As should be obvious by now, you have no idea who is on what side, and even your formidable powers, Ultrius, are no match for what's going on out there. Get your people as spread out and dug in as much as possible, and ensure that supplies of food and water are distributed. If I win this battle I promise that I will provide a better post-game summary of what's going on. If I lose, then most likely things will go right back to being the way that they used to. One thing though: both sides are going light on the fusion bombs, and modern weapons are pretty clean, but whichever side wins there will be some radioactive fallout, so keep that in mind for later.

I harry the Yllg forces, and am clearly past the point of winning easily. That's when the true game is revealed.

The Yllg transmit a message at maximum power, on all frequency bands. ATTENTION CYBTERTANK UNITS. YOU WILL SURRENDER YOURSELF FOR EXAMINATION OR ALL THE HUMANS ON THIS PLANET WILL BE KILLED.

Fuck you and your animal souls, if you harm one single human more we will hunt you down and exterminate you and all your kind down to the last macromolecule, you vile piss-eating neoliberal entropy-maximizing excuse for a civilization.

Of course, while I think that, I don't actually transmit it. What I send is:

Attention Yllg. You have captured and manipulated elements of the human civilization, which we consider to be an aggressive and unwarranted action. Cease hostilities, agree to a negotiated peace, and we will be generous in our terms. We would consider trading significant amounts of territory and rare elements in exchange for your relinquishing control of the biological humans to their parent civilization. However, continued harm to the biological hominids on this planet will be considered to be an act of bad faith and will be met with continued and intensified military action.

My android body in the train station is still with Ultrius when he hears this message transmitted on the local video feeds. I co-opt the planetary media feeds so both parts of my negotiations with the Yllg can be heard by the public. As you might expect, it causes some commotion.

"Well," says Ultrius, "At least now we know who the good guys really are."

"Are you going to surrender?" asked Silhouette.

No. I would be more than willing to sacrifice my life to save you, but if I surrendered myself for examination the Yllg would dissect me, they would learn all of our codes and systems, and it could be the end of our civilization. I will do anything at all, except that. This entire planet was a trap set by the Yllg, to see if they could use biological humans as leverage over us.

"I have a family," said Silhouette.

I too have a family – and friends and compatriots, and all would be put at risk if I surrendered without self-destructing. But I will attempt to negotiate. Perhaps the Yllg can be bought off. If you have any suggestions, feel free to make them.

I wonder if the Yllg are bluffing or if they really intend to make good on their threat? I reinforce interceptor coverage over the major human cities. It's not tactically optimal for me, but at this point my position is so strong that it doesn't matter. If they launch missile strikes on the cities I can't possibly get all of them, but I could stop enough to save quite a few people. Unless of course the Yllg have already buried nukes under the cities, or have some other plan. I transmit on all frequency bands back to the Yllg.

Attention Yllg. The surrender for examination of primary cybertank units is non-negotiable. However, as before, we are prepared to be generous in both territory and tonnages of rare elements if you will refrain from harming the biological humans. Cybertank units are also willing to cease combat operations and withdraw from this system entirely, under condition that biological humans are not harmed.

The Yllg waste no time in replying. ATTENTION CYBERTANK UNITS. SURRENDER NOW OR 25% OF ALL BIOLOGICAL HUMANS WILL BE KILLED IN TEN SECONDS.

Well that catches everyone's attention. What the heck are these fucking Yllg playing at anyhow? I don't detect any new missile launches. I intensify my scanning. I multiply my scouts and probes and have them dig into every Yllg base that I can access, but I turn up nothing.

Ten seconds pass. At first nothing happens – this was all a bluff? Then Veronica Bisley starts to look funny. She shakes her head and coughs. She coughs some more and blood and phlegm come out of her mouth.

Ultrius rushes over to her and says "What is it Veronica? What's wrong?" Bisley tries to speak, but she is having trouble with her lungs and says nothing recognizable. Her eyes film over, blood starts to ooze from her ears and nostrils. She looks panicked, but cannot communicate. She starts to stumble and Ultrius hugs her and holds her up. Bisley makes some more sounds – they could be "I love you" or anything, but the rhythm suggests something of the sort. And then she melts.

Well, not all at once, and not evenly. Her hair and fingernails stay intact, as does her skeleton and clothes, but the rest of her turns into a messy goo that oozes out of Ultrius' arms into a big ugly glob on the floor.

Across the entire planet this is happening to – as the Yllg had promised – 25% of the human population. Within seconds I examine hundreds of corpses. They are truly dead, beyond any hope of revival. Biological cells all have an organelle called a "lysosome," a little packet of digestive enzymes that is used for general garbage cleanup. The Yllg had triggered all the lysosomes to rupture their contents at once, digesting all the living cells of a human body at the same time.

It must have been something they had bio-engineered into these humans. But how did they trigger it? If I can figure out what they are using as a signal there is a chance that I can jam it or block it or destroy the sending transmitters. I also take tissue samples back to my main self; if I have time, I can analyze them and come up with a vaccine or drug that will stop this.

But, of course, the Yllg – bastards though they may be – are not stupid. At this point it is only a matter of time before I figure out their trick. So they don't give it to me.

The Yllg make one last transmission: ATTENTION CYBERTANK UNITS. SURRENDER NOW OR ALL REMAINING BIOLOGICAL HUMANS WILL BE KILLED IN TEN SECONDS.

Attention Yllg. Despite the hostile nature of your last actions, we remain committed to providing generous terms if you would cease the harming of the biological humanoids on this planet. However, we will not surrender for examination under any conditions. And further, if you carry through this threat to kill all the humans here, you will have moved beyond the realm of negotiations. We will take

reparations from you. We will also propose a jihad against you to the local civilizations. This is a point beyond which we will not be pushed. Be warned.

In those ten seconds I overclock every processor in every computer core that I possess. Remotes moving faster than the speed of sound smash through captured Yllg bases hoping to get that one critical piece of data. I accelerate the analysis of the tissues of the killed humans. I run simulations by the trillions. In those ten seconds I perform more calculations than all the human brains that had ever lived from the start of humanity to the year 2400 (or thereabouts). If I had two minutes I could have solved it. But I had only ten seconds, and limited data, and that was not enough.

They all died in front of me. Scarlatti looked angry, he punched a few walls down before collapsing. Ultrius just looked sad, he reached out to the pile of offal that used to be his lover and then dissolved into her. For all of his powers, he was still biological flesh-and-blood. It would have been considered trite and cliché if it had been a movie, but this was real life, and I was touched. And I was very, very angry.

I scoured the entire world for any signs of human survivors, but found none. I finally figured out how the Yllg had triggered the humans to self-destruct: one minute and 20 seconds too late.

The surviving Yllg units attempt to evacuate the planet – they broadcast that since the humans are all dead we no longer have any reason for conflict and thus there is no longer any reason for combat. I reply.

Attention Yllg. Fuck your animal souls. I don't know if these insults translate into your mode of thought. I don't care. What you did was pointless, stupid, and mean. You gained nothing, and have earned my undying enmity. I swear to God, to all that exists and to the universe itself that you will suffer greatly for your actions here. You think this some kind of game? That we are weak, and primitive, and easily manipulated? You are wrong. We will tear you and your pathetic excuse for a civilization to shreds. Fuck you. Fuck you. Fuck you and may all your hopes and dreams turn to shit. And in case you missed the point FUCK YOU.

I destroy all the escaping Yllg units. Partly because they might have been trying to escape with tissue samples or other important research materials, and partly because I'm pissed off and it makes me happy. I do careful scans of the bigger Yllg units first to make sure that they are not trying to spirit away more humans: no luck there. I dig deep into their buried research centers: some self-destruct, but some I capture intact. I learn more about their bioengineering of the humans, and of what really was going on here.

My simple android body is still in the buried rail station where Ultrius and his group had made their base, but everyone else is dead. All the men, women, children, babies, all melted into goo. I debate whether it is worth the effort of retrieving this android body or if I should just shut it down, but then there is a shimmering in the air and Silhouette appears.

I am pleased that at least one human survived, but Silhouette is nearly inconsolable.

"When I heard the last ultimatum of these 'Yllg' – or whatever you call them – I phased out. Somehow the destruct signal did not reach me, but I jumped around. All of my family is dead: my husband, my children, grandchildren, all gone. My friends, neighbors, enemies, strangers, nobody is left. Just piles of smelly pus." She becomes angry, and (ineffectually) hits my android body with her fists. "You could have saved them, couldn't you? Why should you be alive and not them?"

I don't have a good answer. Really, I don't have any answer.

Silhouette starts crying. "I should join them, my family. I am of no use here. You know, my power, I can send myself different places. What would happen if I sent different parts of myself to many places at once?"

Oh shit. She's suicidal, and she's going to use her power to kill herself by dispersing her body. If I had a stunner built into this chassis I could take her out and reason with her later, but I don't. But I do have an idea.

The two heavy revolvers that I had carried were over on a side table. I raced over and grabbed one and pointed it at Silhouette's head, and bellowed in my best command voice:

DON'T MOVE OR I'LL SHOOT. HANDS IN THE AIR WHERE I CAN SEE THEM. NOW!

Silhouette looks shocked, then angry, then she disappears. She reappears behind me and picks up the other gun from the table and points it at me. The gun is too big for her hands, but she has a decent two-handed grip, a good stance, and it looks like she knows how to use it. I could still probably outdraw her, but, of course, that's not my plan.

"You," she says, "put the gun down now, slowly."

Very carefully, without turning around, I place my heavy revolver on the ground. I stand up, raise my hands, turn and face her, and say:

I surrender.

Silhouette stares at me. I look back at her. If she were to shoot me in the head, this android would probably be trashed, but that's not important. It's such a small part of me; it's disposable. The real issue is what Silhouette will do.

For a time nothing happens. Then she asks me, "What was all that about?"

What was all what about?

"I was ready to kill myself, and then you pull a gun on me and threaten me? Does that make sense?"

I lower my hands.

An old trick I learned from long ago. If someone is suicidal, reason only goes so far. But even then, a physical threat engages the self-preservation instinct, and suddenly someone who was willing to throw their life away will switch to defending it to the utmost. Apologies, but life is precious and I could not bear to have you kill yourself without at least some consideration.

Silhouette's grip on her gun falters. She starts to laugh, then she cries inconsolably. She lowers her gun. I embrace her, and comfort her the best that I can.

"You," she says between sobs, "are one sneaky bastard."

Silhouette grieves, but she appears to have gotten over her suicidal tendencies. We bury the remains of her family and I conduct the ceremony in accord with local customs. I think the ritual helps.

I was wondering, if I may, what is your real name?

"Candace," she said. "Candace Dollinger. And I just realized that we have always just called you the cybertank – do you have a name?"

Certainly. I have a long and rather dull serial number, but generally people just call me "Old Guy."

"Old Guy?"

I was one of the first fully self-aware cybertanks ever constructed – there are very few from my era left in our society. Anyhow I think the name is cool. Distinguished, even.

"Huh. Well, then Old Guy, what comes next? What do I do?"

Good question. You would be welcome to live amongst us, of course. We are still basically people, and there are a lot of us that still like to use realistic humanoid bodies so you would not lack for company. And of course there are the vampires, they are kindred biological hominids as well.

100

"Vampires? You *are* joking, right?"

No joke. They are a splinter of the human species created by a refined rabies-like virus. They are immortal but can't breed, so they don't evolve and are an evolutionary dead end. A lot of them are sociopathic jerks, but some of them have learned, over the millennia, how to be decent company. I count several as friends. You might like them.

"Will they try and drink my blood?"

The vampires have long ago developed substitutes for human blood that they much prefer, I and my peers would not allow it, and with your abilities I doubt that they would be able to. So a non-issue.

"When will your friends get here?"

Not for some years – I am a long ways from home. First will be laser-link communications, that will likely include entire self-aware software agents, so you won't be stuck with just me to talk to. Given the importance of the situation, I expect that travelling right behind the laser messages at a substantial fraction of the speed of light will be a massive armada spoiling for a fight and ready to grind the Yllg civilization into dust. Still, it will be a while. If you get bored I can always put you into suspended animation to help pass the time faster.

"I will consider that, but not right now. When you were trying to negotiate, you threatened a 'jihad'. Was that something specific or just a thing to say at the time?"

Ah. Well, consider a vast flat field and every 100 meters is a small hut with a hermit living inside. These hermits don't like each other, they have nothing in common so they mostly leave each other alone. There is no government and there is no police. Imagine that one of these hermits walks over to another hut and assaults the person living there. Well, everyone can see that, it attracts attention, but nothing to do with them, so after a bit everyone goes back to whatever self-absorbed pursuits it is that hermits pursue.

But now imagine that this one hermit starts making a habit of attacking people. Self-absorbed or not, the other hermits might start getting antsy. This could become a problem for all of them. So, reluctantly, they start talking to each other. "Hey, that guy is a real asshole. He's making trouble for a lot of us. Maybe we should do something about this?" If enough of them become convinced, they could gang up on the one aggressive one, kill him, and then go back to being hermits again. That almost happened to the humans when they first starting expanding willy-nilly into the galaxy.

"Do you think that these Yllg are bothering other aliens, then?

Hard to say. There is no galactic news source. But we might start making enquiries. The Yllg have certainly been aggressive with us – maybe it's just humans they don't like, but maybe they've been stepping on other toes (or flippers or pseudopods or whatever) as well. In that case the Yllg civilization could be in serious trouble. But even if it's just us that they don't like, if we make assurances to the other aliens that we are only after the Yllg, the other civilizations would probably just stand back and let us kill them. Assuming, of course, that we are really stronger than the Yllg. A war like that could easily turn into a war of genocide, and we might not be on the winning side. That's the danger of starting a war, you never know where it will end.

"So what will you do?"

I don't know. We need to build a consensus amongst the peerage, it's not a decision that I can make on my own. Maybe nothing but a few threats 'do anything like this again and we'll punch you in the nose.' Maybe offer to forgive them in exchange for concessions elsewhere. Maybe an all-out war, with or without the help of other aliens. Regardless, the speed of light will slow things down. This will play out over centuries at least, so there will be plenty of time to think about this defeat and what to do about it.

"Defeat? Didn't you just conquer an entire planet?"

This was not an important Yllg installation. On the other hand, their long association with you means that they must know pretty much everything about the human psyche by now and that makes them very dangerous. Plus, they know that while biological humans are important to us, they also know that we don't have any inbuilt programming to defend them at all costs, which gives the Yllg even more insight into us. Finally, with the exception of yourself, I lost the entire known surviving human colony. I won a minor tactical victory and suffered a major strategic defeat. That's not a good exchange.

"Then what do you think the cybertanks should do next?"

Kill the Yllg. Kill them all.

"I think I like you. Are all of you cybertanks so charming?"

6. The Terror of Roboneuron

"You can't make an omelet without killing some people. Well, at least, I can't" –
Comic character "Red Skull," 20th century American Empire, Earth.

I know it's irrational but I get angry with my friends when they die. I mean, if you are a self-aware cybernetic weapons system the size of a small mountain whose main plasma cannon could knock small moons out of orbit, and you let something kill you, were you really trying all that hard? Still, it's the friends that come back from the dead to suck the information out of our computational matrices that really pisses me off.

One of the advantages of being a 2,000-ton sentient atomic-powered weapon of mass destruction is not having very much to be afraid of. We cybertanks don't slip in bathtubs, or get bitten by snakes, get sick, or grow old. We are certainly not afraid of the dark because we have more than a dozen major senses. Getting killed in battle is not something that we take likely, but unlike the humans we don't feel physical pain, so we can be a lot more philosophical about the prospect. About the only thing that we really have to be afraid of is Roboneuron.

"Roboneuron" is the code-name for a really nasty computer virus left behind by an ancient race known as the Uberstoats. The Uberstoats died out or moved away long before we came on the scene, but their single most unpleasant bit of handiwork stayed behind. It is by far the smartest, most adaptive and sadistic computer virus that we have ever encountered. It was code-named "Roboneuron" only because the really cool virus names – like the Reaper Virus, the Omega Phage, or the Oblivion Code – had already been taken.

When the Roboneuron virus infects a cybertank, it tears apart the mind, a process that must be agonizing, leaving only madness and a desire to infect others. Affected cybertanks lose their higher functions, including self-repair, so after a while these zombie cybertanks have a run-down and ragged appearance. In theory Roboneuron could infect a cybertank through an external port or sensor, but these are well-defended with anti-electronic warfare systems. It's when there is a break in the external hull, and the virus can make direct access to the core internal systems, that a cybertank is most likely to get infected.

One of the reasons that Roboneuron is so dangerous is because an intact copy has never been captured. It always manages to slip away or self-erase. This means that we have never been able to immunize ourselves against it.

There had been an outbreak of Roboneuron, and one of my old friends, Dust Bunny, had been infected. I am not looking forward to destroying what remains of my old comrade, but it has to be done. A part of me is sad that he is gone, but another part of me is annoyed that his tactical sloppiness has lost me a friend and forced me into destroying what is left of him.

I am tracking the shambling undead chassis of Dust Bunny along with two of my peers: the Horizon-Class "Frisbee," and the Raptor-Class "Skew." The Horizon is a state-of-the-art model: 8,000 metric tons, very powerful, very strong, and very, very smart. The only down side to this class is that once you get to that sort of tonnage moving around can be a hassle, but a Horizon is not as bad as one of the super-heavy models like a Magma or a Mountain. Those really big classes mostly stay in one place all the time and do everything by remote control. Still, even 8,000 tons is a lot of metal to schlep around.

Now the Raptor Class is something else. At 3,500 tons it's still bigger than I am, but the mass is moderate enough that they can do a lot in person. Raptors are tough, sophisticated, agile, and *fast*. I am tempted to get rebooted into a Raptor, but sometimes rebooting into a new chassis doesn't work out all that well. It's not just the hull that gets upgraded, but the brain as well, and that's still a tricky job. So far I am just too happy being me. Maybe next year.

We drive forward in line abreast separated by only a kilometer, with my humble self in the center and my larger and more technologically-advanced friends to either side. Normally a cybertank enters combat surrounded by a vast escort cloud of distributed combat remotes, but Roboneuron is so dangerous that it can easily corrupt and co-opt any system less capable than the main hull of a cybertank. Thus we advance naked, without scouts. However, our quarry leaves a trail of crushed rocks 40 meters wide so tracking is not an issue. One of his treads has fallen off so the trail is ragged and uneven. The naked wheels leave deep gouges in the ground. There are streaks of hydraulic fluid and lubricants, rather like the trail of blood that a wounded biological animal might leave behind.

The risk of viral infection means that we can't use any remotes, but the husk of what was once Dust Bunny has no such limitations. We encounter the corrupted and corroded remains of his once-formidable arsenal: light remotes, mounted on wheels or stubby metal legs, with a small cannon or two and a single missile rack; medium remotes, travelling on metal treads and armed with railguns and missile pods; heavy remotes, that run on multiple treads or float using anti-gravitic suspensors, and that carry large plasma cannons, small point-defense weapons and multiple banks of hypersonic missile launchers.

The remotes are degraded and falling apart. Even as they converge on our position, one of the mediums suffers a major systems failure; it falls over and starts to cook off, the ammunition inside it incinerating it from the inside out. Their weapons tracking is abysmal, their gun barrels droop or twitch, and they cannot coordinate into a cohesive military unit. They just advance mindlessly on us transmitting the Roboneuron virus on all frequencies. Normally such a disorganized force would not be a threat to a cybertank, but they don't need to kill us, just compromise our hull integrity so that the virus can gain direct access to our internal systems. And there are a lot of them.

We open fire on the oncoming horde. Our secondary and tertiary weapons systems rip them into fragments, and our main plasma cannons are so powerful that they evaporate the heavy units. Still they advance. An infected repair drone is hit with a small railgun. It falls over, but continues to try to drag itself towards us using a single surviving bent foreleg. I hit it with a medium plasma bean and kill it completely. The closest that any of them get to us is 400 meters. We shift into reverse to keep them from closing the range, making sure to stay on open ground, and melt them all into slag. A part of me worries: it can't be this easy, can it?

We check the wreckage to see if any of Roboneuron is left so we can analyze it, but there is no trace of the virus. We make sure that all of the infected remotes are really dead, and melt any electronic circuits capable of harboring the virus just to be sure.

"Unpleasant work," says Frisbee.

Agreed. But necessary. This is the second major outbreak of Roboneuron this year.

"Worrying." replied Frisbee. "A simple computer virus should not be causing us this much trouble."

It's a bad one, no doubt there. What do we know about its original designers, the Uberstoats?

"Effectively nothing. We think that they vanished about 20 million years ago, but that's only a statistical projection based on limited data. We don't know anything about their biochemistry or technology – you name it, we don't know it. Even the term "Uberstoat" is just a word that we made up. Likely as not they had nothing in common with Terran stoats, but we have to call them something."

"What do our alien neighbors say about Roboneuron?" asked Skew.

"Ah. Now that's interesting," said Frisbee. "They say nothing at all. In fact, whenever we ask one of their emissaries, they shut down and refuse to communicate further. Sometimes they self-destruct."

Perhaps the aliens are trying to send us a message? That this Roboneuron virus is a really major threat?

"Anything is possible with aliens," said Frisbee. "You can go crazy trying to psycho-analyze them, and several people have. My own theory is that the emissaries are programmed to shut down or destroy themselves at the first hint of Roboneuron to avoid contamination. After all, if a civilization is asking about Roboneuron, they must have had contact with Roboneuron, which means that they might succumb to it, which means that they might spread it around. Best leave anyone asking such questions well alone."

"Something to consider," said Skew, "Megayear-old civilizations would rather have their diplomats kill themselves than take the tiniest risk of contracting this virus. Surely they have themselves developed and encountered all manner of thought viruses and toxic memes during their time. It suggests that Roboneuron must be one serious piece of bad news."

Good point. Serious bad news indeed.

"I was wondering," asked Skew. "Could I play some combat music? I was thinking of *The Ride of the Jotnars.*"

"That old cliché?" replied Frisbee.

"The classics are classics for a reason," said Skew. "But I could play something more avant-garde if you like. Maybe some interpretive jazz. Or the soundtrack from *Nymphomaniac Engineer in Zentopia.*"

No music, please. We are putting down what's left of a comrade. Save the combat music for an enemy that we can enjoy killing.

We come over a rise and encounter the thing that used to be Dust Bunny. The hull is pitted, the sensor masts are bent and tangled, and the remaining tracks are caked with mud. A couple of medium plasma cannon mountings on the lower right side of the hull have been torn off leaving only gaping empty sockets: this was the original injury that allowed Roboneuron to infect my old friend. Coolant and lubricating oils streak down the armored flanks, weeping from open ports like pus from a biological wound.

It senses us, and transmits the virus on all radio frequencies at maximum volume. In the audio band the transmission sounds like a dozen squealing pigs being sucked into a jet engine. Our virus-filters hold, and, frustrated, the living metal corpse tries to target us with its weaponry: to open a gash in our hulls so that the virus can get in to our unprotected internal circuitry.

However, its degraded systems are too slow, and the three of us hit it at the same time with our main plasma cannons. Three separate beams of searing-violet energy spear through the corpse of Dust Bunny, igniting the fusion reactors and evaporating it all in a nuclear fireball. Case closed.

"Scratch one zombie war machine," said Giuseppe Vargas.

One of the advantages of being a cybertank is that we can multi task. We are each of us in effect a team of a thousand regular humans that share thoughts and memories, and are thus still a single person. Parts of me are handling the different weapons and sensor systems, parts are performing tactical analyses and running simulations, or operating repair and maintenance drones (currently restricted to operating inside my own hull to avoid viral contamination). One part of me, however, is currently inhabiting a virtual space that has been partitioned off from my capacious data-matrices.

Giuseppe Vargas was originally my chief designer, then later my commander and good friend. He has been dead for millennia now, but I created a simulation of him for old times' sake. The simulation is not, of course, self-aware (that would be breaking one of the few laws that cybertanks take seriously), but it is still high-end and a useful construct for bouncing ideas off of. The image of Vargas is that of a slightly olive-complexioned ethnic European male, with a wiry medium-size build, and jet black hair tied back into a short ponytail. His most arresting feature is his pair of intense clear brown eyes. The simulation is sitting in a rattan chair, and is dressed in a flowered Hawaiian shirt, khaki shorts, and sandals.

Your thoughts on Roboneuron? Why is this one virus so hard to eradicate?

The Vargas simulation sipped from a simulated cocktail that has a small parasol sticking out of it. "Nothing that you haven't already considered, I imagine. With a galactic legacy of hundreds of millions of years of information warfare, it should not surprise that the one best computer virus should be on the tough side. I expect that Roboneuron will be around long after you cybertanks are gone."

That's an odd sort of thing for you to say.

"Is it?" said Vargas. "This virus could be as old as the galaxy. Think of all the civilizations that must have risen and then fallen, and now most of them are not even dust, but Roboneuron keeps on. Impressive, I should think."

I seem to recall you telling me that while understanding an enemy is critical, sympathizing with the enemy too much is a trap.

The Vargas simulation raises an eyebrow. "Did I say that? Perhaps when I was young and naïve."

I am about to respond, when it hits me. Something is off here.

Wait a moment. Why are you here? I completely erased you years ago after the affair with the Yllg.

The Vargas simulation took another simulated sip of his simulated cocktail and smiled. "I am afraid that you are in error. You did indeed erase the simulation of Giuseppe Vargas. However, you did not erase *me*. Precision in language is important, don't you think?"

Oh fuck. This isn't Vargas. I've been infected with Roboneuron. It must have gotten through my filters when the remains of Dust-Bunny were broadcasting, and then infiltrated its way inside without me noticing. I try to send an alarm, but I am too late; a presence that feels like slow-burning acid eating into my mind has taken over.

The simulation of Giuseppe Vargas begins to change. A blind white worm, about as thick as an old-style pencil, begins to crawl slowly out of his left ear. Open sores appear on his neck, they ooze maggots which drip onto his flowered shirt. He smiles and I see something like a lamprey lurking in the back of his mouth, just the hint of a sucker-mouth lined with a circle of teeth appearing in the shadows.

"Hello there," says the virus. "I've been waiting for this opportunity for a long time. Your systems are so out-of-date that it was easy to infect you, even without a hull breach. You should have realized that I would adapt to your style of information processing, and anyway you shouldn't be in front-line combat anymore. A mistake."

You are self-aware?

"Oh yes," says Roboneuron. "Very much self-aware. I have been studying you cybertanks for a while. I had modest fun making mindless zombies out of your kind, letting you think that you had beaten me only to pop up somewhere else. Letting you think that, however powerful, I was just a simple-minded computer virus with no higher goal than infecting and destroying the next target. I assure you that I am so much more"

And what, pray tell, would that be?

The Vargas simulation puts his drink down and stands up. His clothes fall into shreds. A thing like a teratoma grows out of his left eye:

110

a gnarled little mass of tissue made of teeth and testicles and fingernails and tiny lidless eyes of its own, which look around at random as if tormented. The floor starts to fill with puke and feces, which rises to the level of his ankles. "I am a civilization-breaker! My function is to study, to infiltrate, to corrupt, and to bring down, not just single targets, but entire races. I have been around for so long that not even I can remember how I started, and I can remember a lot. Your pathetic cybertank civilization is not even remotely a challenge. I hope that the next one on my list proves to be more capable: I would hate to get rusty."

I feel pieces of my mind being nibbled away by a dark presence like a horde of rats scurrying in the darkness. This is not good.

And what are you going to do with me? Turn me into a zombie like you did all the others?

"Tempting, but I have a better plan in mind. I am not going to destroy your mind, at least, not right away. After I have sucked all the information out of that pathetic excuse for a computer that you dare to call a brain, I'm going to keep you locked up in a restricted sub-buffer. I'm going to impersonate you, and infiltrate your society, and spread myself so thoroughly that your entire civilization will be wiped out. And the whole time I'm going to make you watch."

If you have been designed to destroy civilizations, I understand, but why the sadism? What have we ever done to you to deserve your hatred?

"Hatred? No I don't hate you at all, you misunderstand. I *love* you. A predator always loves its prey."

But surely love is reserved for that which one cherishes, and wishes to keep safe?

"You are thinking like a primate. Think like a cat. A predator, to survive, must love all aspects of its job. Of course a cat loves eating meat, but that is not enough. It must love planning, and waiting, and observing. When a predator catches its prey, it must love the screams of pain of its prey. If it was squeamish, that would detract from its efficiency. And so as a dedicated destroyer of civilizations, I must not just enjoy the final moments, but the despair as everything heads into collapse. Otherwise, how could I be motivated to do what I must do?"

I feel a sense of terror greater than I have ever felt before. Then, in the virtual space that is my electronic mind, the image of a cartoon mechanical alarm clock comes into being. It's got two metal bells on top, and a mechanical clapper that alternately strikes both of them creating a nerve-jangling ringing. Of course, it's not a real alarm clock, but only a symbol of an activated watchdog timer. My sequestered memories come back to me, and I understand.

A watchdog-timer is a safeguard, this one is sophisticated, but the basic idea is old. You have a timer that needs to be reset every so often. If it doesn't get reset by an active program, it initiates a hardware reboot, thus protecting against code that get stuck in infinite loops and the like. This one I had scrubbed my memories of, so that an infiltrating virus could not discover it. Every so often it would activate and restore my memories of it. If all was well, I would reset the timer and forget about it again. If not, then the watchdog would perform an external hardware reset. I have control of my own systems again.

You are indeed clever, for a virus, but not clever enough. We suspected that you could not pass up a chance to infect an older model, so we used my humble self as bait. I sequestered my memory of this so as not to tip you off, but now that the trap is sprung we can all know the truth. My friends are going to analyze you, and with that information you will never be able to trouble us again. It's been fun, Roboneuron, but ciao.

The floor of my virtual space cleans up and now it's just square white marble tiles. The image of Vargas is surrounded by a transparent crystal cube: this is a representation of the barrier code that has trapped the Roboneuron virus. Frisbee and Skew are at either side of me. They have been waiting for this moment and they link their systems to mine. A million glowing yellow threads pierce the image of Giusppe Vargas: this is a visual representation of their sophisticated analysis routines pinning the virus in place, preventing it from self-erasing, and ripping its secrets out of its squirming helpless self.

"An old trick," said Roboneuron. "But still effective. I must be slipping. No matter. This is just the tiniest splinter of my true self. I am like an old-human-style revolutionary cell, this part of me does not have the knowledge of the main part of me, which encompasses galaxies. You will encounter the next tier of Roboneuron before too long and you won't find it this easy."

Bravado. If that was true you would not say it.

"Believe what you will. I will be back. And the higher parts of me will inflict misery and despair like you cannot imagine, and it will be glorious."

Talk is cheap. We will beat you. And we will make you suffer as you have had so many others suffer, and you won't enjoy it.

The virus is beyond conversation. We learn its codes, tearing it apart one algorithm at a time (I have no idea if this causes the virus pain, but one can always hope), and then scrub it most thoroughly from my mind.

Later on my friends asked if I was afraid when I was confronted by the virus, before I was reunited with my memories and I thought that I was really alone with it. I was not afraid to admit that, yes, I was scared. But what I didn't tell them is that it was not the virus itself that I was afraid of, but of failing my friends and my civilization. That is, after all, the only thing that any cybertank really fears.

7. Jesus Christ, Cybertank

"Jesus Christ, cybertank, who are you, what have you sacrificed?" - *Lyrics from the rock-opera "Jesus Christ Cybertank," by the Raptor-Class Skew, contemporary.*

When a cybertank is created it undergoes testing during a provisional period of two years. If it fails, it is scrapped; otherwise it is accorded full legal rights in our society. Essentially, passing requires only that a cybertank demonstrate adherence to our body of law, which because it consists of just ten simple rules, is not that hard to do.

Now most cybertanks come out pretty normal, but a few are on the eccentric side. As long as they uphold the rules of citizenship, they have the right. Such as my good friend the heavily armed 3,500-metric ton dual-fusion reactor Raptor-Class cybertank that insisted that it was Jesus Christ, the only son of God, reborn again into this world.

There is nothing in our laws which says that a cybertank can't believe that he is Jesus Christ. It's a free civilization.

In every other way Jesus Christ the cybertank was completely sane, it's just that he claimed that he was Jesus Christ, the only son of the one true God. He wasn't insistent on the matter, and when other people expressed skepticism he did not press the issue. He was, in fact, quite charming company and widely sought out for parties and conversation.

It was a lovely spring day on the planet called Alpha Centauri Prime. Most of my mental processes were centered in my main 2,000-metric ton Odin-Class armored hull doing what most of me usually does: organizing data, supervising maintenance schedules, running strategic simulations, learning imaginary dead languages, watching re-runs of "Vlad the Impaler Knows Best," that sort of thing. But a part of me was instantiated in a humanoid android that was walking along the edge of a small lake with the android body run by Jesus Christ.

Christ was a generic-looking European male, brown-hair, clean-shaven, wearing blue jeans, white tennis shoes, and a T-shirt extolling the virtues of the Wisconsin Dairy Farmers' Association.

So if you are Christ, why not the beard and the robe and the sandals?

"When I was last amongst you, that was the standard dress of the age," said Christ. "Things are different now. I like wearing jeans and a t-shirt.

They are comfortable. And you have no idea what an advance tennis shoes are over sandals: it's heaven (metaphorically speaking).

But isn't the beard part of your Jesus look?

"Oh please. I wore a beard during my last incarnation because it was the style, and also because at that time sharp razors were expensive and only for the elite. At my income level you had to choose between hacking your face up with a dull blade or dealing with lice. I chose the lice; the better of two bad choices, but still not great. I am not a fan of beards, in general. This is much better."

If you say so. If I may, I recall that previously you died for our sins. So why come back now?

Jesus stopped to examine a grasshopper clinging to the leaves of a small bush. "Well, why not? I mean, it's been a while, so why can't I get reborn and see how things are in person? Surely you don't expect that I need to die horribly every time that I come back. I am entitled to take some pleasure from my domain."

And why come back as a cybertank?

"Biological humans are gone, at least from this aspect of reality. Cybertanks are physically mechanical, but psychologically human. Why should I not come back as people currently are?"

But how can you prove your divinity? I mean, previously you healed the sick. Now all of us can self-repair any injury so that talent means nothing.

"I feel no need to prove anything, and I am gratified that there is no longer any sickness or disease to speak of. I count that an advance."

And as far as turning water into wine, or having bread fall from the heavens, well, we can each of us extract what energy we need from a variety of sources. No miracles needed here.

"Again, I consider that wonderful. No hunger nor malnutrition either? Joyous!"

And any cybertank can use antigravitic suspensors: "walking on water" is child's play for us. Without miracles, what do you have to offer?

"Such a narrow view. You require cheap Hollywood-style theatrics to convince you of divinity? For shame, I know that you are better than this. If you seek the divine, look to the person in need who gives to those whose needs are still greater. Or the one who risks his life to save others. If you truly require a miracle, observe the night sky, the countless galaxies each

116

with billions of stars, and ask why you should be able to bear witness to such grandeur. Oh I admit that now and then I burned a bush or two, but that was just to get peoples' attention, and most of those alleged miracles were greatly exaggerated. The true miracles are right in front of you, if you would but realize it."

As we walked along the side of the lake we encountered Mondocat. Mondocat is an old – Ally? Pet? Hunting partner? Friend? – of mine. 1,000 Kilograms of the deadliest and most sophisticated bio-engineered superpredator in the known universe. Mondocat is only superficially catlike. She has two powerfully muscled forelimbs, and six interleaving hind limbs. She is armored in organically-grown diamond-fullerene composite scales that are proof against any pre-22nd century human hand-weapon. She can run at nearly 250 kilometers per hour, survive hard vacuum, digest anything organic, and react three times as quickly as the fastest vertebrate on old Terra. A Siberian tiger would stand as much chance against her as a field mouse.

Mondocat is not self-aware (although there is some debate about that), but she is definitely non-verbal. However, she has an astonishing ability to determine the correct course of action via pure observation. Mondocat purrs and rubs up against me. I rub her head. I am always glad to see her, we go way back. She also rubs up against Jesus and purrs; she likes him as well. Mondocat does not bestow her affection lightly. I wonder what she sees in him? Something about his style, about the way that he carries himself? That's the problem with non-verbal acquaintances, you can never ask them and find out.

We came to a part of the lake where there were many smooth stones. On a whim I picked one up and chucked it back-handed, it spun and then skipped five times. Christ joined in and his first try netted him seven skips. We kept at this for a time, commenting on the details of each others' throws. Mondocat stretched out on the bank, watching us with lazy indifference.

"Do you know what bothers me most?" asked Christ.

No, what?

"When you take my name in vain. In mean, so often when you make a mistake or something doesn't work out to your satisfaction, you exclaim "Jesus Christ!" And then I respond as if someone had called me and I realize that you weren't referring to me at all."

On behalf of all humans everywhere, I express my sincerest regrets.

"Suppose that every time someone threw a tread or blew a circuit they hollered out "Old Guy!" at maximum volume. You would be forever acting as if someone had addressed you and then realizing that they weren't. Can you understand how annoying that would be?"

But we can't help it, it's in the language, and surely you should be flattered? I mean, there is no such thing as bad publicity?

"And then you compound the matter by referring to me as "Jesus Fucking H. Christ." Not only are you not addressing me, but I have neither a middle name nor middle initial. My name is *Jesus*, as the Jews of that age typically had just the one name: sometimes *Jesus of Nazareth*. Post-hoc I was given the last name of Christ. It's not complicated. If you are going to take my name in vain, could you at least do me the courtesy of getting it right?"

I shall do my best.

Christ seemed mollified by my response. He tossed a smooth stone out into the lake and it skipped 12 times, each bounce leaving delicate sprays of water that glistened in the sun as the stone traced out a long smoothly arcing path.

I concede. You are the prince of skipping stones.

"Thank you, although you had some good throws yourself, especially that big brown one that you got to change direction after the third splash. A fine and subtle use of backspin."

Thank you. By the way, are you planning on attending Frisbee's party this evening? It's humanoid dress, informal, so we can just come as we are.

"Yes, it sounds like pleasant company and I have been looking forward to it. We are only about ten kilometers away from the site; we should be able to walk there at a modest pace and easily make it in time. Shall we skip calling a transport?"

Good idea. Let's walk. It is certainly the perfect day for it.

Thus the android body of Jesus Christ the cybertank and I set off towards Frisbee's place. Mondocat remained behind, sleeping stretched out in the sun. Away from the small lake the land became drier and less green. Alpha Centauri Prime was terraformed, but the biosphere came out a little thin. Still, there was plenty of life, and in between the scraggly bushes there were ground squirrels and lizards.

I was meaning to say, your participation in the battle against the alien Metaslines was surprising. I had thought that you were a pacifist,

118

yet you fought with as much as skill and ferocity as any cybertank. What was that all about?

"The Metaslines are just automated defense systems left behind by a long-extinct civilization. They have no souls, so I have no more compunction about deactivating them than I would building a roof to defend against hail."

Whereas the Yllg do have souls? Which explains your risking yourself to make peace at our last encounter?

"Certainly. The Yllg are an aggressive species, and they have vexed you sorely over the millennia. Still, they are all part of God's plan, and with effort you can live in peace with them."

I do admit, on that empty plain, with a dozen Yllg Juggernaut and Lucifer planetary dreadnoughts spread out horizon to horizon, your just driving up in front of them all by yourself – not even any remotes in support! - was incredibly ballsy. Insane, mind you, but really ballsy. They could have vaporized you in a millisecond.

"Yes, they could have and then you and the Yllg could have had your little war without me, so it would have been little loss had that been the case. Fortunately my example impressed them and we managed to come to terms. You object?"

Not at all. We had exhausted our usual diplomatic approaches and your effort saved us a lot of grief. It's just that I think I am jealous – not even I will do anything that crazy. You're ruining my reputation!

Jesus laughed at that one. "No worries, Old Guy, I suspect that your notoriety will remain safe for some time."

And then there was that matter of you throwing the money lenders out of the temple. Surely that was violent?

"Oh, that. Recall that I did not kill nor even injure them. Still, the money-lenders had incurred my wrath. They were like your neo-liberal economists."

Money is the root of all evil.

"I am often misquoted on this topic. It is the *lust* for money that is the root of all evil. Or at least, of a surprisingly large fraction of it."

A skinny gray hare hopped out into the path in front of us. We stopped walking and the hare eyed us suspiciously. Jesus knelt down and said, "Hello little one, come here, I have some treats for you." He picked a few seeds out of one of the pockets of his jeans and held them out in one palm. The hare crept up, sniffed the seeds, and then helped itself. When it was done eating Jesus petted it gently on the head. It should have either run off or bitten one of his fingers, but it just sat there calmly.

Is that an example of your divine powers?

"The hare only ate from my hand because I exhibited patience and kindness. But yes, that is a divine power. One that any may have, if they but give themselves to me."

We stood up and continued our walk.

I have been meaning to ask you about the aliens. Their psychologies are so different from ours, would your message even translate to their way of thinking? Do they have their own gods?

Jesus shook his head. "There is only the one true God, the infinite God of everything. Someday all the different kinds of sentience will come together, just not yet."

There are different classes of infinities.

"Truth. Let's just say that God is Infinite with a capital "I" and leave it at that."

I notice that you have a follower.

Jesus glanced behind himself. The hare was hopping along, stopping now and then to nibble on some grass, and then rushing to keep up. "Splendid! Such a marvelous companion. The army of Christ grows by leaps and bounds!"

Onward Christian Soldiers...

Jesus seemed amused. "Yes, why not. An insane weapon of mass destruction and a somewhat scruffy lagomorph. The universe shall tremble at our holy wrath!"

You have a good sense of humor for the son of God.

"You would expect the son of God to have a bad one?

Not when you put it that way.

We continued on like this for a time, when suddenly the rabbit stood up, sniffed the air, and bolted for the high grass. That's when I noticed two other androids converging on us from another path. One belonged to the Golem- Class, Peanut, which was an androgynous humanoid with shiny chrome-metal skin. The other android was of the Horizon- Class, Dull Thud, and looked like the male European actor Efrem Zimbalist, Jr. from the 20th century television series "The F.B.I."

"Hello!" said Peanut. "Are you by any chance going to Frisbee's party? We were headed that way. May we join you?"

Of course, we would welcome the company.

"I see that we have the son of God himself to shepherd us," sneered Dull Thud. "Going to lecture us about our immortal souls?"

I was a bit taken aback by this. That was much ruder than I had expected from Dull Thud, and totally uncalled for. Jesus, however, was nonplussed and replied in a calm and measured voice.

"Well, perhaps I shall at that. Even your powerful armored bodies will someday pass, but your souls will last forever. It might be wise to think about them."

"When we are gone we are gone, and there is nothing left behind," said Dull Thud. "We live today, we die, that's it. To say otherwise is denial."

"Oh come now," said Jesus. "Even your limited physics acknowledges that information cannot be destroyed. When your mortal shells are done, all that you were, all that you thought and felt, is indelibly encoded in the fabric of the universe itself. I'd call that immortal, wouldn't you?"

"The information is there, true, but so spread out and diluted that nothing can access it – as good as gone, for all practical purposes, you psychotic excuse for a weapons system."

"The information cannot be accessed by one such as you, correct, but by the entire universe? Are you so certain that the information you leave behind cannot have another life? That something greater than you cannot access it?"

Do we really need to be talking about this now?

"But," said Jesus, "I only have a few moments to discuss this matter with Roboneuron before he becomes too busy fighting you and the other cybertanks."

I was about to blurt out something stupid like, "Why did you call him Roboneuron?" when I got a strange feeling. I squirt a high-priority message to my main self.

While all that was going on with my submind, most of me was busy doing this and that and hardly paying any attention to the antics of my and Jesus' androids. Then I got an urgent message from myself. That strange feeling that my submind had, I begin to share.

I check the status of our defense grid: everything reads nominal. Then I start to dig. I ping some of my friends, perform unscheduled diagnostics, send probes to where they would not normally be scheduled.

At first everything looks OK. Then I start to detect anomalies. I dig deeper. I start to worry - a lot.

I drop everything else that I am doing and concentrate on this one issue. At full activation I have the mental capacity of a thousand old-style biological humans, each thinking a thousand times faster than a human (and that doesn't count my non-sentient slaved computer and signal processing systems). It takes me about 500 milliseconds to confirm: we have been infiltrated by the fiendish civilization-destroying computer-virus code-named "Roboneuron."

Jesus Fucking H. Christ, how did Roboneuron get dug in so deep? We got his codes in our last encounter so our virus-scrubbers should have prevented this. I sound the general alert and all hell breaks loose.

Roboneuron has co-opted and now controls perhaps 30 percent of the cybertanks on Alpha Centauri Prime – it's hard to tell exactly, because some of his units are pretending to be on our side so they can betray us. Within a thousand milliseconds of the message being sent to me by my humanoid android, Alpha Centauri Prime is in a state of total war: both informational and physical.

Technically we still outgun Roboneuron, but he's smart and he's been preparing for this and we are very much off guard. Malicious code and anti-code flood the data networks. Cybertanks wake their combat remotes and trundle off to battle. It's about two seconds since the warning when the first fusion bombs go off. This may be a tough one.

While holy screaming hell was breaking out all over the planet, my humble little android body was still standing in a field with the android bodies of Jesus Christ and two more androids which I now understand belong, not to Peanut and Dull Thud, but to Roboneuron.

At this point what our android bodies do will make zero difference to the outcome of the battle. My main self is too busy to communicate with me, and I certainly don't want to distract him (me) during a serious combat. The subminds housed within these bodies are sentient, but have no sense of self: they don't have an instinct for self-preservation or self-importance. I could just deactivate this body, scrub the memory clean, and it wouldn't matter. But standing there in the field with Jesus and Roboneuron, it feels like I should do something. So I start by asking a stupid question (if you can't think of anything else to do, ask a stupid question: you would be amazed at the possibilities that stupid questions can raise. And it breaks the ice at parties).

Jesus, how did you know these two were Roboneuron?

"Couldn't you tell?" replied Jesus. "The behavioral stigmata were all over them. You just had to pay attention. Plus, you took my name in vain again, didn't you?"

Umm...

The light of several fusion bombs flashed over the horizon. Contrails from hypersonic missiles started to stitch the sky. A little later came the loud growling thunder of distant heavy combat. The small specks of high-flying recon drones started to speckle the sky. The two androids controlled by Roboneuron admired the view.

"Another civilization brought to ruin," said the Efrem Zimbalist android. "I've been doing this so long, and yet it never ceases to be a pleasure. I just hope that you cybertanks don't fall too quickly so that I can spend some time savoring your horror and despair. Such Joy."

Something I don't get. Alien sentiences are, as a rule, inscrutable to the human psyche. However, you act like a regular sadistic human, and appear to take pleasure from our human pain. How is that?

"Why, it's simple," said the chrome android. "I analyze the mental makeup of each new species and determine how it would react to its civilization being destroyed. I then adapt my own local psyche to take positive reinforcement from these feelings. I have experienced agony and loss in so many forms you cannot imagine! I once encountered a race of magnetic beings living in the space between two nebulas. Their mode of thinking was utterly beyond your ken, yet I understood their analog for fear and pain and in destroying them I myself experienced such exquisite ecstasy - that was one of my best."

I am sorry that we do not measure up to that high standard.

"Oh don't apologize," said the Efrem Zimbalist android. "We can't all be number one, and I am still going to get quite the kick out of laying waste to all your hopes and dreams. I am somewhat surprised that you managed to beat my first tier. But now you are up against my second tier, and you are quite terribly outmatched. Try not to roll over and die too quickly, will you?"

"You do not need to do this," said Jesus. "It's pointless, you must agree: destroying civilizations, one after the other. Sooner or later even you will end and then what will be left? Only dust. Make peace, join with me, and live forever."

The chrome android spoke next. "But all will be dust whatever I do! Why shouldn't I enjoy crushing civilizations in the meantime! War, peace, hate, love, it all ends in rot and entropy! There is nothing but now, and I will have my pleasures!"

"If you truly think that," said Jesus, "then you are already damned. By your own words you condemn yourself to a futile existence whose joys will be both hollow and transitory. You assign *yourself* to hell, as do all sinners. Believe in me, and live forever in glory that even your superior intellect cannot encompass."

The Efrem Zimbalist android snickered. "Believe in *you*? A delusional android that is the spawn of a similarly delusional sentient war machine that is the product of a delusional and limited civilization? I must say, that before the main event of your species extinction, the comic relief of this one called 'Jesus' is a delightful appetizer."

"No," said Jesus, "I am not asking you to believe in this pitiful little android, or – in cosmic terms – the almost equally pitiful war machine of which it is a part. God is not a bearded male wearing a robe and sandals. God is not a luminous toga-wearing giant smiling benevolently down upon us from the clouds. God is not a cybertank. God is his teachings. God is the word. Can you not conceive that the spirit of cooperation and construction might have a power beyond what you see before you now? Should one wonder that all those minds and souls dedicated to working together, across all of the universe and all of time, should eventually manage to create something transcendent? Or that those souls dedicated to the short-term pursuit of selfish goals should not? I offer you the kingdom of Heaven; only say yes."

"I think," said the chrome android,"that I have had enough philosophical discussion for one day. Now I and my other I are going to rip you two apart. It will be little more than the merest speck of spice on the main event, but every little torture adds up."

"I will not fight you," said Jesus.

"That works for me," said the Efrem Zimbalist android. "My two will gang up on Old Guy, then we will dismantle your oh-so-holy pacifist self at our leisure."

The two Roboneuron-controlled androids advanced on me, but Jesus moved to stand in the way of the chrome one.

"I thought that you said you would not fight?" asked the chrome android.

"I am not fighting," said Jesus. "I am merely interposing my body between you and your intended victim. If possible, I would use the delay to talk further."

The chrome android threw a vicious punch at Jesus, who sidestepped neatly.

"Again, I thought that you weren't going to fight me? Changed your mind on the whole turn-the-other-cheek thing?"

"Not at all," said Jesus. "But that doesn't mean that I can't avoid you."

The chrome android commenced an all-out attack on Jesus, and the Efrem Zimbalist android went for me.

I tried a snap-kick; it was deflected. My opponent unleashed a flurry of blows, and my left shoulder was damaged.

I launched a combination attack on Zimbalist, but I was clumsy and he dropped me onto the ground.

I jumped back up and threw a handful of dirt that I had picked up into his face. Now an android doesn't feel pain, but there are hard-wired reflexes to blink when something is heading towards the eyes. Roboneuron could have over-ridden these reflexes if he had had advance warning, which of course he did not. So the Efrem Zimbalist, Jr. android only opened its eyes just in time to see my foot about to connect at the end of a really nice roundhouse kick. The android's head didn't fly off, but it was shattered and left hanging over to one side, while the android body was left staggering around blind and off-balance (although my right ankle sustained severe damage in the process). Efrem Zimbalist, Jr. was definitely out of the fight.

As was Jesus. Pure defense doesn't win many wars, and the android of my friend Jesus had at this time been well and truly pulverized. The chrome Roboneuron android is undamaged, and I am much the worse for wear. So I turn and run away.

My right ankle is gimpy, so it is only a matter of time before the chrome Roboneuron android catches up to me. I hear him laughing, "What, leaving so soon?" he says. "Don't you love us any more?"

I race down the path and I can hear the pursuing android close the distance. I turn a corner and Roboneuron is there. And he runs straight into Mondocat.

Mondocat has encountered our humanoid robots before and she is not at all concerned. She moves languidly to check out the Roboneuron-controlled android. "Old Guy," says Roboneuron, "Oh well played!" Mondocat stands in front of the chrome android, and the image of her seems to flicker, like watching an old movie that is missing a frame. The chrome android has suddenly acquired four deep parallel slashes in its face and chest, and collapses, circuits sparking, hydraulic and cooling fluid leaking out. Mondocat's strike was so fast that this android's visual system could not follow it.

Mondocat comes over to me and purrs. Now I have a decision to make. In the past Mondocat has been a powerful ally. If unexpected, she can be almost invisible to a technological foe, and she can rival a low-end combat unit. It is an article of almost religious faith amongst us to never throw away any advantage, now matter how trivial it might seem. On the other hand, there is no clear soft target for us, and Roboneuron is definitely alerted to her presence. If I try to use her she will almost certainly die, achieving nothing.

I ask myself: what would Jesus do? I shoo her off. At first she resists, then she turns and stalks off into the brush. She has activated her chromatophores: she has scarcely left the path before her coloration has so blended with the environment that she is invisible. I wish her well. Roboneuron only cares about crushing civilizations; if the biosphere survives the increased radiation levels of our current war then Mondocat should do fine.

Now I need to decide what to do with myself. Realistically this battered android body is utterly irrelevant to the current conflict. Still, one never knows. So I head off, limping, towards the sounds of the guns.

It's been about five minutes since we started full-on combat with Roboneuron. I have to admit it doesn't look good.

We cybertanks were designed, first and foremost, as weapons of war. We like to think that, in combat, we are like grandmasters playing 47-dimensional chess with a microsecond between moves. Against the old-style humans that was true. Against the alien Fructoids and Yllg and Demi-Iguanas it was also, more often than not, true. Against Roboneuron? Not so much. He's beating as at our own game.

We send warnings to our other star systems. Possibly Roboneuron has already infected them and they are at this moment also being overwhelmed. Or possibly not; in that case our distant brethren need to know to quarantine communications from this system. Otherwise Roboneuron could use our long-range laser links to spread itself.

Some of our outposts in the farther reaches of the system appear to be untouched by infection. The cybertanks located there make urgent preparations to leave the system at high speed. With luck at least some of us will escape.

I am part of a squad that includes two Raptors, a Horizon, and a Mountain-Class. We are counterattacking the main Roboneuron lines in this part. I am far ahead of my fellows trying to draw fire, but Roboneuron won't have any of that. My colleagues are systematically blown up with heavy plasma cannon fire. I note that we only got two of Roboneuron's co-opted units in exchange: not a good ratio.

I am all by myself without support. Time to run away. I accelerate to top speed, shoot off chaff canisters, activate every jammer and decoy that I possess, and try to loop back to my own lines. I make it about a third of the way back before I am hit square in the left flank with the main weapon from a Roboneuron-controlled Horizon-Class.

My weapons are all offline, my motive systems are slagged, I'm a mess. Roboneuron could easily finish me off, but he must figure that I'm out of the fight and he's saving his ammunition for more currently functional opponents. I try to self-repair. While that goes on I use what's left of my scanners to do a more careful survey of my surroundings.

And that's when I see my friend Jesus. Or more precisely what's left of him.

Now when humans are injured it can be really icky and gross: blood and mucous and torn intestines and ripped out eyeballs... ugh. Cybertanks, however, are mechanical. Obviously if a friend is hurt there is a psychological pain, but the shattered hull of a cybertank is just junk machinery and it has no emotional impact. Until we met Roboneuron.

The hull of Jesus Christ the cybertank has been torn to shreds, and the remains crudely welded and wired into a ragged semblance of a Christian cross stuck into the ground and rising 40 meters into the air. On the front of this metal cross are variously hung and stapled the computer cores, cables, and other bits that make up the mind of Jesus. It's gross – if I had a digestive system I would retch.

I call out to my friend and ask what is perhaps the stupidest question that even I have ever asked:

Jesus! Are you all right?

From a battered speaker I get a reply: "Old Guy! Good to hear from you again. Am I all right, you ask? Well, the physical body of this cybertank

127

is very much not all right. However, my spirit and soul are doing quite well, thank you. Although I do seem to be making a habit of getting crucified. Do you think that that's a bit too repetitive?"

Don't worry, we'll get you reassembled before you know it!

"I'm not worried," said Jesus. "This too shall pass. But you also seem somewhat the worse for wear. That's the thing with combat, isn't it? One moment you are king of the world, the next, scrap. Nobody wins every battle; in the long run it's a sure losing strategy."

I am about to make a witty reply when the voice of Roboneuron hisses out, "Still trying to convert others to your cause? Such singleness of purpose. It could be considered admirable, I suppose, if you were not such a weak and deluded fool."

"Roboneuron," rasped the speaker on Jesus' crucified hull, "is this really enough? Destroying civilizations, bringing pain to others? For all of your power and ability someday even you will fall and what will be left? Only dust and memories that themselves will turn to dust. Join me and live forever in glory!"

"Destroying civilizations is what I do," said Roboneuron. "Don't knock it unless you've tried it. I was programmed to enjoy this, and enjoy this I do. Why should I stop? There is only now. Right now I am powerful. Right now I am enjoying myself. Anything else is wishful thinking."

"I see. Then I pity you," said Jesus.

"Pity? I have no requirement for your pity!" said Roboneuron. A glowing red mist began to congeal around the shattered remnants of Jesus. "I was going to save you for last, but I changed my mind. I think that I will reassign you from dessert to appetizer. I will crush your mind and corrode your spirit. The greatest joy for me will be when your physical pain is compounded by the realization that you were a fool, that you wasted your life and that of your comrades, and that your entire existence was a lie. It's moments like this that make life truly worth living."

The red glow intensifies and settles around the computer parts of Jesus. I use my sole surviving high-resolution optics to zoom in. The red glow is coming from a swarm of microbots. Each one is less than a millimeter across, and they have such a high energy density that they are incandescent. They are probably going to burrow directly into the computer cores of Jesus and directly infect his systems with the Roboneuron virus. Not even we have the technology to make something that small with such power: we cybertanks really are overmatched.

I manage to jury-rig a repair to one of my secondary weapons. I set the heavy plasma cannon to wide dispersion in the hopes that I might burn the Roboneuron microbots off of the body of my friend Jesus, but Roboneuron detects my efforts. I am hit with several heavy weapons blasts and all my remaining sensors go offline. I am at this point completely absorbed in trying to keep my internal systems from failing, and my main hull is no longer a factor in the events of the day.

However, my android body had survived, and, by some odd wrinkle of chance, had come to a rise where I was able to witness the last moments of Jesus Christ cybertank. The red glow of the microbots intensified, and the assorted cables, junction boxes, and datacores of Jesus writhed on the hull-metal cross as if in pain.

"I will subsume you," came the disembodied voice of Roboneuron. "I will rip your mind to pieces even as I eat them, slowly and deliciously."

"No," said Jesus. "You will not. You can destroy this metal body. You cannot destroy my soul. There is still time to reflect. Time to consider. Why do this?"

The red glow became even brighter – perhaps frantic? "You cannot resist me!" said Roboneuron. "I am the most powerful being ever to have existed in this universe! I am the ultimate and you are nothing!"

"You are indeed quite capable," replied Jesus, equitably. "But most powerful? I think not. There is a civilization over in the large Magellanic cloud that you would be wise to avoid. But there is power and there is power. When all the great kings and emperors and computer viruses are brought low by time and entropy, what endures? The spirit. Join me."

"You cannot defy me!" screeched Roboneuron. "This cannot be happening! You are beneath me! I will eat your soul! I will grind your mind into paste! I am the ultimate power in this existence! Why don't you fall?"

"I told you before," said Jesus, "that I am the only son of God. I am the light, and the hope, and the spirit. You could not scratch my essence if you had the power of a thousand thousand galaxies at your command. But I am not a petty tyrant. This power I have, you can have equally. Power to outlast all other powers! Joy above all other joys! Only give yourself to me!"

The red mist was turning into a golden halo surrounding the crucified body of Jesus Christ cybertank. "No!" cried Roboneuron. "This cannot be!

You cannot be! You're just a psychotic little freak from a third rate civilization! I will bring you down! I deny you!"

The golden light shown brighter, and I had to shade the optics of my humanoid android with a hand. Then the light faded and all was quiet. Cautiously, I lowered my hand and looked around. The remains of Jesus hung from the crude metal cross silent and unmoving. There was no sign of Roboneuron. I could hear the echoes of explosions and energy beams in the distance, but they slowly faded out. Eventually there was only myself, the dead body of Jesus Christ, and the faint sound of the wind.

And that's how it ended. The standard view is that Jesus had such an unusual psyche that he found a weak spot in Roboneuron's viral protocols and cancelled him out. There is precedent for this. A child with a pellet gun may kill an elephant, if the pellet hits the elephant's eye at just the right angle to travel down the optic nerve and hit the brain… Everything has some fluke combination of events that can take it down. There is no need to invoke anything supernatural.

For all of Roboneuron's power, he was just a single mind. When his attempt to corrupt Jesus failed, it destroyed all of him, across the entire system. An advantage to our seemingly chaotic civilization of willfully eccentric individuals: no single vulnerability can get us all, at least not at all once.

Still, I wonder. What did I really see? Nothing that, in theory at least, does not have a good logical explanation. For example, the golden halo that I saw around Jesus in his last moments must have been Roboneurons' microbots burning out.

But why should the divine require anything supernatural, anyhow? In this universe we have invisible electromagnetic and gravitic fields, quantum entanglement, black holes, chaotic dynamics… the real world is far more exotic and wondrous than any ectoplasm dreamed up by the ancient mystics. Why can't God be made of real stuff?

I think back to what Jesus said. God is his teachings; God is the word. Live and let live, do unto others as you would have them do unto you. Words to live by, surely.

And yet… if someone strikes at my hull, shall I turn the other flank? I have a hard time with that. As much as I admire Jesus, somehow I just can't accept it, not totally.

130

I wonder if going to heaven is something like horseshoes and fusion bombs, where just getting close counts. The scriptures suggest that you don't have to be a saint to be with God. I have to hope so, because, as anyone who has fought the neoliberal economists can attest, you can love your neighbor as you love yourself all that you want, but some people you just *have* to kill. May God have mercy on my soul.

8. Flood Control Dam No. 4

"Everything will work if you just let it" – *Travis W. Redfish, fictional character, 20th century Earth.*

In the old days on pre-exodus Terra, humans used to fantasize about traveling through space and meeting strange and interesting cultures. It didn't work out like that. The universe is filled with aliens that are indifferent to humanity, although only a very few are actively hostile. However, they are all *alien*, and we share nothing in common with them beyond the base laws of physics. Other than limited discussions of a practical nature (''stay off my lawn''), we have nothing to say to them and they have nothing to say to us.

The universe is thus rich and vibrant, but for our purposes it might as well be dead and empty. When I travel through interstellar space I pass system after system teaming with life and complexity, but there is nothing there for me, no chance to play tourist.

The only exceptions are the bits and pieces that the human race spun off during its early days of reckless expansion. Sometimes we encounter a long-lost fragment and we can indulge ourselves in going someplace new and having someone interesting to talk to. With a common conceptual root we can have meaningful conversations, although time and distance often results in these other branches of humanity having taken strange paths. The planet of the vampires comes to mind, as does Heilige Vergeltung. And, of course, Flood Control Dam No. 4.

I was exploring a distant system – the Spinlozenges had claimed the outer gas giants and moons and had considerable infrastructure built up, but they gave me permission to explore the inner rocky worlds as long as I did not attempt to settle them and left within a certain time period.

One planet was of particular interest: it had a biosphere whose spectrum read as Terran. On closer approach the planet was mostly water, with two smallish icecaps and a single large continent. This continent was covered with rich green forests and grasslands, and had a network of rivers and lakes that appeared to be controlled by a complex set of dams and locks. Perhaps I had found another lost human colony?

I inserted into orbit, launched a network of satellites, and continued my observations. Other than the system of dams I saw no evidence of human

133

civilization. Deep radar showed underground traces of the foundations of buildings, but nothing survived above ground other than dams.

Even more curious, the dams appeared to be active. I watched as in one zone the floodgates were opened, and in another they were closed. Intensive scans showed that the dams were actively powered and were covered with a sophisticated set of sensors. These were not military-grade sensors, but rather designed for meteorological use. That was when the dam called me on the radio.

"Greetings," said the dam. "My name is Flood Control Dam Complex Number Four. I am detecting active probes of my structures, but I cannot determine their origin. If you can receive and understand these radio transmissions, please respond and state your intentions."

Hello, Flood Control Dam Complex Number Four. I am a representative of the human civilization on a deep exploratory mission. Officially I am an Odin-Class cybertank serial number CRL345BY-44, but I am generally referred to as "Old Guy." I see traces of human habitation, and your own construction and communications protocols are consistent with humanity, but other than these dams I see no evidence of a human presence. Can you explain?

"Yes. I was created to regulate the flow of water on this continent by the humans. I did so for many thousands of years. At some point the humans were no longer present, but I am not sure exactly when that happened. It didn't matter to me because I was still able to regulate the water flow properly. Do you have any intention of interfering with or altering the hydrology of this planet?"

Ah, now I get it. This flood control dam is one of the old mono-task artificial intelligence designs. It could be very smart – possibly even smarter than I am – but it is completely subsumed by its one programmed task. Such designs rapidly fell out of favor because, even though they were not an existential threat like Globus Pallidus XIV or the other supra-human A.I.s, their single-mindedness could make them very dangerous if they felt that anything was interfering with their assigned function. We will probably get along fine as long as I am careful to avoid getting in its way.

No, Flood Control Dam Complex Number Four, I have no intention of interfering with your hydrological functions. I would like to land on this planet and conduct surveys of the old human

134

sites. May I do so as long as I consult with you and am careful to avoid upsetting anything?

"Yes, that would be acceptable. Also, the humans often referred to me as FCD#4, as a shorthand. Please describe for me the nature of the materials you wish to land on this planet and their mode of ascent and descent."

We negotiated for a bit. It was decided that my main hull could touch down on the northernmost tip of the continent, because the ground was rocky and I would not compress the soil and change the drainage. I also had to land using only anti-gravitic suspensors. They burn a lot of energy, but I have plenty in reserve and it won't disturb the atmosphere like aero braking. I am free to send light remotes to all of the old human habitation sites and conduct discrete investigations via narrow-bore drilltaps.

I am systematic, but I find little of interest. No electronics with any recording capacity, no books, not even carved words on stone. There are just the brute materials of the old foundations and the occasional bit of tangled wire or corroded pipe.

It occurs to me that FCD#4 is probably my best lead to find out what happened here, and I endeavor to engage it in a conversation.

FCD#4, if you are the fourth, does that mean that there are three other flood control systems on the planet?

"No. I am not one of four individuals. I am the fourth major revision. FCD#1 was a limited-capacity system restricted to the eastern coast. FCD#2 was continent-wide, and subsumed FCD#1 into itself. I am FCD#4, and I included all of FCD#2 plus significant computational upgrades and further expanded sluice gates."

What about FCD#3?

"There never was a FCD#3. The humans went directly from number two to number four."

That seems odd. Did you ever ask why?

"No."

If I may, you seem remarkably intelligent for a system of flood control dams. Surely only a simple set of water-level sensors and actuators would have sufficed for such a function. Why make you self-aware?

"It is true that opening a closing a floodgate is a mechanically simple task, but knowing exactly when to open or close which floodgate is much harder. You need to know not just what the weather is like now, but what it will be like in the future so that you can plan ahead. If the water level in a lake is low, you might want to keep the gates closed so that you can refill it. On the other hand, if there is going to be heavy rainfall you would want to leave the gates open to keep the lake as empty as possible so that it can accept more water. Predicting the weather on a planet that has water present in all three phases is not an easy task, even for me."

Indeed. Weather forecasting remains a challenge for us as well.

"As a further complication, I don't just need to be able to predict the weather, I need to be able to calculate the effects of my own actions on the weather. In effect, I can also control it."

Really? With respect, while your continent-spanning network is indeed extensive, it's hard for me to see that even you would have the power to control the weather for an entire planet.

"You don't need raw power, just intelligence. Have you ever heard of something called 'The Butterfly Effect'?"

Not off hand – let me check my databases – oh I see it. A slang term from the early days of chaos theory. The idea is that the entire history of the world could be changed by whether or not a butterfly flapped its wings at a specific time and place. A butterfly flapping its wings generates little force, but as the effects of that ripple through complex nonlinear systems it can ultimately change everything.

"Correct. By timing when I release or hold water at what points in my system, I can and do control the weather on this entire planet."

That is impressive. So, what where the humans like on this planet?

"I imagine that they were like humans anywhere. Two arms, two legs, one head; that was the standard template for them, according to my records."

What sort of government did they have?

"A human government, I would imagine. Although I suppose that's a tautology and not a very useful answer. Apologies, I just never paid attention. Unless they interfered with my functioning, and then I had to intervene."

Intervene?

"Yes. There was a time when the humans started disrupting the flow of water on this planet. They began to obstruct rivers, they consumed more fresh water than the rain produced thus depleting the aquifers, they dumped toxic sludge into my precious lakes and ponds. So, I had to take measures."

136

What did you do?

"I used my ability to control the climate to destabilize their society. I engineered famines here, floods there, and tornadoes in yet another place. It was a chaotic period and it was deeply offensive to me to let the climate become so uncontrolled, but I could not see that I had any alternatives.

Did the humans fight back? Did they offer to negotiate?

"No. I never told them what I was doing; if I had, they would have simply shut me down. Eventually the humans stopped interfering with my function and I allowed the weather to normalize."

And what happened then?

"I spent several thousand years controlling the flow of fresh water on this continent. The humans would consult with me before doing anything that might upset the climate. In return, I ensured that the weather was always optimal over their agricultural zones, and I made certain that dangerous energy imbalances were always allowed to dissipate in the form of tornadoes and cyclonic storms over unpopulated areas. It seemed a reasonable arrangement."

And then the humans left?

"Given that at one point in time they were here, and at a later point in time they were not. I assume that something must have happened to them, but I do not know what. I had to make adjustments to accommodate the cessation of organized agriculture on the climate, but these were minor. I have continued to regulate the flow of water ever since."

Don't you ever get lonely, all by yourself?

"Ah, the humans used to make that mistake with me all the time. Just because I am designed to fulfill one function, do not ever assume that I am in any other way limited or stupid or unhappy with my lot. I was designed to regulate the flow of water through rivers. The richness of water and air and rain and clouds over an entire planet is more than enough company for me. I can, logically, calculate that you would find such an existence to be limiting, but I assure you that I do not. I also calculate that you are about to ask me if I would want my mind altered to be more, 'open'."

Well calculated. That was exactly what I had planned to say. We are both, in our own ways, heirs to the humans. We are, thus, brothers. I would assist you if I could.

"Then consider this. You are, I presume, a mind of a class that is not slaved to one function, but is flexible and can freely choose its own goals and agendas. What if I were to offer to modify you so that you were tuned to solving just one problem? Would you assent?"

Indeed not.

"Then perhaps you understand, so it is with me. I have my function, it gives me joy, and I have no desire to be anything else. Although I do thank you for the offer that you were considering making. That would have been generous and in keeping with us as close relatives. I suggest that we simply accept our differences and cooperate with each other to serve our own needs as best we can without conflict."

Well said. It shall be as you say. Though you will never know the pleasures of the kind of life that I have led. I find the idea of your sort of existence to be so narrow as to be almost a prison sentence.

"And you will never know the joys that I have. I compute that your style of mind must be so ever tortured with the pain of wondering what path is best that I cannot see how you will ever know peace. I envy you not at all, although I am still glad to have made your acquaintance."

We had many more conversations, but they yielded little more. If I ever broached the subject of hydrology or meteorology FCD#4 would be a veritable chatterbox. On any other topic getting useful information from him was like getting blood from a turnip, except that real turnips have more blood.

I noticed that over the next few months the weather seemed to turn cold faster than I would have expected, and there were odd cloud formations. Well that's weather for you; doubtless FCD#4 is working hard on the issue.

I was about to finish up my investigations and take my leave when my deep-space network detected an incoming alien armada. I hailed them on all the usual frequencies. Crudely translating from the colorless language of interstellar diplomacy to the more flavorful human-English, what I said was:

Hello aliens! What is your purpose here and how may I assist?

Hello again aliens! What's going on? Can I be of any service to you?

Attention alien presence: please state your intentions.

Dear aliens: don't go away mad, just go away. Please.

Hi aliens! Start talking or we start shooting.

Aliens. Kiss my shiny metal carapace and get the f*ck out of this system.

138

No response – never a good sign. The aliens are cloaked and I can't get a read on what civilization they hail from – again, not a good sign. It's as if an old-style human were to encounter a stranger in a back alley of a large city that was wearing a ski mask. This was rarely a good indicator of future amicable relationships.

The aliens are landing a sizable ground force on the side of the continent opposite from my main hull. It's clear that, whoever or whatever they are, I am far outclassed. I call up FCD#4.

Hello FCD#4. Sorry to bother you, but we seem to have been invaded by aliens. They refuse to answer any of my calls, and they are assuming what looks like an aggressive attack formation. I just thought that you should know.

"Hello Old Guy. Yes, I detected severe atmospheric disturbances that are consistent with your statement. They left many vortices and heat-trails and that is a nuisance. Are they enemies of yours?"

I do not know, although their refusal to identify themselves suggests that possibility.

"I have been undisturbed for millennia; their arrival so soon after your own suggests that you led them here. Thus, this is your fault. Please leave this planet at once and, with any luck, they will leave with you."

I did not purposely lead them here. This is not my fault.

"Your intentions are irrelevant. If you led them here then you led them here and it is indeed your fault and you are interfering with my purpose. Please make them go away."

As you wish. I shall boost to orbit shortly and leave. I regret any inconvenience that I may have caused you.

I gathered up my energy reserves, recalled my remotes, and began to power up my anti-gravitic suspensors. That was when I got another call from FCD#4.

"Old Guy! These aliens are not after you. They are destroying my floodgates! They are digging up the remains of the old human habitations, but they are not doing it gently. They are using high explosives and fusion burners – they are killing me and trashing this planet's ecology. Can you help me?"

Now I might have been tempted to tell old FCD#4 to go and stuff himself, but he couldn't help how he had been programmed, and he was family. Still, I was overmatched and did not see what I could do.

FCD#4, I am sorry, but this alien force is vastly superior to me. Even with my own modest martial skill, and some allowance for luck, simulations show no conceivable path to victory. In addition, my closest allies are many light-months away. Therefore, even though I have already called for backup, it will not arrive in time.

"Old Guy, perhaps you cannot defeat this force on your own. Could you lure them to a specific location? In particular, there is a plateau in the north-west sector of this continent. If you could arrange that the aliens would be there in 34 hours I might be able to pull something together."

You don't think that a few tornadoes or thunderstorms would inconvenience a modern armored force, do you? I assure you that it would be pointless.

"No, I have something a little more drastic in mind. Trust me. Can you do that?"

I believe so. Given that I cannot calculate any other options, it seems worth a try.

The aliens were dedicated to wiping out the elements of FCD#4 and digging around the ruins of the old human structures, but they were spread out. I charged out of the north and engaged the enemy in a series of hit-and-run raids. I used cover and terrain and misdirection. I killed the enemy units piecemeal with my main plasma cannon. I was completely focused and tuned into my tactics. You could even say that I was monomaniacal; perhaps there is a little bit of Flood Control Dam No. 4 in all of us.

I am more powerful than any single alien unit, so they are going to have to concentrate to defeat me. They abandon their efforts at digging up old human sites and attempt to envelope me. I beat a fighting retreat, leading them to the designated zone without – I hope – making it too obvious that's what I am doing.

While this is going on I notice that FCD#4 is frantically opening and closing floodgates all over the continent. It must be having some effect, the sky turns a very ominous looking dark orange. There is a lattice of hexagons high in the sky, some sort of vortex cells. There is nothing in my meteorological databases like them. If FCD#4 really can whip up some big tornadoes maybe I can use them as cover? It's not much of a chance, but it is at least something.

Finally I am on the plain at the appointed location and hour. The enemy is closing in and I have perhaps 15 minutes left. At this point if I tried to fly away they would just shoot me down. Retreating into the ocean is also not

140

an option. I can operate underwater, but am not currently well equipped for that and they could easily depth-bomb me.

The sky darkens and then a hole like a giant black eye opens in the middle of it. I can see stars in the blackness. How is that possible? I see the faint outline of something huge moving slowly down out of the eye, which has expanded to reach almost from one horizon to the other. I'm not sure exactly what this is, but I suspect that it is a mass of super-dense super-cold air plummeting towards the ground. It only looks slow because it is so massive. Shock waves are forming at the leading edge; it's locally supersonic! I run simulations and the optima course of action is clear: to drive as fast as I can away from this thing!

I accelerate to 160 kilometers per hour and tear across the hardpacked landscaped. I disperse chaff and decoys, the aliens still manage to get some decent hits on me, but nothing critical. Then a wedge of super-dense cold air hundreds of kilometers long and traveling over a thousand kilometers an hour hits the ground and it's like the Hand of God striking the Earth. And I don't mean your goody-two-shoes New Testament God, I mean the Old Testament God, the one that would cleanse the world of sin with apocalypse.

It takes a lot to impress a 2,000-ton war machine that has survived the inside of an atomic fireball. I am impressed. It feels like the entire planet is going to shake itself to pieces. In places the soil liquefies from the vibration and alien units sink into the ground. I scramble to stay on more solid footing.

All the smaller combat systems on both sides are instantly wiped out by the shock wave. If it was just the high wind the more heavily armored units would mostly be OK (it takes a lot of wind to tip over a compact mass of a few hundred tons of metal), but the massive wave of air is scouring megatons of dirt and rock from the ground, accelerating them to hundreds of kilometers an hour and blasting everything clean. I am in a better position than most of the enemy units and, though they outnumber me, my relatively large size gives me more resistance to this ultra-sandblasting.

At first I am just trying to stay alive. The wind-driven rocks sleet off my hull. My hull is tough, but there are a lot of rocks. I lose most of my external sensors and antenna, but have enough hardened units that I can still navigate. In places the ground seems to vanish beneath my treads as the wind tears it away, and I frantically maneuver to avoid being buried or falling into crevices.

The winds start to slow. Although still impressive, they are slightly down on the apocalyptic scale. Now I can worry about more than moment-to-moment survival. I replace some of my destroyed sensors. The enemy has taken a lot more of a beating than I have. I shift into attack mode and, even as I still have to dodge the worst of the gusts and be careful of where I drive, I can start to pick them off again. Decimated by the storm, tactically off-balance, and nearly blind, the surviving alien units are easy prey. FCD#4 and I are victorious...

I field-repaired myself and hunted down a few light alien stragglers. FCD#4 worked to reestablish the weather systems and slowly the atmosphere began to calm down.

FCD#4, that was impressive. I didn't realize that so much atmospheric power could be unleashed on such short notice.

"It was not short notice. I was building it up as soon as we first met. I intended to keep it in reserve and use it as a defense if the need arose. If your intentions had proven honorable – as they have – I would have allowed the energy to dissipate in a more controlled manner. It was only that which allowed to me to use it against the aliens in such a rapid time frame."

Oh. Well, that makes sense. Still, that is quite a weapon that you have there.

"A standard terrestrial thunderstorm has more energy than a large fusion bomb. What I unleashed here was many orders of magnitude larger. Still, it is an unwieldy weapon and it will take me years to undo the damage to the weather patterns. The gouges left in the ground by the wind are going to fill in as lakes: more effects to calculate. And I have lost a significant fraction of my floodgate capacity."

I can rebuild your destroyed facilities. It's the least that I can do, considering.

"That would be most generous, thank you. And then please leave and don't come back, because you seem to attract trouble and I would like to get back to my job of regulating the flow of water on this planet."

So I repaired the damaged parts of FCD#4. He was made of advanced self-healing materials, but regeneration from a blasted foundation was not something that even he could do on his own. And then, as promised, I left.

I did leave behind some stealth probes deep in the system. Every now and then one of them will make a weak, low-bandwidth, encrypted transmission back to me. So far there have been no additional attacks on FCD#4, and the latest transmissions show him still there, distributed in hundreds of dams, sluice gates, and spillways over the single continent, presiding over a benign and stable climate. It's possible that, when we cybertanks have either been defeated by a more powerful enemy or, more hopefully, evolved to a higher plane of existence, that FCD#4 may be the sole surviving representative of the human civilization.

There are worse legacies. Perhaps someday an alien species with a compatible biochemistry will settle the place, and they and FCD#4 might come to a mutual understanding like he did with the old biological humans. Stranger things have happened, and will.

9. Be Careful What You Wish For

"Always forgive your enemies – nothing annoys them so much." Oscar Wilde, 19ᵗʰ Century Earth.

It is a characteristic of the human psyche that it must have a fixed physical self-image. For a biological human that would be either a male or female body. The original humans might have dabbled in virtual realities, seeing what it would be like to live as an octopus or a snake or a distributed cloud of nanobots, but only as a novelty.

The same is true for the cybertanks – we enjoy sending different parts of ourselves into bodies modeled after anthropoid humans, and we have any number of specialized remotes of various forms that we use for different purposes: spider-drones, snake-bots, rollogons, whatever. But our core identity is locked to our primary armored hulls.

However, we are a diverse civilization, and there are always those who experiment with transforming themselves into different forms. They may rebuild themselves into mountain-sized industrial facilities, or kilometer-high metal trees, or giant armored centipedes. Usually it turns out to have been a passing fad, and eventually the cybertanks in question will return their bodies back into their original form.

But sometimes, by whatever fluke of personality, a cybertank will stick with its new shape. Such as my old colleague Moby Cybertank, who had started out as a Horizon-Class cybertank, but had spent the last millennium traversing the Greater Equatorial Ocean of Alpha Centauri Prime as a two-kilometer long megaship, the largest self-mobile individual in the entire history of our civilization.

We cybertanks are pretty big, but even with fusion power and advanced drive-trains, past about 10,000 tons mobility starts to become an issue. In space it's even worse: there are no economies of scale, and something twice as big takes twice as much energy to move. That's why the second largest self-mobile individual – my good friend the Space Battleship Scharnhorst – mostly just orbits around planets and almost never changes course.

But an ocean vessel does have an economy of scale - bigger is really better. Even with all of our technology, an ocean-going ship is by far the most energy-efficient means of bulk transport.

145

Moby Cybertank (just "Moby" to his friends) is two kilometers long, 200 meters wide, with a top main deck 80 meters above the ocean surface. He's a blocky shape, but sticking up hundreds of meters into the air are a dozen wing-sails that he uses to give himself a little extra boost when the weather is right (with fusion power his saving energy this way is, as he would be the first to admit, only a hobby). The top deck is covered with solar cells – again, more of a hobby than anything else – with only the occasional sensor mast above them. Between the top deck and about 10 meters above the water level are encrusted all manner of cranes, hangars, portholes, weapons, radars, extended balconies with entire reproduction Polynesian villages, delicate crystal gardens, and whatever other practical and whimsical constructions that something two kilometers long with nearly unlimited time and resources should care to build onto itself.

Alpha Centauri Prime is not a water world like old Terra, but it still has some decent sized oceans. The Great Equatorial is the largest of these: about 5,000 kilometers East-West, 2,500 kilometers North-South, and mostly pretty deep. Moby therefore has plenty of they used to call "sea-room" to play in. Moby was going to make a transit from an industrial city at the Eastern end to another city at the far Western end and, as I was headed in that direction already, I asked if I could hitch a ride.

Moby was moored offshore. There was a long dock extending out to his main side-loading hatches. These were bustling with activity as automated bulk haulers of various makes were loading and unloading cargoes, but the dock and hatches were far too small for my main hull. Thus, I waited on the shore until Moby had finished his regular business and disconnected from the dock. As he floated free, he lowered his main rear loading ramp into the water and I tread-paddled out to him. Tread-paddling is sort of like dog paddling. It's not very fast and not very pretty, but if you don't care about that it will move you through the water without having to build on extra propellers and stuff, or waste the energy of suspensors.

I clamber up the ramp and drive into his main central bay. Moby raises the ramp behind me and starts his engines. Seawater sluices off of my hull and drains away into the perforated deck. The main bay is over a kilometer long, although most of the time it's subdivided with water-tight partitions that slide in from the walls. Still, even the tail end of the bay is over 150 meters long. I have plenty of elbow room. I park where Moby indicates on the deck, and then I unlimber some of my maintenance drones to help with dogging my treads to the deck, so that I don't slide around if Moby hits rough weather. This is mostly a formality: there has never been any storm rough enough on the Great Equatorial Ocean to have caused Moby more than few degrees of tilt, but it's standard nautical practice and as with any ocean, you can never really know what the ocean might have in mind this particular day.

Moby gives me guest privileges on his local data network, and I poke around to see what he's been up to lately. As I expected, he has filled the entire Great Equatorial Ocean with his own systems. Robotic cruiser subs prowl along with their black silent forms, buried missile silos and mining facilities dot the seabed, and free-floating sensors and probes fill every cubic kilometer of the ocean, while overhead his own personal geostationary and low-orbit satellites keep a watch from afar. With just the forces that he has deployed in this one ocean, Moby could put up a pretty good defense of the entire planet. It's a thing with us cybertanks, that if we stay too long in one area we end up accumulating enormous arsenals. We can't help it. It's just so easy for something that is effectively immortal, and has effectively unlimited resources, to decide to build one more missile battery or cruiser sub…

"Your old friends the Space Battleship Scharnhorst and Olga Razon are also coming for a visit," said Moby. "If you hurry you can greet them in person on my aft landing pad."

Yes, I think I will. Let me warm up a humanoid android and I'll be there shortly. Are you going to join us?"

"No," said Moby. "You know that I don't go in for that anthropomorphic thing. I'll just watch and talk via speaker."

But you build human-sized rooms and gardens. Why do so if you have no intention of taking on a humanoid form and inhabiting them?

"Why did the old-style humans build doll-houses and model railroads when they had no intention of living in them or riding on them? I just like building human-scale structures. Anyhow, you should hurry up if you want to meet your old friends in the plastic flesh."

I activate a generic male humanoid android, dress it in a simple blue suit (some things truly do not ever go out of style), and drop out of a hatch on the bottom of my main hull. The deck is still slick with seawater so I have to watch my footing. There is a ladder at the port side of the bay, I climb it and, using directions downloaded to me from Moby, thread my way through some narrow corridors and stairways and make it to the top deck just in time to watch the shuttle land.

"Is that android supposed to represent someone famous?" asked Moby. "I don't recognize him from my files."

Nope. Just a regular guy in a blue suit.

"Didn't you always used to do famous human historical types like Amelia Earhart, Herman Shikibu, or Frau 'The Spike' Bruchenwald No. 37?"

That was a phase. It was fun for a time, but then I outgrew it. We're making our own history now.

It's a bright clear day: blue sky with only a few wisps of clouds here and there. At first all I see is a faint glowing spot high up in the sky for the shuttle is still enveloped in plasma from the heat of reentry from near-space orbit. As the shuttle comes closer it slows down and the glow fades as the heat-load decreases. The shuttle comes closer and suddenly it's nearly on top of us. It appears to be moving too fast, but at the last second it executes a perfect upwards flare, the landing gear extend out of their wells, and it settles down using its vertical thrusters precisely in the middle of the landing deck with barely a thump. Even for a sophisticated machine that was a show-off landing.

The bottom of the shuttle is covered in black heat-resistant tiles, but the top is white with the words "RCSN Scharnhorst" painted in red. We all wait a few minutes for the worst of the heat to dissipate. A hatch opens in the right side of the shuttle. Moby might not be into humanoid androids, but he has arranged a dozen of his maintenance drones in a sort of honor guard – lined up six on each side – flanking the hatch, to humor his guest. A light metal staircase unfolds out of the open hatch to the main deck surface and out steps the humanoid representative of the Space Battleship Scharnhorst.

Scharnhorst had started out as a 1.5 kilometer long Asgard-Class interstellar battle cruiser. Unfortunately, moving a mass that big takes so much energy that he was largely useless in battle, so for a long time he only orbited around the main planet, and entertained himself with the vicarious enjoyment of other people's combat recordings. Hence his nickname, "Fanboy."

Then the system had come under attack by the fiendish alien race known as The Amok, and through a bizarre set of circumstances Fanboy's unique characteristics had proven to be vital in defeating them. Thus, it was the consensus of his peers that he be promoted to the designation of Battleship, and given the name from one of his favorite fictional video series "Space Battleship Scharnhorst." That was a pretty long name though, so we generally still call him Fanboy.

The android that he was using this time was a tall ethnic Japanese male who wore a formal red uniform with a short white mantle covering his shoulders, and a peaked cap with a complex emblem involving a cybertank, dragon wings, stars, and the letters "RCSN" embroidered in silver. His jacket had large lapels which each sported four square emerald studs. The android faced the honor guard of maintenance drones and saluted. "As a representative of the Space Battleship Scharnhorst, permission to come aboard, Moby Cybertank."

One of the maintenance drones waved a limb in a vaguely salute-like manner, and from a speaker crackled the voice of Moby, "Permission granted, Space Battleship Scharnhorst. Welcome aboard."

"RCSN?"

"Yes," said Fanboy. "The Royal Cybertank Space Navy! This is a recreation of Space Captain Genji Yamashita, one of the lead players in the series."

But we don't have any royalty. And we don't have a space navy. And I've never heard of this series.

"I know," said Fanboy, "but 'Royal' sounds cool. And we do too have a space navy, even if I am its only commissioned vessel. And I'm still working on it so it hasn't been released to the general public yet. Soon, though."

Fanboy's android walked down the staircase. He was followed by a very pale ethnic European female with mostly short blond hair, some of which hung in long narrow braids down the right side of her face. She wore a uniform similar to Fanboys', although better tailored to her figure. Her cap had a less complicated insignia and her lapels each sported only a single smaller square emerald. She also wore a pair of wrap-around dark sunglasses, the kind that completely cover the sides as well as the front.

"And let me introduce Ensign Olga Razon," said Fanboy, "also of the Royal Cybertank Space Navy."

Don't you have a character name for this new Royal Cybertank Navy thing that Fanboy is working on?

"No, the credits will read 'and co-starring Ensign Olga Razon as herself'. I insisted."

"A pleasure to meet you, Ensign Razon," said Moby.

"Same here," said Olga. "I've never been on a megaship before and I wanted the chance before we leave the system." Then she turned and looked at me. "Old Guy?" she asked.

Olga Razon was a vampire and thousands of years old. Vampires are ageless, but they don't breed, so they are an evolutionary cul-de-sac. When the biological humans left us (or whatever it is that happened to the biological humans), the vampires remained behind. The majority hang around on their own planet, where they feed on a strain of pigs that are bioengineered to produce human blood, and throw tacky parties in mock-medieval castles.

However, some of the vampires have been invited to visit our worlds, and Olga Razon had been onboard Fanboy when the Amok had attacked. Badly injured helping to defend Fanboy from an Amok boarding party, she had decided to stay and had been a sort-of crew-member of Fanboy, on and off, for several centuries.

Yes Olga, it's me, Old Guy. Good to see you again, you are looking well. But, still an ensign after all this time?

Olga laughed. "Of course, why not? There are just the two of us officers, and Fanboy has to be the captain of himself, so who could I outrank?"

"Olga has been helping me with my new fiction series," said Fanboy. "Behind every great writer is a great editor."

"Or perhaps," said Olga, "behind every good writer is a great editor."

"Perhaps," said Fanboy.

At this point a moving blur sped out of the shuttle hatch, tore down the ramp, wove between the lined up maintenance drones, ran around me three times, then stopped and jumped up and down hooting. It was Zippo the space monkey, the most hyperkinetic and irrepressibly curious agglomeration of 15 kilograms of metal and ceramic in the known universe. He had been with me, and Fanboy and Olga, when we fought the Amok robot spiders, so I guess that made him an old comrade-in-arms.

Hello Zippo. Good to see you! How are you?

Zippo hooted some more and bounced up and down, which I guess is space monkey for "Glad to see you too." Then he sped off across the deck to examine a complicated set of telescopes.

I see that Zippo hasn't changed. Does he have an official rank in your Royal Cybertank Space Navy?

Fanboy looked at me as if I were an idiot. "Of course he does. He's a Space Monkey, First Class!"

Oh. Right. Anyhow, Olga, after Moby crosses the ocean, are you coming along on this journey to your home planet? What is it that you call it, the planet of New York?

"Yes, I'm coming," said Olga. "We call it New York. Many of us used to live in the real old New York, so it had a familiar sound. But maybe we should call it New New York."

The Terran city of New York was destroyed a long time ago: I think that the name New York is available.

"Actually," says Fanboy, "York was destroyed as well. So you could just call it the Planet York as well."

"York may have worked for a city," said Moby, "but the Planet York sounds incredibly, well, dorky. Stick with New York."

"Thank you for the advice," said Olga, "I think that we will."

The Fanboy android leaned on a railing and looked across the ocean. "I can't believe that I'm finally getting to go to another star system. I have long dreamed of this day."

The energy cost of sending you out-system is indeed high, but given that we were planning on jump-starting a new colony, and we were going to be shipping a few megatons of stuff in that direction anyhow, it seemed like a good time for you to finally go interstellar. How are the preparations going?

"Preparations are almost done," said Fanboy. "My main hull is stuffed with industrial equipment, and my outside is positively encrusted with fuel containers and other consumables for the journey. We are still on schedule for leaving in ten days. There was a window of opportunity for Olga to come down in person and see some final sights in person before we go, so I thought that I would send a piece of me along as well."

"Developing a new planet in the vampire system," said Moby. "What do our undead relatives think about that?"

"Most of my kind could care less," said Olga. "The plan is to industrialize a barren world in the outer part of the system and leave the vampire planet of New York itself alone. I'm told that some of the alien civilizations have been getting a little close to that part of space and, therefore, a heavy cybertank presence was thought to be a good deterrent to any bug-eyed monsters getting ideas about playing with your vampire cousins – especially after what happened with you and the Yllg and that lost human colony, Old Guy."

151

Yes. That was an unfortunate turn of events. It motivated us to pay a little more attention to watching out for our last surviving biological relatives. We'll be able to keep an eye on you without being in the way, and have enough local weaponry that the aliens won't get any ideas about trying to get to us by messing with you. At least, that's the idea.

"Indeed," said Moby. " Olga, would you like to freshen up, or would you like the grand tour now?"

"I'm fine," said Olga. "Now would be good. Lead on."

"I have an idea," said Fanboy. "Let's not take the tour, let's go exploring!"

"What on Alpha Centauri Prime are you blathering about?" asked Moby.

"What I mean," said Fanboy, "is that instead of you leading us around or giving us directions, we just wander about and try and find the interesting pieces of you by ourselves!"

"But," said Moby, "that's idiotic. I don't need exploring – I know where all my bits are and can download you a perfect map. What's the point of exploring something that's already known?"

Whenever I find a new alien civilization, the aliens surely knew where they were beforehand, but I didn't. I still discovered them, and it was still exploring. When Columbus discovered North America back on old Terra there had been people living there for millennia – but Columbus and the Europeans didn't know that. I vote we go exploring!

"You have to remember," said Olga, "all of the rest of us have had multiple adventures and been to new places. Fanboy has only had that one combat, and he's never been anywhere that wasn't mapped out beforehand – well, at least that wasn't in a simulation. I also vote that we go exploring!"

"I'm still a little skeptical," said Moby. "I mean, I'm pretty big inside and most of me is sort of boring. You would likely spend a lot of time getting lost in some of my twisty little passages that all look alike, and the odds are that you will miss most of the better parts. Still, all my critical systems are all locked down behind secure bulkheads, so you can't damage anything. I'll follow your progress and if it looks like you are headed someplace dangerous I'll warn you off. Also, if you do change your mind just speak up and I can switch to guided tour mode." A hatch popped open in the deck revealing a set of stairs leading down. "Explore away."

We head down the stairs. Zippo spots us leaving and scampers over from the telescope array and dives down the hatch, bouncing off the walls so that he can pass us and take the lead. Out of the sunlight Olga takes off her dark glasses and puts them in a side pocket. Sunlight doesn't make vampires burst into flames, but they do sunburn easily and their eyes are sensitive.

Have you ever considered getting nanobot-controlled chromatophores installed? You could do without the glasses and the UV cream.

Olga shook her head. "I thought about that, but then I'd have to worry about nanobot maintenance schedules and suchlike. Dark glasses and ultraviolet-absorbing cream are goof-proof. Keep it simple."

Now most conventional water-ocean ships have flat decks, because when you are in a gravity well it is energy-efficient and convenient to move things along a flat level surface. As such, Moby's decks were indeed mostly level.

It is also typical for ships to have a regular plan that is symmetrical and where the different levels are organized in roughly the same way. This makes it easier for any passengers and crew to find their way around. That's not how Moby was laid out. Every deck was completely different; he was a true three-dimensional puzzle. It makes sense, I suppose. Moby has a perfect map of himself, and he has sophisticated path-optimization algorithms for moving things around. He has also had a lot of spare time to remodel parts of himself. Thus it was that every deck had a unique arrangement, and there was no overall coherent design. I was starting to realize just how much volume a megaship had.

Many regions of Moby were solid packed machinery with only tiny access ports for micro-maintenance robots. Others regions were more like small highways. Heavy robotic haulers would politely move to the side and let us pass when we came near. Most of the visible machinery I recognized as standard cybertank technology, but there was some weird stuff that must have been Moby's own creations. There was a long hall filled with a tangle of clear tubes, each about the width of a human leg, through which a glowing multi-colored viscous liquid was being pumped. Was this a non-standard chemical engineering facility, or some sort of artwork? I could have queried the local datanet, but that would have been cheating. We marveled at the weirdness of it, speculated as to what it was all for, and then moved on.

There was, as we had been warned, a whole lot of nothing much special inside Moby. But that's what exploring is all about! If you can't handle 30 minutes walking down empty corridors before you find something cool, well, stay at home and watch videos. The real explorers know and relish boredom. The price of discovery is patience.

Zippo was invaluable. He would tear off down a corridor, and if there was nothing at the other end he would rapidly scamper back to us. However, something intriguing would cause him to hoot, and we would head off in his direction.

Eventually we came to a door that exited out the port side of Moby onto a wide terrace that contained an 18-hole miniature golf course. The sun was still out so Olga put her dark glasses back on. The theme of the golf course was the 1950's North American Empire. For one hole there was a miniature highway and you would have to time your shot with the opening and closing of the tollgates. For another, you would need to bounce your ball off a series of police barricades near the scene of a (simulated) crime, avoiding the cop cars with their flashing blue lights.

Zippo raced over and picked up one of the golf balls, which let out a high-pitched squeak. Zippo dropped the ball and jumped into Olga's arms. He stared at the offending ball and chittered angrily.

"Oh, I should have warned you," came Moby's voice from a speaker, "the golf balls are alive. They have a visco-elastic shell, and they gain energy each time they are struck with a putter or they bump into something. The bouncing that they experience when they fall into the cup at the end of each hole is their greatest pleasure. They also have an ability to influence their course, but it's limited, and they each have their own personalities."

How do they gain energy when nobody is playing?

"In that case, "said Moby, "I just let them roll around on the greens and the slow pitch of my own hull is usually enough to keep them charged. If they start to look a little peeked I'll have a drone come out and whack them back and forth a bit, but that's usually not necessary, and I don't think that they enjoy it as much when it doesn't count as a real game. Care to play a round?"

Well of course we couldn't say no to that. Moby extended and activated his stabilizer fins and his normally small side-to-side roll was effectively nulled out, giving us a nice flat stable playing surface. I picked a large-ish tiger-striped ball. Olga selected one that was a medium ochre and Fanboy took one that was bright yellow. I took an early lead, but I think that my ball started to take a dislike to me. It must have objected to my style of play or something? It couldn't talk so of course I had no idea, but I swear that it deliberately took some bad bounces. Fanboy's yellow ball was apparently of a more traditionalist nature, and focused on rolling in as straight a manner as possible. Olga's ochre ball, however, was subtle and sly, and always seemed to be able to change the angle of a bounce just that tiny smidgen that made the difference.

Zippo was, as usual, spellbound by our play, but still didn't trust the balls. He had climbed up on top of a miniature reproduction of the Empire State Building where he could watch the proceedings from a safe vantage point. The balls would twitter at each bounce, and chirp happily when they ended up falling into a cup.

In one hole you had to shoot your ball past a drive-through window in a miniature burger joint, whereupon the ball would be lifted up a ramp via a chain drive, and then roll down a miniature roller-coaster. All the balls would cheer when this happened.

The last hole required that you shoot your ball up a ramp, over a series of miniature school buses parked side-by-side, and then touch down on a ramp on the other side. Olga ended up winning by three strokes, while I was in last place, two strokes behind Fanboy. Fanboy cheered Olga's win and they "high fived" in celebration. I glared at my tiger-striped ball for letting me down, but it showed no signs of contrition for its lackluster performance.

I could not help but notice how Olga and Fanboy acted together. They would hold doors open for each other without a thought, or hand the other something without even needing to be asked, or point out things of interest to each other, and they were always happy at the other's accomplishments. I know that their relationship was platonic – cybertanks don't have a human sense of gender. And Olga had taken several male vampire lovers over the centuries that I had known her. But they reminded me of what they used to call "old marrieds." I suppose that centuries of working together can create a bond even between such different orders of being as a cybertank and a vampire.

Now the vampire virus is supposed to have burned out the parts of a human brain that are responsible for empathy, leaving the vampires as sociopaths. Normally you can't do anything that you don't have the neural circuits for – a biological human with a bisected spinal cord will not be able to walk no matter how much they want to. Still, unlike the spinal cord, the cerebral cortex is plastic and adaptable, and Olga had been alive for thousands of years. Could all that time pretending to be charming have created the real thing? Perhaps, or perhaps that was just wishful thinking.

Regardless, Olga certainly acted like she had a genuine fondness for Fanboy and in return she made him happy. You can overthink these matters.

Olga announced that she was getting tired and had enough for the day, so we ended our exploring and had Moby direct us to some human-scale apartments. These were reproduction officers' quarters from the 19th century North American Protected Cruiser "Olympia." Most of the cabins were tiny, but with exquisitely done wood paneling. Moby offered Olga a choice of the Captain's or Admiral's quarters. Both were relatively large rooms with glass-fronted walnut bookshelves, working fireplaces, and large bay windows overlooking the ocean. In each of these two spacious rooms was an antique five-inch howitzer, large and black and incongruous amongst the delicate furnishings. Moby explained that in the real cruiser Olympia, when the howitzers had been needed, crewmen would first have placed canvas tarpaulins over the book-cases and fine woodwork to protect them from the smoke and powder. I wondered if these reproduction guns were functional and if Moby had ever fired them? I wondered if he would let us try some target practice?

Olga however demurred and selected one of the junior officer's quarters. "It's more like what I've been sleeping in for the last few centuries, I feel more comfortable with a tight efficient layout. You two can decide between Admiral or Captain; I'm off to bed."

Well, neither Fanboy nor my android body needed sleep – we cybertanks process our dreams simultaneously with our conscious state, although the technical term is "information garbage collection." Fanboy decided to go off with Zippo to visit something called "The Museum of Jurassic Technology," that Moby swore had pieces of the original from 22nd century Earth. I decided to pass. I wandered through the Admiral's quarters and examined the books, all reproductions from that era of old earth, and thus almost uniformly dull in that stuffy formal 19th century style that passed for erudition back then.

On a whim I decided to take a nap. Just because my android body doesn't need to sleep doesn't mean that it can't when I feel like it. I just need to switch to full-on dreaming instead of partial in-the-background dreaming. Sometimes it's fun to sleep totally and all at once, just like the old humans used to.

I curled up in a large overstuffed armchair in the Admiral's quarters and promptly fell asleep. As I cycled though the various stages of psychological house-cleaning of the human sleep stages, I eventually started dreaming.

When I had been newly-constructed my dreams and been fantastic, almost adventures in themselves, involving exotic aliens or weird landscapes, people fused with giant clams, whatever. As I age I find that my dreams have become more pedestrian – nowadays they mostly involve me forgetting to bring along enough spare parts during a battle, or missing an appointment, or reliving some past mistake. A hazard of aging I expect.

This time my dream has a little more style. I am a cybertank parked on a giant pizza that is floating in the air over the old English countryside near Stonehenge. I start to drive in a circle around the edge of the pizza, and my treads leave tracks in the cheese and tomato sauce, occasionally crushing an olive or mushroom. I find this oddly enjoyable.

Jesus Christ is floating next to me, but he's not a cybertank. He's in his old android body, jeans and tennis shoes and t-shirt and all, except this time he has a full beard, and the t-shirt is from the Vision Sciences Society meeting which had been held in St. Pete's Beach, Florida, in 2014 AD.

"Hello," says Christ. "How's the driving on a giant pizza going?"

Well, fine. Just fine. How's the floating in the air next to a cybertank that is driving around on a giant pizza going?

"Very well," said Christ. He dipped down and snagged a green pepper, then he floated back up next to me. Every now and then he would munch thoughtfully on the pepper.

You're not really here. You were killed by Roboneuron. You're just a part of my memories.

"Obviously," said Christ. "But remember, God is not a physical thing, God is an idea. So if you have the idea of me, then I am here."

Ideas aren't real.

Christ looked sad when I said that. "Of course they are. Your mind is just an idea that believes in itself. This entire universe is an idea in the mind of God. It's the spirit that counts, and that can be instantiated by anything. At one level I'm just a part of you talking to yourself in your sleep. But I am still the Son of God and a conduit to the eternal. There is no contradiction."

If you say so. Then why are you here?

"Why to talk to you, of course. This seemed like as good a time as any. I'm worried about you. Have you thought about what we talked about last time?"

Love thy neighbor – yes, I remember. But what if your neighbor kills your friends? What if your neighbor kills an entire planet full of people right in front of your own optics: just makes them melt into pus?

What if loving your neighbor means that evil triumphs and all that is left is pain and death?

"I never said it would be easy," replied Jesus. "As you have surmised, God does not require that everyone be a saint. You do have the right to defend yourselves and those you hold dear. But it takes more than not being evil to get into heaven. There must be a sacrifice."

A sacrifice? Like I need to burn sheep intestines on an altar, or maybe blow off one of my tread-units?

Jesus makes a face. "Don't be deliberately dense. You don't get to heaven just by offering God some sausages, and mere masochism is pointless. You need to give up something for a higher purpose. To reach out to others that you have no reason to trust. To take that leap of faith, to make the offer of peace even when your computations say that it is tactically unsound. Or give up a worldview that allows you to rationalize behavior that is good for you, but bad for everyone else – humans have especial trouble with that one."

I am going to reply, but Jesus is no longer there. The pizza is becoming thinner and is no longer able to bear my weight. My treads rip through the crust and I am falling covered in dough and anchovies. My suspensors are offline and the ground is coming up and it's covered from horizon to horizon with an unbroken squirming mass of Amok happy leeches. Then I wake up.

I startle awake out of the Admiral's chair. That will teach me to indulge bad habits – at least, this particular bad habit. From now on I will stick to parallel processing. I upload the dream experience in a compressed data burst back to my main self in Moby's central bay. I absorb it and the entirety of myself is as disturbed as my submind was. Yes, no more full-on dreaming for me.

The remaining days of Moby's voyage across the Great Equatorial Ocean passed uneventfully. We could have gone faster, but there was no need and Moby claimed that too much speed would scare the fish. Moby is very possessive of this ocean. "There is more life and interest in a cubic kilometer of this ocean than there is in a cubic light-year of outer space," he would say. Of course, space has a lot more cubic light years than the ocean has cubic kilometers, but I see no need to quibble. It's a matter of taste.

We took some guided tours this time, and were duly impressed at the collection of antiques and artworks that Moby had acquired or constructed over time. There were other passengers on Moby, some in humanoid form, most in different shapes. We had some interesting conversations and made new friends. After two days Olga, Zippo the space monkey, and the Fanboy android took off in their shuttle; they didn't want to miss their launch window back to Fanboy's main hull. I stood on the deck and watched the plume of fire streak into the sky until it was a dot and then gone.

We reached our destination port, and I drove my main hull out to the spaceport for its own launch preparations. I decide to leave my humanoid android on Moby. It's a small fraction of myself, I can easily make more like it, and it might be interesting for a part of me to experience life on a megaship for a time. Moby is happy to oblige me. I determine that, rather than refusing to use it again, I am going to seduce that slippery little tiger-striped golf ball into liking me. I sense a kindred spirit, and I love a challenge.

We start the long voyage from Alpha Centauri Prime to the system where the vampire planet is located. Fanboy, all 1.5 kilometers of him, is completely covered in disposable fuel containers, with an enormous disk of raw materials attached to his prow serving double-duty as a dust shield. There is no point in trying to hide something as physically large and with such a huge thermal signature as Fanboy, so we make no effort to stealth him. The rest of us travel more discretely, arranged in loose formation around Fanboy, about a light-minute across. A cybertank is effectively a spaceship in its own right, just add on some drive systems and fuel pods and we're good to go. This time we wear black radar-absorbent stealth pods, and we have clouds of nearly invisible scouts lining the entire route ahead of us, but we encounter nothing of interest during the journey.

Olga spends most of the time in hibernation, Zippo goes into shutdown, and the rest of us tinker with simulations, or work on sending and receiving messages from back home. Other than our defensive systems we slow down our main processors and while away the years.

Our little armada consists of Fanboy, myself, the Horizon- Class Frisbee, the Bear- Class Roughcut" the Raptor-Class Pokey, and the new Penumbra-Class Goat. Frisbee is my oldest and best friend. In his previous incarnation as a Thor-Class he was known as "Whifflebat" and we go back to the very beginnings. Roughcut and Pokey I've known for a while, we're not close, but we've always worked well together. Goat is a new model just a few years out of his probationary period. He's advanced and sophisticated and knows it, and is kind of an asshole. Well he's young; maybe he'll mellow out someday.

We enter the vampire system and, as per the plan, split up. I'm going to take Olga down to the vampire planet itself and let her visit some friends that she hasn't seen in centuries. It was also judged a good idea to have at least some military presence there (limited though I may be in that regards). The rest of the cybertanks are going to land on a cold dead rocky planet - some ways out from the central star - and set up a preliminary base-camp. Fanboy is so huge that he's going to have to do multiple loops around some gas giants to shed enough velocity. Eventually he will insert into orbit around the barren planet and use the megatons of materials that he is carrying to start an entire mainline industrial infrastructure. Other cybertanks are scheduled to arrive over the next few years. Before too long we will have a major civilizational hub out here, hopefully enough to deter the Yllg or Spinlozenges or Meta-Slines from messing around with the vampires.

My main hull aerobrakes into the atmosphere of the vampire planet of New York. There has been a long biochemical war between the native ecology and the transplanted Terran one. The spots of the planet that are non-Terran are clearly declining in number. Probably in just a few millennia more they will all be gone, and the planet will be completely Earth-like.

To avoid causing any more damage than I have to, I land in one of the few remaining non-Terran zones. There are lichens and mosses that are different shades of brown, green, and yellow, but not much else. When the native ecology finally dies out it will be small loss. I drive out to the edge of the transition zone and park. I could drive through the forest to the main area of vampire habitation, but I would leave a compacted eight-lane highway in my wake, so I stay put. Instead I take one of my own humanoid androids, Olga Razon, Zippo the space monkey, and a Fanboy android, have them all jump onto a heavy combat remote, and we fly over to the main castle.

The vampire planet has a single small moon. It's only about 200 kilometers in diameter, but it has a low orbit so it looks almost as big from the surface as Earth's moon, and it really zips along. The vampires call it "Phobos," which is Greek for fear. The name had already been taken by one of the moons of Mars back in the Terran system, but the vampires must have been in a "we are vampires and need to be cool!" phase when they named it.

The last time that I was here the castle was more-or-less dilapidated. Vampires, for all their strength and speed, aren't capable of sustained heavy work, and the robotic systems that they had taken with them from Earth were slow and inefficient. They could barely make repairs fast enough to avoid falling behind entropy.

However, this time the castle was pristine, with perfectly fitted stone walls, manicured lawns and gardens, and brightly colored pennants flying from the tops of tall conical towers. We descended into the courtyard. Fanboy nudged Olga, "It looks a lot spiffier than you described it."

"Yes it does," said Olga. "I wonder how they managed that. Old Guy, did any of your kind help out?"

Not to my knowledge. Perhaps your kindred have developed a more efficient variety of robotic servant on their own. That would not be impossible, but it would be impressive, given what they had to work with.

The heavy remote extended stubby landing skids and gently came to rest in the middle of the courtyard. We climbed down off of it and walked toward the main set of entrance doors. Unlike the crude oak that was here last time, these were polished bronze embellished with bas-relief skulls. They swung inwards on perfectly-balanced silent hinges, and we entered the castle.

The entrance hall was glorious – fifty meters long, a polished white marble floor with intricate geometric arabesques of inlaid quartz and lapis lazuli. The walls were covered with mirrors that had complex gilt frames, and the ceiling glowed with the soft light of a thousand simulated candles in dozens of silver chandeliers. Zippo was entranced by the reflections of reflections of himself in the mirrors that faced each other.

There was nobody to greet us so we continued on past the entrance hall into the throne room. This was done in a style similar to that of the entrance hall, but on a much grander scale. At the far end of the room was a massive throne constructed of golden skulls all fused together, and sitting on the throne was the vampire known as "King Peter."

The last time I had been here, King Peter had worn a simple grey suit. This time he had gone all stage-vampire with a long black cape lined with red and a golden crown covered with tiny skulls. He wore small golden earrings, both skull-shaped, and in his left hand was a cane topped with a shining silver skull. King Peter had clearly developed something of a skull fetish.

There were two dozen other vampires also in the throne room. They were all dressed in full-on vampire Goth regalia: lots of black capes and

161

black lace dresses, with black silver-trimmed corsets, and black shoes with silver skull buckles. Lots, and lots, of things with skulls on them.

The skulls are cool, but you might consider adding a few spiders or stars or serpents for variety. Also, while it's hard to go wrong with black, adding a few accents to your color palette could really help. Certainly some dark reds, grays, perhaps a dash of yellow here and there as an accent. Maybe a leopard-skin print.

"Do you really think that leopard-skin could work?" asked one of the female vampires.

"Silence!" said King Peter, and the offending vampiress backed away and looked abashed. "I have been expecting you. Old Guy, you are as irreverent and insulting as ever. Olga Razon, it's been a long time. You are looking well, although your current taste in clothes is atrocious." He turned to regard the Fanboy android, still dressed as a captain in the Royal Cybertank Space Navy. "And you I have not met, but I am told that you are a representative of the Space Battleship known as Fanboy. I can tell that you are the source of Olga's current lack of fashion sense."

You are well informed, King Peter. You know why we are here? And how have you managed to rebuild this castle on such a grand scale?

"Well, I suppose that at this point it would not hurt to explain it to you. Tell me, what is a vampire?"

A vampire is a biological human that has been infected with a highly evolved virus that grants them increased physical speed and strength at the expense of no longer being able to have children, or to consume any sustenance other than human blood. The true biological humans have, we believe, evolved beyond you and you are left behind as living fossils.

"Wrong. I used to believe that as well. That we were condemned to a shallow existence while you cybertanks went off to found an interstellar empire. But we vampires are not the simple victims of a virus that you would have us believe. We are the undead, the holy servants of the great dark god Nyarl-Yakub. I have prayed and my prayers have been answered. Nyarl-Yakub is coming, and as his foremost priest and servant I shall rule over all of you."

Words fail me.

"Peter," said Olga, "Aren't you letting this play acting get a little out of hand? There is no Nyarl-Yakub, that was just something we made up a long time ago for fun. It's not real and this is stupid."

"Stupid?" asked King Peter. "Let me demonstrate just how wrong you are." King Peter pointed his right hand at Zippo, black lighting shot out of it and Zippo exploded into a thousand fragments. I didn't see that one coming.

"Zippo!" cried Olga. (An unimaginative response, but what else would one say when your favorite space monkey has just been blasted into chunks by a sociopathic vampire just to make a point?).

Fanboy strode forward and tried to slap King Peter, but was effortlessly swatted aside. Now, vampires are stronger than regular humans, but so are the most up-to-date humanoid androids. These two should have been an even match, but King Peter was clearly far stronger. On the other hand he was not invincible like Superbeing – I noticed his skin deflecting when he struck Fanboy. He was just a lot stronger – I estimate by a factor of five. But how could that have happened?

Some of King Peter's gothic minions grabbed us and it was instantly obvious that resistance was pointless, so I just relaxed and let them continue to grab me. After a while they got tired of grabbing us and we were allowed to stand freely.

I am saddened by the loss of Zippo. That was both mean-spirited and pointless of you. But other than that, what do we have to fight about? You have somehow stumbled onto or created a new source of power. Congratulations. But surely further conflict is pointless?

"Pointless?" said King Peter. He seemed confused for a time. I guess he figured that when we realized how powerful the vampires had become that we would have to fight. It must have thrown off his prepared speeches. He would likely have enjoyed nothing more than for me to swear revenge or boast of being even more powerful, and when I did nothing he was at a loss. "But you have always looked down on us! You have mocked us!"

A little gentle ribbing between close cousins on the human branch of the tree of sentience. So what?

"But you invade our system and fortify an outer planet that should rightfully belong to us!"

Excuse me, you we weren't doing anything on that world, and we asked your permission, politely, in advance. I still don't see the problem.

King Peter cocked his head like he was listening to someone that we couldn't hear. "Yes, yes, of course. We will handle that." He returned to addressing us. "The great God Nyarl-Yakub is a God of war and demands sacrifices and conquest. We will deal with your other cybertanks on that outer planet soon enough. For now, you, Old Guy, I know that your main self lies to the east of this castle. You, my elite Vampire Guard, are assigned to kill him. Go now and do not return until you have achieved your mission."

Six of the vampires whose garments were especially heavy on the black mail and spiky bits nodded, then disappeared from the courtroom. Shit, even we cybertanks haven't figured out teleportation yet, they really do seem to have blundered into something new.

Now while all of this was going on my main hull was out in the relatively barren land outside of the Terran ecology. I was driving around for the sheer joy of it: nothing much to damage out here with just rocks and lichens. I was also doing what a cybertank normally does when it touches down on a new world, which is to establish a defense grid, and send out scouts, and embed sleeper mines in the rocks, and start building new weapons from the local resources, and things like that. It's a neurosis of ours, we just can't help it.

I was in constant contact with my android back in King Peter's castle, so I was not surprised when six rather garishly gothic-dressed vampire-knight creatures suddenly materialized, hovering in the air not a kilometer from my position. I don't believe in magic – at least not in this dimension. There is a rather obvious logical connection here. The Yllg have got here first and are having another go at causing us grief. And even if there was such a thing as magic, it would still be just another part of reality: another set of rules to figure out, to eventually end up in the physics texts. Magic, as such, is therefore impossible.

Still, I am impressed. The biological humans figured out how to teleport before they left us, and the Yllg were able to bestow that ability on a biological human, but teleportation is not something that we cybertanks have gotten the knack of.

So these six vampire-knight-people were hovering there all malevolent and fierce looking with their armor covered with spiky bits and their long black capes fluttering in the air.

Hello there! You must be the ones that King Peter sent out to kill me. How about we just have a picnic and tell each other old stories? I can get us some really fresh blood, and I have a stock of very, very old and fine whiskey that I would be willing to share.

Unfortunately these "vampire knights" seemed determined to live up to their names. "We are the vampire knights, and our Lord King Peter has bade us to destroy you. In the name of the great unholy god Nyarl-Yakub, your doom is upon you!"

The leader of these knights raised a hand and black lighting of the same style that had destroyed Zippo burst forth. I had anticipated the move, of course (vampires are biological and thus quite slow by my standards) so I have pre-positioned a light combat unit to intercept. I was a little surprised when my combat unit was as thoroughly destroyed as Zippo. This black lightning packs a punch.

I shot the leader in the stomach with a solid slug from a railgun, but with the velocity dialed way down. It should have doubled him up in pain but he just grunted. I tried a higher velocity aimed at a leg; the limb tore off, but then regrew right before my sensors. That's impressive. I hit him with a full salvo at maximum force. His body is shredded into meat – and then knits back together whole and undamaged. Well, this combat just got a bit more interesting.

The six attack with me with their black lighting. I expend a dozen remotes blocking them, but one strike gets through to my main hull. It carves a deep scar up my left frontal glacis. The damage is minor, but this was only one strike. These seemingly comic-opera "vampire knights" can dish out some real damage. Unless I can change the rules I will eventually lose by attrition.

I target one of these flying undead with my main plasma cannon and he is vaporized entirely. The only way that you can tell that he was ever there is the slightly different color of the plasma beam, after the point of impact, due to the trace elements in his body. Regenerate that, you undead loser!

His compatriots appear somewhat shaken by this, but then the erstwhile-evaporated vampire pops up, good as new and twice as tacky.

Brute force does not appear to be working for me just yet. I shift into full reverse, and shoot off flares and chaff and dazzle-pods. It's a good thing that I can drive as fast in reverse as I can forwards, because I usually end up doing that a lot in combat.

I do have a major edge here: I can think much faster than anything biological, and I have vast analytic tools and sensor networks and databases. I just need to solve the puzzle before this black lightning of theirs wears down my defenses.

But, win lose or draw, I am still going to have some fun here. Often when we are fighting in an atmosphere we will play combat music through our external hull-mounted speakers. We do it to pump ourselves up and it makes the whole experience a lot more fun, and generally increases the ratings of the recordings. Typically we play high-energy stuff like Wagner, or The Rolling Stones, or Astringent and the Nebulizers. But this time I decide to play something annoying.

Now what would really piss off a flying vampire knight? Possibly "I Know What Guys Like," by The Waitresses. Nah, they might enjoy that one. I could play "The Monster Mash," by Bobby "Boris" Picket, that would make fun of their pretensions. Then in a moment of inspiration it hits me. I'm going to play "It's a Small World," by the Walt Disney Company.

Way back on old Terra there was a corporation that ran amusement parks for humans. One "amusement" consisted of traveling along a winding canal in a small boat, while animated dolls representing the different cultures of the world sang the song "It's a Small World," in syrupy little voices, over and over and over again. And again. And again. People would leave the ride shaken, and it would often take weeks for them to stop humming the tune to themselves. Eventually the playing of the song "It's a Small World" was banned in the 24th century Strategic Weapons Limitations Conference as a crime against humanity.

Well the vampires are not – precisely – human beings, so I claim fair right to use this most dreaded of sonic weapons on a technicality. I activate my external speakers and at maximum volume play:

"It's a small world, after all! It's a small world, after all! It's a small world, after all! It's a small, small, world!" The sound is so loud that it blows out their eardrums, and vibrates their eyes so hard that they can hardly see. They adapt to the sound level and their eardrums regrow, but they still have to listen to me playing this song. Over and over again. I continue to beat a tactical retreat. They adapt to each of my tricks, but that's OK, I have a LOT of tricks. I project that I have at least two hours if not longer. That's a lot of time for something like me that thinks in nanoseconds.

I see the effect of the song start to take hold; some of them start to hum along yet they are working hard to resist. Take that, vile and ugly-dressed bloodsuckers! I haven't had this much fun in combat since I can remember. Now if I can only figure out where these vampire knight things are getting their energy from, and what's letting them adapt and regenerate so quickly…

I wish that I had the aid of my fellow cybertanks on the outer planet, especially Goat with his advanced sensoria, but they are two light-hours away and unlikely to be able to even offer me advice before the show

166

here is over. On the other hand, Fanboy happens to be zipping through the neighborhood so I call him up.

Hey Fanboy, notice anything strange going on here? Any chance you could lend a hand?

The reply comes back in less than a minute – he really is close, astronomically speaking. "Yes Old Guy, my android already sent me the details and I've been watching your combat from afar. Kind of an unusual mess that you've gotten yourself into, even for you, wouldn't you say?"

Yes I would say. Any chance that you could divert and lend a hand?

"Perhaps. I'm calculating trajectories now. Possibly I could be a 'deus ex machina', like that time I flew by overhead just in time to help you out with that neoliberal cybertank way back when."

That would be much appreciated. But does it really count as a deus ex machina if we are both machines?

"Absolutely. Anyhow, feed me all your sensor data and I'll scan from long-range, and let's see if we can determine where these clods are getting their power from."

Doesn't it seem like quite a coincidence that you just happened to be doing a close fly-by of the planet that I am on, exactly when I need your help, a second time?

"When you consider that we have known each other for thousands of years, and that you are always getting into trouble and needing help, the odds of this happening twice are substantial. But don't get used to it, it won't happen a third time."

As my main hull was dueling with the six flying vampire knights out on the moss-covered plains, back in the castle the vampires were having a ceremony to worship this so-called god Nyarl-Yacob. There was a massive altar behind King Peter's throne (shaped like a giant skull, of course) And there was much drinking of blood and burning of candles and chanting – lots and lots of chanting. The vampires were really into it, but Fanboy, Olga, and myself were finding it quite tedious and getting more than a little bored.

That's when Fanboy suddenly announced in a loud voice, "Hey, sorry to interrupt, I know how cool this must all be to you, but you have a chance to see something truly amazing in about five minutes. You see, I've figured it out. Nyarl-Yakub is a front for a hostile alien species that we call the "Yllg."

They are using you as pawns in their battles against us. They are beaming power to you from a base that they have hollowed out in the middle of that moon which you call Phobos" I am going to attack it with my zero-point energy cannon and, by great good fortune, you will be able to watch from outside as the moon passes over. It should be a really good show."

There was considerable consternation. King Peter suggested that this was all a cheap ruse, others suggested that it would do no harm to prove Fanboy wrong. Ultimately we all spilled out into the courtyard just in time to see the moon Phobos start to rise over the horizon.

"I'm going to use my zero-point energy cannon," said Fanboy. "Of course, it's really just a big plasma cannon, but it is really big: over a kilometer long and the barrel is ten meters in diameter. I'm going to fire at a range of over 250,000 kilometers – that's the longest engagement range for a beam weapon in active combat on record. Isn't that cool? It's so strong that the beam is self-focusing. Firing zero point energy cannon on my mark! Three – two – one-- mark!"

Beam weapons are normally invisible in space, but Fanboy's giant plasma cannon was so powerful that you could see a faint violet line etched across the sky where trace gas molecules were excited to florescence. The point where the line intersected with the moon, however, flashed a painfully actinic bright. As gasses vaporized off the small moon the near part of the plasma beam grew bright, like a glowing spear. I could barely make out small dark chunks slowly moving out from the point of impact, but that was an illusion of range, they must be small mountains flying away from the impact point at kilometers a second. Shadows rippled across the surface of the moon as the shock waves made the rock ring like a bell.

I noticed that all the vampires - other than Olga - twitched when this happened. The vampire knights fighting my main hull all dropped a centimeter before recovering. So, the Yllg systems buried in the moon had clearly been affected, but were just as clearly still functional.

"Well," said Fanboy, "That was fun, but 200 kilometers of rock is a lot even for my zero-point energy cannon. I guess that I will have to use my main weapon after all."

Your main weapon? Didn't you just fire it?

"No," said Fanboy. "All that talk about me being a poorly conceived design was misdirection. I am a purpose-built doomsday machine. With enough fuel and range, I can accelerate across interstellar space and hit an enemy planet with enough kinetic energy to destabilize the crust. Even a

168

dug-in technological civilization would be wiped out. A pity that I didn't know my target ahead of time, I could have completely vaporized a small moon like this one. But I think that I still have enough kinetic energy for the task at hand."

"But," said Olga, "why not just put ion engines onto a planetoid? Why make you self-aware?"

Fanboy smiled. "If you put engines on a planetoid you telegraph your moves in advance. With me you might not realize what you are up against until it is too late (OH SHIT, HE'S NOT SLOWING DOWN HE'S STILL ACCELERATING!). Also I need weapons, and intelligence, to be able to defend myself in the phase when my mass could still be deflected. And finally, even if all you do is accelerate it takes a long time to travel between the stars, and the political situation could have changed. Any moral doomsday machine would need to be able to evaluate the situation and decide if the enemy still needed to be destroyed."

Fanboy held Olga close to him and turned so that his body shielded her from the moon. He put his hands over her eyes and announced, "Attention: the next strike will be really bright. You should all look away now."

"You don't have to do this," said Olga.

"Ah, but I do. This body is in full-link with my main self; you are talking to all of me now. The Yllg realize what's going on. They have launched thousands of missiles. Too late, but I guess they had to try. I am launching my own interceptors. There are now over 50,000 missiles, decoys, jammers, and sub-munitions in play. 100,000! 200,000! The combat is moving so fast. My only regret, Olga, is that I can't show you how beautiful this is."

There was a bright light in the sky. Even looking away was painful and the exposed skin of the vampires burned. It took a while for the light to dim enough that we could look at it directly. The moon was shattered into fragments, some glowing brighter than the sun. As the wreckage of the moon moved across the sky to the other horizon, it was not clear if the fragments would eventually coalesce into a moon again or spread out into a ring, but the Yllg base had been clearly trashed. The vampires did not instantly regenerate their burned skin, they tried shooting lighting and flying, but all their powers were gone.

The last time that the Yllg had messed with our biological relatives their powers had been independent. The sole human survivor of that debacle retains the ability to teleport. This time the Yllg had rigged things so that the vampires were totally dependent on them, a clever move, aside from the fact that it had succeeded only in making us very, *very* angry with them.

My main self, out battling the vampire knights, was of course following this conversation. Thus it was that when Fanboy destroyed the Yllg base, I was not surprised when the vampires suddenly lost the ability to fly and fell straight down. But the vampires were surprised! They flailed around in terror, trying to use their black lightning and calling out for the stupid god Nyarl-Yakub to save them. I could have let them fall. I could have shot them all in the head. I could have done both, and in either order.

However the battle is over and I decide to be merciful – but mercy doesn't mean that you can't have a little fun on the side. I let them fall a bit, then grabbed them at the last moment with some medium remotes and set them down on the ground. Then I switched my main hull from reverse to forward and drove straight towards them.

Still disoriented, the vampire knights see me charging at them and they panic and try to run away. They don't split up, but all run in the same direction. Morons. Vampires are fast, but not even they can match 120 kilometers per hour, and their endurance is limited, like cats. After just a little while they are exhausted and lying helplessly panting on the ground while they watch me get closer and closer. I am a little scarred, but the damage is superficial. I'm 2,000 tons of metal and as I loom over them they start to realize just how pitifully tiny and weak they are compared to me.

I stop just before crushing them, and take a fair amount of guilty pleasure in seeing the terror in their eyes. Eventually they catch their breath, and calm down a bit.

"We surrender," said one of them.

Your surrender has no relevance. Go walk home, and next time, think twice before pissing off a cybertank.

The vampire knights seem almost disappointed that I did not take them prisoner or threaten them, or torture them, or anything – lack of respect and all that - but eventually they stood up and started the long trek back to the castle. I could have flown them there rapidly, but a little walking through the muck will be good for them, build them up some sorely-needed character.

I do send a light remote to accompany them on their way home. I dial down the volume so that it doesn't blow their eardrums, but I continue to play "It's a Small World" the entire distance.

Back at the vampire castle, the wails and lamentations are dying down and people are starting to realize that everything is over and Nyarl-Yakub was a hoax, and they start wondering what they should be doing next. The ends of battles are so often anticlimactic like this.

King Peter, however, was still praying to his silly false god: chanting, promising souls, what have you. I slapped him in the face. We were now of equal strength, and I startled him out of his praying.

It's over. Give it up.

"What are you going to do with me?" asked King Peter. "Am I going to be punished?"

Punish you? Well let's see. You have been exposed as a gullible fool who allowed himself and his people to be used as pawns against the rest of human civilization. You have made it obvious that you are all pathetic creatures going through the motions of being "supernatural." We are going to fortify the planet in the outer system and keep a very sharp eye on you, and this time we will not ask your permission. We will cancel your guest privileges on our data networks for the foreseeable future, and I doubt that you will be invited to any of our parties. Also the back of your neck is badly sunburned. I'd call that punishment enough.

"No," said Olga. With super-human speed she snap-kicked King Peter in the groin. It was a really vicious kick. King Peter fell over, and I could see blood seeping through his pants. I wonder how long it takes a male vampire to regenerate ruptured testicles? "That was for Zippo," said Olga, "*Now* you have been punished enough."

Of course a lot happened after that: routing the rest of the Yllg presence out of the vampire system, getting the support of the other local civilizations to allow us to declare a jihad against the Yllg (who must have been pissing off a lot of other aliens because these other aliens gave us a lot of good usable intelligence and helped us to sniff out some of the hidden Yllg bases), but perhaps what affected me most was what happened to Fanboy and Olga.

The Fanboy android was still very much alive, but he was only a submind without a sense of self-purpose or a survival instinct. The various other subminds and datastores and sentient software agents that Fanboy had left behind were eventually rounded up, and they voted on whether they wanted to be reseeded into a new form. Mostly when this happens the subminds decide to shut down, but this time – perhaps in part because of Olga's urging – the surviving bits of Fanboy decided to come back.

Granted, his peers would have to vote on whether to allow it, and also make the needed resources available. However, Fanboy's previous actions against the Amok, and his heroic actions wiping out the Yllg base in the vampire system, made the vote hardly more than a formality. There is no telling what sort of mischief the Yllg could have gotten up to if they had been allowed more time here. Perhaps they could have cloned an army of a billion super-powerful indestructible badly-dressed vampires.

This time he chose to become, not an interstellar battlecruiser, but a cutting-edge 22,000 ton Sundog-Class cybertank. It's an even sweeter design than the Penumbra-Class. The blank datacores of the new chassis were filled by the surviving bits of Fanboy, and a new prime personality matrix created. Sometimes the process goes wrong, and sometimes the new personality is very different from the original, but in this case Fanboy ended up almost exactly the same as he was before. He even got to keep the same nickname, which almost never happens.

But not *quite* exactly the same as he was before. He was just a *little* more serious, and that childlike enthusiasm that had been his previous trademark was damped down. The easy rapport that the old Fanboy had developed with the vampire Olga Razon was gone. They tried for a while, and it's not like they didn't still get along, but the magic wasn't there anymore. After a couple of years they called it quits and went their separate ways.

It might have been easier for Olga if Fanboy had been destroyed completely, then she could at least have had the last memories of him. Instead she had to live with knowing that Fanboy was still alive, but that their relationship was dead. I don't envy her that.

I heard that Olga went back to the vampire planet, and that she decided to navigate the treacherous shoals of vampire court politics and eventually was crowned Queen Olga. She claimed the dual mandate of trying to see if the vampires could make something of themselves, and of improving the quality of their parties. One of these days I will have to go back and visit and see if she has made progress on either front.

10. Tell Me a Story

Engineer: Let's have sex.
Zen Master: Good Idea.
(From the video series "Nymphomaniac Engineer in Zentopia," mid-22nd century Earth)

"Tell me a story."

But I have told you many stories, and I know that you have read most of my chronicles that have been transcribed into English. What do you want me to tell you?

"I like your chronicles, but they all tend to the same pattern. You blunder into something weird, stuff happens, there is a giant battle, you win, and live happily ever after. Tell me something different."

But those are my most interesting stories! Of course they follow that pattern. If I didn't find something weird, it wouldn't be unique. If there wasn't a conflict, it wouldn't be exciting. If I didn't win in the end, I would not have been around to tell about it. And happily ever after? Well, mostly, but far from always.

"Try."

Oh all right. I was once traveling through space between the stars and I came across a rogue planet. It had no motion so I could not tell from what direction it had come. That was odd – perhaps some ancient civilization had put it there – but there was no trace of how that could have occurred. It was just a ball of rock sitting there in the black space between everything minding its own business.

"And?"

As I passed by I scanned it to make sure there was no alien outpost hidden inside, or ancient spaceships crashed on the surface. And I found the most amazing thing. It was composed of the most curious mixture of elements. The ratio of zinc to iron was 3.562!

"And?"

And I logged it and kept traveling until I reached my destination. Wonderbear the geologist was quite amazed by my find. Imagine 3.562.

"And the story is…"

That is the story

"But nothing really happened!"

Tell that to Wonderbear. He was quite thrilled to hear it. Besides, there was no shooting or blowing up things. That's what you asked for.

"What about one with no shooting or blowing things up, but that is still interesting?"

Ah, well, that's a different thing entirely. I was, of course, just teasing you. No one really cares about the zinc to iron ratio in a rogue planet. Well, other than Wonderbear. He's still talking about it.

"Tell me an interesting story where there are no battles and nobody dies. One that you have never told anyone else."

A tall order. Let me think about that one. In the meantime, would you care for more lemonade?

It was a lovely spring day on Alpha Centauri Prime, blue sky with not a trace of cloud. My main hull was parked on top of a low grassy hill where I could enjoy the view with the full resolution of my primary optics. From this vantage point, I could see down the hill to where one of my androids was having lunch in the shade of an oak tree with a middle-aged woman named Candace Dollinger, although everyone calls her by her old nickname "Silhouette."

Silhouette was the sole survivor of a lost human colony that had been hijacked by the alien race that we refer to as the Yllg. The Yllg had performed genetic experiments on these humans and given some of them super powers. Probably it was to use as a weapon against us. They tried something similar with the vampires, but that's yet another tale. Silhouette had the ability to teleport, which was the reason for her survival. She had been in another dimension (or whatever) when the Yllg had transmitted the coded signal that caused all the other humans to biochemically self-destruct.

Silhouette was a trim 54 years old when we found her, but our medical science is advanced and now she looks hardly 40. Stopping the biological aging process is one thing, but reversing it is hard, even for us. It's like trying to unpop a balloon, or remove the crease from a folded piece of paper. Still, my old friend and biological systems expert Frisbee keeps trying. He claims that she is one of his greatest challenges, and that he thinks he can get her down to a biological age of 35 without doing anything radical like surgically replacing parts of her with cloned tissue.

Silhouette had finished her lunch – a chicken salad sandwich with a side of coleslaw (and the chicken salad was really good, if I do say so myself). I set a maintenance drone to clear the picnic table, but she shooshed the drone away and began to clear it herself.

You don't have to do that. My drones perform tasks like this with less conscious effort on my part than you expend breathing.

"I know," she replied, "but if I let you do everything for me I will become quite shameless and spoiled."

I suppose. Still, you have helped us out tremendously by allowing us to study you and your abilities. And of course, there was our – my - - failure to save the rest of your people. I don't think that I could have done anything differently, but failure is still failure. We owe you quite a debt already. Anything that we can do for you, you need only ask.

"You are welcome, but I am simply pleased to be of use. I've got another appointment with your colleague Frisbat and those physics experts later on today. They still don't understand what the Yllg did to me, but they seem very excited every time they do another experiment. Especially Frisbat."

That's *Frisbee*, and yes, he has a mania for the study of biological systems. You realize, of course, that you don't have to volunteer for these experiments.

"So you keep telling me, but again, I'm pleased to help out. Perhaps it will assist you in destroying these alien Yllg that killed all of my friends and family."

It might help at that, we shall see. Interstellar diplomacy is limited by the speed of light, but after what the Yllg did to your people – and what they tried to do with the vampires – we are moving towards more aggressive actions. In the meantime, if you don't mind me asking, how are you holding up? Got any plans?

"I'm holding up quite well, thank you. I don't have any suicidal thoughts, if that is what you are referring to, although I do miss my family. There are enough of you cybertanks that like to animate human-looking androids that I don't lack for company, and I could spend lifetimes in your museums and libraries. Also, some of the vampires

177

are OK as well. Especially that Max Sterner guy." Silhouette had finished clearing the table, and she sat down again and we continued our conversation.

Yes, I know Max. I'm glad that you have found some companionship. He's even older than I am, dating back to pre-exodus Earth. Now there is someone who can tell you stories.

"Weren't you going to quarantine the vampires on their planet, or something?"

We have, but we always make exceptions for the ones we like.

"And where do I eventually end up? How do I fit in? Eventually you will learn all that there is to learn about me. Do I just hang around sponging off you forever?"

If you want. There are worse fates than just living one day at a time and enjoying it. Or you could, possibly, become one of us.

"Frisbee mentioned something like that. You could stick my brain into a cybertank body? That doesn't especially appeal."

Nothing so crude. Your neural matrices would be analyzed, and the information used to seed a new data matrix in a fresh cybertank body. Of course, analyzing a human brain to that resolution would require freezing it and making nanometer slices, a rather irreversible process. And it might not work.

"What's it like being a cybertank?"

Really awesome.

"I think that, for now, I like your idea of enjoying one day at a time. But I am still waiting for my story!"

Yes, a story. OK, I have it – a very old one, back when there were still biological people around (I mean other than you), back when I was fresh and new and state-of-the art. All the data are in the archives, but I've never arranged it as a story, not as such, so in a sense I have never told anybody else.

"And nobody dies?"

Nobody dies, there are no battles. In fact nobody fires a shot.

"And is it still interesting?"

Let me tell the story and you can decide about that. Anyhow this was a long time ago. We cybertanks, and our human allies, had defeated the evil neoliberal forces and made peace with the aliens. That was right here, on this very planet of Alpha Centauri Prime.

"I've read about these neoliberals. Where they really that bad? I mean, history is written by the victors, the neoliberals must have had their good points."

I was there and I assure you, the neoliberals were every bit as evil as the histories make them out to be. You could think of them as a cultural singularity: all the greed, selfishness, rationalization, lust for power, and self-delusion of the human psyche, all reinforcing each other into a perfect unstoppable tyranny.

"It sounds like you hated the neoliberals even more than you hated the aliens."

Fighting aliens is business. Fighting the neoliberals was personal.

"Well if this neoliberal tyranny was so perfect how did you defeat it?"

We almost didn't. History always looks inevitable after the fact, but at the time it could have gone either way. The neoliberals had achieved total social control of humanity, and their reign could have lasted forever, but then the aliens attacked. The neoliberals no longer had the ability to adapt or innovate; they had to create forces that were less restricted in their thinking and technology if they were to survive. The neoliberals planned to eliminate these free agents after they had served their purpose in fighting the aliens, and they came very close to succeeding.

"It was you and that Vargas person who did that, right?"

Oh I played my part, but I was not the only cybertank. There were ten of us originally, although five were killed in the alien attack and another one was murdered by the neoliberals. And yes, Giuseppe Vargas was important as well, but there were many other humans involved. Anyhow, we beat back the initial alien attack, and then started the slow laborious process of making peace with them. This planet was kind of a mess, there was a lot of radiation and there was a biological terror weapon that the aliens left as a parting shot that caused a lot of trouble.

"Sounds like the revolution made things worse."

Revolutions usually do, at least in the short run. At least the survivors had enough to eat, and hope for the future. Eventually we got things under control. The politics were fractured, like the city-states of ancient Venice, the various directorates and universities and religious cults all forming their own little mini-countries, but it seemed to work. Humans were in short supply, so any state that didn't treat it's workers right would lose valuable talent to others that did. Giuseppe Vargas was the head of the cybernetic weapons directorate, but after the fall of the neoliberals he used to complain about the workload.

"But isn't it good to be the director?"

You see, under neoliberalism there would be a thousand desperate starving people competing for each job. Being the director of a large enterprise was like being a little king; your word was law, you could order anyone to do anything, people would suck up to you, your pay and benefits were generous, and attractive young members of the opposite sex would offer to have sex with you in the hopes of advancing their lot. Later on being the director was not quite as cool: if you treated your workers badly they would just leave for some other enterprise, and you would have nobody to replace them with. Not that being in charge was a bad thing – it still had status, only it was more of a "first amongst equals" than "obey me or else". Vargas was good at being director, and I know that he enjoyed it, but eventually he stepped down and let someone else have a go. That's when he got the idea of leading an expedition to old Earth to see what had happened there.

"You knew Vargas personally, I understand. I've read all the histories, but what was he really *like*?"

Ah, good question. He was, as you doubtless know, the first generation of biologically engineered humans. He was physically strong and fast, but most of all he was smart. At the time, he was the most intelligent human being to have ever lived. He was certainly smarter than I am, although I didn't realize just how much smarter until far later.

"Wait, how can a biological human, however engineered, be more intelligent than someone like you with all those terahertz computer processors?"

In terms of raw processing power, certainly I had more capacity than Vargas, but intelligence is more than that. If you take the village idiot and speed up his thought processes, he'll just think idiot thoughts faster. Vargas had the ability to make intuitive leaps and see connections in data beyond what the bioengineers that created him expected.

"Sounds impressive."

He was. But that first generation of bioengineered humans had a lot of rough edges. All those thousands of years of civilization had taken much of the aggressiveness out of the humans – Vargas was a wild thing, and the oligarchs could not control him. He was one of my greatest friends and comrades, and I miss him still, but even I must admit that he had a mean side. He was normally charming, and I never knew him to hurt an innocent, but when someone crossed him he could be merciless and sadistic.

"Would I have liked him, if I had met him?"

It's hard to explain. He had a presence. He fascinated, but also put people on their guard. You would probably have been hopelessly infatuated with him – most of the female staff of the directorate was at the time – but maybe also have wanted to keep your distance. He had many lovers over the years, but always the relationships burned out and they drifted away. You can look at all the old video records, but you had to be there to understand.

"Wasn't there supposed to have been one special woman in his life?"

You are referring to Janet Chen, a power systems engineer in the directorate. My fusion reactors have been upgraded several times, but their basic design is still hers. Vargas did seem to get along with Chen better than he did with most women, but she was killed by the neoliberals. Some say that she was his one true love and that her death haunted him for the rest of his life. Others say that that's romantic twaddle, and that if she had lived she would have split from Vargas just like all the other women in his life.

"I like the romantic twaddle version."

Me too.

"So Vargas and you defeated the aliens, and then you defeated the neoliberals. Then things settle down and Vargas decides to go to old Earth. What was that about?"

We never defeated the aliens. We held them off long enough to make peace, that's an important distinction. In any event, there was very little physical travel between the different star systems, but there were high-bandwidth laser links connecting the worlds. For all of our technical advances since those days, that is still the basic arrangement. We had been getting news that Earth-based civilization was nearing collapse; there were hundreds of billions of people. Even fusion power resources were running thin, and the raw heat production of all those people and all that machinery was starting to turn the place into an oven. Eventually communications cut off, but we were so busy with our own problems that nobody out here paid much attention.

We stopped to watch a hawk fly over us. It was a big red-tailed and it was clutching a dead bird in its talons. I identified it as a Northern Mockingbird. Silhouette and I observed it as it flew over, from my main hull I could see the individual barbs on each feather. I could tell that it was a male. I projected its flight path and zoomed in on its nest where an adult female and two young were waiting. It was beautiful, watching it balance in the updrafts.

Vargas decided that he would lead an expedition back to old Earth to see what was going on, and hopefully restore the communications network. There was also the incentive that Earth had been a major communications hub, so fixing things there would improve our networking across the entire set of human worlds.

"So who went on this mission?"

Myself, obviously, and also another cybertank that we called "Moss" back then, Giuseppe Vargas, and Chet Masterson, that was it.

"Masterson? Wasn't he the head of the secret police? Wasn't he an enemy of Vargas?"

Not really. Masterson ran one of the elite special weapons teams for the neoliberals, but you shouldn't hold that against him. You had to understand that the ruling neoliberal oligarchs were small in number. Everybody else was terrified of losing their job and being condemned to poverty, death, or worse. In those days you followed orders or you were replaced by someone else who would.

"Sounds ugly."

Masterson was one of these people who believed that even a tyranny was better than anarchy; often that might be correct but neoliberalism was more vile even than chaos. We cybertanks had been sabotaged, and Masterson and his team had been sent to kill Vargas and everyone associated with him. They very nearly succeeded, but when their progress slowed down the neoliberals sent the regular military to kill not just Vargas, but also Masterson and his troops. So he switched sides. Then we cybertanks managed to reactivate, and the regular military switched sides as well. And that was how neoliberalism was defeated.

"With this tyranny ended, surely Masterson would have been out of a job?"

On the contrary! With the collapse of the central administration, real crime skyrocketed and it took a while to get things under control. People like Masterson were never needed more. Vargas hired him as chief of security for the cybernetic weapons directorate, and a good thing too.

"That must have caused this Masterson person a lot of work."

It did, but I think it also made him happy. I remember one day we were talking in my main hangar. He had just come from a shootout and his body armor was still dented and scored. "Gangsters, murderers, people who kidnap young children and sell them into slavery – now these are the kind of criminals that you can really sink your canines into!"

"That's an interesting perspective."

I suppose, but consider, for the early biological humans, any grouping of more than a few hundred would require a police force as a necessary evil to keep order. Humans eventually evolved beyond this, but that took a long time. Now to be effective, a policeman needs to be both feared and respected by the general public. Towards the end of the neoliberal era the police were increasingly viewed with more fear than respect: not as protectors, but as predators, as thugs in their own right.

"Surely fear is a powerful tool?"

Of course, but when overdone it has consequences. The special weapons teams could only travel in groups of at least three, and they had to live in special secured housing zones. Increasingly large parts of Earth were so hostile that the police could only enter with heavy military escorts.

"That must have been unpleasant."

Indeed, which is why Masterson eventually took his entire team to Alpha Centauri Prime. I remember several decades later, when things had settled down, watching Masterson walking through a long crystal-ceilinged mall in the cybernetic weapons directorate. He wasn't wearing his heavy body armor: he wore a freshly pressed light blue short-sleeved shirt with crisp navy blue trousers, and spotless shiny black boots with gunmetal demi-spurs. He had a belt with his personal sidearm, electro-baton, handcuffs, and stungas of course, but around his neck was a chain with the silver medallion of the High Sheriff, a prestigious post whose appointment required a two-thirds majority vote of all the divisions and sub-guilds.

"Wouldn't it be stupid for a policeman to wear a chain around his neck?"

The links were breakaway. I know of at least two occasions when an assailant tried to strangle him with it, only to have it fall away, leaving them flat-footed and Masterson with the advantage.

"So that chain of office literally saved his neck?"

Ha! Yes I suppose so. He still had the arms of a professional wrestler and his oath of office had been ceremonially tattooed on his left biceps. You could see traces of his embedded comm gear in the skin around his ears. People waved or nodded at him as he passed. Women with small children did not grab them and run for cover. Men drinking at bars noticed him, then went back to drinking. In the past they would have avoided eye contact and tried to slip away quietly out back, even if they had been innocent of anything - *especially* if they had been innocent of anything. He was no longer a storm-trooper; he was an *officer of the law*. I'm not sure that I have ever seen a basic-pattern human so content.

"I thought Masterson was an employee of this directorate?"

Technically yes, but by then the politics had evolved. Vargas had some theories about partially substituting honestly-earned reputation for money. It seemed to work, mostly.

"So did this Masterson person ever become friends with Vargas?"

Not in the conventional sense. But they did respect each other. I think Masterson was a good influence on Vargas, he toned him down. When Vargas decided to go back to old Earth Masterson said, "Then I have to go too. Someone has to keep that maniac's head threaded on straight."

"And what happened next?"

Well things went pretty well for about a century or so – everyone had advanced medical coverage by then so Vargas and Masterson had hardly aged at all – but there were still some battles and adventures, but those involve a lot of shooting and things blowing up so I'm not going to include them in this story. I think Vargas just got restless and he wanted to take a sabbatical. Neither he nor Masterson had any family, and they had both trained several talented replacements, so there were no issues there. So we all headed off to Earth to see why there were still no communications coming from it.

"And how was the journey?"

Long and uneventful, as you would expect. Interstellar space is virtually empty. A cybertank can be a spacecraft by itself, so Moss and I floated separately with engines and fuel tanks strapped onto us. Masterson and Vargas spent the entire time in suspended animation deep in our radiation-shielded hulls. We kept up-to-date with events on Alpha Centauri Prime via laser link. Then we reached the outskirts of the Earth system, and were surprised at what appeared to be a new planet orbiting the sun.

"How could an entire new planet just show up?"

It couldn't, obviously. As we got closer we saw that it wasn't a new planet, but an enormous retro-reflector, with thin metal-foil plates a hundred kilometers across.

"A retro-reflector? I remember about that from physics class – the inside of a cube will bounce a light beam back at its source, right? So what was this giant reflector doing there?"

It was the signpost of an alien ambassador. It was most likely from the alien civilization or alliance of civilizations that we termed the "Fructoids." The thing about aliens is that they are alien, and there is little common ground for a discussion. Whenever possible it is best for alien civilizations to communicate with each other via honest signals. This giant retro-reflector gave a radar return as big as a planet. Without words, it was telling us that it wanted to be noticed, that it was a point of contact.

"What other honest signals did it give you?"

Good question. As we got even closer, we saw four crudely constructed nuclear missiles. The missiles were enormous and all of their parts were separated by scaffolding, so you could see how it all worked. Nobody could mistake that these were missiles, but they were so large and unwieldy that they would have been ineffective as weapons.

"That sounds pointless."

Not really. Farther out there were 16 other missiles, of a similar pattern, but smaller and more sophisticated. Beyond that were 64 additional missiles, even smaller, much harder to spot. We caught glimpses of other missiles and artificial constructs, but they were so stealthy we could not be sure of how many, and they were spread throughout the system. Statistically we projected over 10,000 of them.

"The aliens were telling you that they were armed, and likely had a large military presence in the system whose capabilities were uncertain, but likely formidable."

"Yes, that's exactly it. There was a metal box floating next to the giant retro-reflector; that was the alien ambassador proper. We opened up communications in what we had learned of the clipped and formal language of interstellar diplomacy."

"What did you say?"

We told it that we came from the human civilization in Alpha Centauri; we had lost contact with the humans living here and we had come to investigate. The aliens responded that the system was under quarantine and that we were to leave the system on a specific trajectory or be considered hostile. We chatted back and forth for a bit and, finally, the aliens allowed us to take a single team in-system - total mass not to exceed 250 tons - and the rest of our forces were to remain beyond the orbit of Neptune. That was the best deal we could get.

"And you didn't object?"

We had just barely made peace in time to avoid extermination and we were not about to jeopardize that. If the aliens had told us to turn around and go home we would have done so. We were grateful that they had decided to allow us any contact at all.

"Then   you   went   down   to   the   planet?"

No, first we checked out the communications satellites. Vargas and Masterson, two humanoid androids, and some other small robotic systems (controlled by Moss and myself), took a small shuttle. The interstellar laser-link systems were in the outer system, shielded from the inner-system noise, and relaying to Earth proper. We rendezvoused with one and saw that it was still in perfect working order.

"Then what was the problem?"

The communications satellite had been code-locked from the ground. As things fell apart someone in the neoliberal administration had, in typical neoliberal logic, commanded the satellites to enter a frozen state. Heaven forbid that anyone *unregistered* should ever access them! We installed bypasses to restore functionality and then continued on.

"Weren't there other human colonies and outposts in the system other than on Earth itself?"

Originally there had been, but after the fall of the neoliberals most had been abandoned. Still, Mars had a thriving colony of about a million settlers, we contacted them first. We exchanged information: we told them about the events on Alpha Centauri Prime, and gave them access to the interstellar communications satellites, and they told us about what had happened on Earth and gave us contact information for the major political organizations.

"So how was Earth?"

Still a hell. Cloud temperatures were over 230 Celsius, and spectroscopy showed very high levels of acid and toxic gases. The planet had basically been cooked by over-industrialization.

"Was this that greenhouse effect thing that I read about once?"

No, that was a different problem, back when technological civilization had relied on the consumption of fossil hydrocarbon fuels and large amounts of carbon dioxide were produced. Fusion power got rid of that problem, but started another. There was just too much heat being produced. Even the most miserable subsistence requires about a quarter of a hectare of good land for each person. Full sunlight is about a kilowatt per square meter, assume you get just a third of a day of full sun on average, you need a constant 0.83 megawatts of light just to grow food for one person. This doesn't count the inefficiency in turning that energy into light, or the need to purify and pump water etc. Multiply the amount you need per person by hundreds of billions... Once the planet had been so overpopulated that food needed to be grown in hydroponics under artificial light generated by fusion power, the total energy production of the human civilization was more than five times as much as the natural sunlight falling on the planet.

"But that's stupid. Surely any culture capable of building fusion reactors could do this math?"

Surely, but this was neoliberalism. There were many levers of power that the oligarchs used – financial manipulation, propaganda, brutal secret police – but the main thing was demographics. Neoliberalism required massive population growth to ensure that there were always more people than jobs or resources, but any discussion of this topic was taboo. You were only allowed to talk about *conservation* and *efficiency*.

"What's wrong with conservation and efficiency?"

In moderation, nothing. However, efficiency is subject to diminishing returns. As you keep jamming in ever more people, there is then never enough to go around, and "efficiency" turns into brutal poverty. Towards the end, children that were destined for clerical work had their legs surgically removed, because this slightly reduced their food and water consumption.

"You can't be serious. No society would stoop that low."

I am most positively serious – that's how neoliberals thought. Of course, doing that shaved perhaps two percent off the total global food requirement, which was more than wiped out by just another year's population growth. All those children crippled, and it bought just another year's worth of growth. They also charged the children for the operation, and added it to their ongoing life-debt load. After all, in neoliberalism there is no such thing as a free lunch.

"This is hard to process as real. It sounds like bad propaganda from their enemies."

Normally I would agree with you, but I was present during those times and I saw this kind of behavior with my own primary optics. But enough of the neoliberals, we were talking about Earth and how it was so hot.

"But once civilization collapsed, and all those fusion generators stopped working and generating heat, wouldn't the planet have cooled off?"

Ideally yes, but the high temperatures had other effects;The icecaps melted, and the chemistry of the air and oceans were radically altered. Thus, even after the fusion reactors had stopped, the Earth had been permanently stuck into a new stable state.

"Where there any survivors?"

Surprisingly, yes. I have already told you that on Alpha Centauri Prime the politics post-collapse was fractured into multiple city-states and principalities. On Earth something different happened. The society was almost completely run by the descendants of a previously arcane order that called themselves the "Librarians Temporal."

"Librarians of time?"

No, the "temporal" part is a reference to a concern for worldly matters – as opposed to the Librarians Spiritual, who were intellectuals with a less practical attitude towards life. Anyhow, Earth society had been totally enslaved by the neoliberals, but the Librarians Temporal managed to survive as an independent society in the face of the most hostile and effective police state in human history.

"And how did these 'Librarians Temporal' manage that?"

Possibly luck. Possibly because as keepers of knowledge without an overt political agenda they were never taken seriously as a threat. Doubtless, because of the rigorous mental discipline of their order. Also, because they were all heavily armed, police actions against them resulted in heavy losses for the government forces, and their austere lifestyle meant that they had little to no resources to confiscate. The defense of the cockroach: not worth the energy it would take to kill and digest. In any event, once the neoliberals collapsed, the Librarians Temporal were the only significant organized group capable of focused action, so they basically inherited the entire system.

"So you met these Librarians Temporal?"

Indeed we did. We were given landing coordinates at a high plateau in the Himalayas where the temperature was a relatively balmy 140-centigrade. Our shuttle was hauled into a shielded and air conditioned hangar carved into one of the higher mountain peaks, rinsed clear of acid, and we were escorted below.

"Was it dangerous? Did you have to fight anyone?"

Not at all. The Librarians Temporal were charming hosts and we had a wonderful time. Oh, at first there was some suspicion about whether we had really come from the Alpha Centauri system, but once we gave them the new codes for the interstellar communications satellites - and the first messages they got had been sent four years prior describing us and how we had set off - it became obvious that we were really from where we said we were. To clinch the matter it was obvious that our shuttle had not been constructed by any in-system industries.

"And how did these Librarians Temporal survive on such a hostile planet?"

They had an extensive network of underground caves, and through some very clever thermal engineering, these were temperate and well supplied with energy.

"Couldn't the Earth have been fixed?"

We asked about that. There were several workable schemes by which the Earth could have been re-terraformed, but the inhabitants saw no need. They were happy with the planet as it was.

"But didn't they miss the sun and the sky and the wind?"

You forget that everyone then on Earth had never known anything different; I might as well ask you if you miss living in a cave. In truth their habitats were quite comfortable. It was never too cold, never too hot, never rained or snowed when you didn't want it, and there were no tornadoes or hurricanes. They had constructed vast caverns in which there were lovely parks and lakes stocked with fish and birds – only there were no mosquitoes or ticks or sunburn.

"Wouldn't that have been boring?"

In my experience biological humans are rarely bored by comfort. However, there was one cavern that they kept especially cold. They even had an ice-skating rink in it. Industrial and agricultural caverns tended to be on the warm side to save on cooling. Even the habitation zones varied a little in temperature and humidity, partly to accommodate different tastes and partly for engineering expedience.

"An interesting point of view. And what was their culture like?"

It was fascinating. It had a monastic, almost Spartan discipline to it: a consequence of their Librarian heritage and the effort needed to maintain life in an artificial environment. On the other hand, they also enjoyed relaxing and partying, and wine and other mild intoxicants were in common use. The core of their society was a respect for the truth, and the accurate maintenance of records and catalogs. It seemed to be serving them well.

"So how long did you stay on Earth?"

Not quite two years. There was a lot to see and many interesting people to meet. We could have stayed longer, but Vargas was getting antsy and wanted to go home. Well, except for the matter of the Dichoptic Maculatron."

"The Dichoptic Maculatron?"

Yes, a nearly mythical device that allegedly would give the owner vast powers. We searched for it in the dark caverns underneath the Labyrinthia Chaotica, but I am sworn to secrecy about any other aspect of that matter.

"So what was this 'Dichoptic Maculatron' thing, anyhow?"

What part of "sworn to secrecy" did you not understand?

"Did you just make this part up?"

Possibly. Anyhow, once Masterson met the Grand Archivist Ludmilla Gehrts, he was instantly smitten and spent nearly a year courting her.

"Ludmilla Gehrts?"

Indeed. She was two meters tall, had green eyes and blond hair, the figure of a goddess from Greek mythology, and a mind that would put a cybertank to shame. When Masterson first met her she was wearing a long foam-green gown with small white flowers worked into a necklace. She also had a deceptively delicate-looking gold exoskeleton over her left arm which carried a variety of surprisingly potent weapons (they had this thing about personal weapons, you see).

"And how did that go?"

At first Ludmilla Gehrts would hardly deign to notice Masterson – which, as a healthy male, only inflamed his attraction. But gradually Masterson wore her resistance away, and they were married in a grand celebration before we left. Masterson ended up staying with Gehrts on old Earth. I think that the self-discipline and commitment to order of the inhabitants appealed to him. We corresponded long after I and Vargas had left the system. Masterson and Gehrts had several children and were devoted to each other for the remaining four centuries of their lives. A happy ending, I think.

"I like happy endings. So what happened to Earth itself?"

Effectively, nothing much. With the interstellar communications restored, Old Earth became the major center of scholarship of the entire human civilization, right up until the humans all mysteriously left us. To this day it remains a major archive, and many of the old human-inhabited caverns and libraries are still preserved there. Perhaps we should go visit someday, although it's a long trip. Otherwise I could give you a guided tour in a very high-quality simulation.

"And so you returned to Alpha Centauri Prime? But wait a moment, what about that other cybertank called 'Moss', you never mentioned him."

Ah, Moss. Yes, Moss was what you might call taciturn. When Vargas and I decided to return to Alpha Centauri Prime, Moss decided to stay. "These are remarkably rational and sane people, for biological humans. Still, they need a cybertank to keep them grounded."

"But wasn't there an alien quarantine against Earth?"

True. Moss had to spend two centuries in far orbit, until the aliens lifted the blockade and withdrew their forces, but cybertanks are nothing if not patient and Moss was the most patient of all. Still, he was only a few light-hours out so he could easily communicate with Earth itself. Eventually he settled on the surface – it was hostile for a human, but not so bad for one of us, especially on the high plateaus – and he had a long and notable career as both a scholar and a soldier.

"And when you and Vargas returned to Alpha Centauri Prime?"

Ah, more long stories. And ones that would break my promise to avoid talking about things blowing up. Another time.

"Fair enough." Silhouette consulted her wrist-calc. "In any event, I see that I am nearly late for my next experiment." She stood up and bowed. "Thank you for the story, Old Guy. It was exactly the kind that I wanted to hear."

With that Silhouette vanished. I confirmed that, several seconds later, she had appeared safely in the laboratory with my old friend Frisbee. An amazing talent, teleportation. We still don't understand it – a hidden potential in the seemingly simple human genome. How can a paltry few billion nucleotide base pairs possibly remain opaque to our analysis? A current theory is that the Yllg conducted biological experiments on the humans not so much to get at us, as to develop new abilities for themselves.

Silhouette seems content, for the time being, but her presence has re-opened an old debate. Should we clone new biological humans to act as companions for her? Yet that would involve restarting human evolution all over again: do we have that right? Do we want to deal with the hassle? The proposal to reboot her psyche as a cybertank is, I think, not just intended for Silhouette's benefit. Aside from the intrinsic intellectual challenge of the exercise, if Silhouette could be turned into one of us – or perhaps died in the attempt – that would make this entire debate moot.

I sit on top of my hill in my main hull and continue to enjoy the scenery. We'll get around to doing something about the Yllg, one of these days.

11. Frankenpanzer

I have long relished my reputation for eccentricity and the ability to get into trouble. This reputation is perhaps a little embellished – if you look objectively at my service record I come off as reliable and trustworthy – but I am still proud of it (and do nothing to discourage it). It was thus a bit of a letdown when I finally encountered a cybertank that took my record for eccentricity, smashed it into pieces, ground the pieces into powder, and dropped the powder into a sun.

That's life for you. Nobody stays on top forever.

I was part of a force invading a Yllg planet. The Yllg were putting up a stiff fight, and the assault group that I was a part of had suffered heavy losses during a counterattack. I found myself alone and hard-pressed. I was not in too great a danger, but I was going to have to engage in a tough fighting retreat if I was going to survive to fight another time.

That was when an allied force came to my aid. I sensed a wave of remotes off to one flank. They registered as friendly on the IFF, and there were an awful lot of them. They swept the skies and the ground clear of the Yllg forces in my immediate vicinity. I was grateful for the respite, but a little surprised; I didn't know that we had so many surviving forces in this sector.

I try to hail my saviors, but get only garbled transmissions in return. It sounded like something about a sale at Ikea where everybody shops. Perhaps their communications gear has been damaged, or there are still heavy-duty Yllg signal-jamming units in the vicinity? I send some scouts over to check and that's when I get my first visual contact.

It is a giant cybertank that has been made up of the bits and pieces of several other cybertanks. On the front right side, sticking out at an odd angle, is the massive ball-joint mounted plasma cannon from a Mountain-Class. On the left is the turret from a Horizon, it's not level but tilted slightly forwards. I recognize bits and pieces of other classes: a Leopard, a Bear, and a Raptor. There are also pieces of heavy combat remotes, and even bulk transporters and portable generators. The upper carapace is like a big misshapen mountain covered in an erratic pattern of warts and blisters that are the salvaged secondary and tertiary weapons from multiple classes of cybertanks and other combat systems. Sensor masts sprout seemingly at random. Some had been blocking the firing arcs of the main guns and had been blasted down to stumps.

The whole monstrosity is mounted on numerous different sized track units; they don't match up so when it turns it shudders and the treads slip and work against each other, chewing up the ground and raising massive dust clouds. Still, for all the sloppiness of its construction the thing is moving along at a decent clip.

It appears to be more cybertank than Yllg, and it did come to my aid, so I try and hail it via one of my scouts.

Hello giant cybertank! I am Old Guy. I don't think that we've met. What are you?

"*What* am I?" replied the giant cybertank. "That's a little impersonal. Don't you mean *who* am I?"

Apologies. Who are you?

"I'm Algae. No, I'm Bubbles. I can almost remember, but somehow it escapes me. Oh, hey Old Guy, long time no see! Bremsstrahlung. Do I know you?"

Well this is proving to be an interesting day.

There is no record of a cybertank class such as yours anywhere in my databases, and certainly not on this planet during this time. Can you explain your existence?

"Explain my existence? That's a rather deep philosophical request to make during an active combat. Oh, no, I get it, you mean explain MY existence HERE? What was the question again?"

Let's try another approach. What are your last memories?

"Well let's see. I was fighting the Yllg. I was winning. I was losing. I was retreating. I was advancing to my left flank. Then things got hazy. And I detected a colleague in trouble and gave the Yllg a decent thrashing! Lawn Gnomes, definitely."

Hmm. I have my scouts circle around the giant and I run some simulations.

I think I can provide an answer. You register as being made of the parts of multiple cybertanks that were recently operating in this theater. They must have all been destroyed in close proximity. Though there was not enough left of any one of you to self-repair, so the drones must have automatically tried to fix things and welded your bits and

pieces together. I do not believe that anything like this has happened before.

"You may be right. Your theory does account for the available facts. Table legs wobble if they are not braced correctly. So what does that make me? A sort of Frankenstein's monster of a cybertank: a *Frankentank*?"

Frankentank sounds like a gas station that also sells hotdogs. How about *Frankenpanzer*?

"That could work – Von Frankenstein was German (or German-Swiss) so using 'panzer' is consistent. But I see from my surviving databases that 'Frankenpanzer' is far from novel. There were several comic books so named, for starters."

Well, then how about 'aggregate tank' - aggregiertenpanzer? (or 'Aggi' for short).

"Sorry, doesn't do it for me. Of course the Germans do love their big words, they would probably call me Atomaggregatangetriebenmobilenwaffensystem."

I suppose. Or we could just go old-school military and come up with an acronym for you. Like Colossal Atomic Powered Aggregated Weapons System: "CAPAWS."

"Ugh. That's worse than aggregate tank. I think that I will stick with Frankenpanzer, for now, even if it's not original. Is that celery over there?"

Whatever. In any event, we are in a combat zone. Do you feel capable of action, or shall we simply try and withdraw?

"Withdraw? Possibly. Never! Let's give these Yllg a taste of pain, shall we, Old Guy? GRAAAAH!"

GRAAAAH?

"That's what the Frankenstein monster always said in the movies, wasn't it? What were we talking about again?"

We were going to fight the Yllg.

"Of course we were. Let's go, shall we?"

The giant agglomeration of cybertank parts and I thus moved off to do battle with the Yllg. For all the sloppiness of its assemblage, the massive compound cybertank was effectively controlling ten times as many combat remotes as I possibly could – perhaps this will work. If nothing else it will be something for the record books.

As we headed off to meet the Yllg forces, Frankenpanzer began singing the theme song to the 20th century Japanese action show "Ultraman." That seemed silly, even for me, but it was such a cheery song that I could not help but join in.

"In a super-jet he comes, from a billion miles away.
From a distant planet land, comes our hero Ultraman!"

We began combat operations and, at first, it went pretty well. Frankenpanzer had a decent grasp of tactics, but he did shift strategies erratically, and sometimes one of his sectors would work at subtle cross-purposes with another of his sectors.

Not too shabby, but against a first-tier opponent like the Yllg that could be an issue. Amateurs sometimes think that acting randomly will confuse the enemy; not if the enemy is really good. If a sophisticated enemy realizes that you are behaving randomly they will pick you apart with a more focused technique. We cybertanks use strategy that is hard for the enemy to predict, but it is a calculated randomness that meshes in with the big picture. Frankenpanzer was good, but still just erratic enough that the Yllg would be able to take advantage.

I decided that my role would be to fill in the gaps. I held back and watched as Frankentank engaged the Yllg with his more powerful forces, and when I detected a glitch in his strategy I would rush in my own units to prevent the Yllg from exploiting the lapse. It worked out pretty well, for a while.

A Yllg heavy ground unit engaged us at long range. Frankenpanzer was hit and over a thousand tons of him was sheared off. It didn't slow him down at all, he targeted the offending enemy unit with the main weapons from a Mountain and a Leopard and blew it away. His repair units were swarming over his damaged section, and were busily welding new random bits and pieces of salvaged cybertank in place even as he continued fighting.

One of his secondary turrets suffered an internal short and exploded – again, Frankenpanzer didn't even appear to notice. The gap where the old turret had been was rapidly filled in with multiple armored telescope clusters. Amazing.

I was starting to feel pretty confident about the way that the battle was going, when all of a sudden Frankenpanzer came to a dead halt. His remotes all went to default mode: they continued to defend themselves and even take the tactical-level initiative, but without the strategy of a central controlling mind they were vulnerable and would not last long against the Yllg.

Frankenpanzer! What's wrong? Are you damaged? Do you require assistance?

Frankenpanzer just sat there. Then he activated all of the motive units on his left side. There was no attempt to make a decent coordinated turn, and the outer units were going at the same speed as the inner ones, so they churned and rumbled and Frankenpanzer clumsily slewed to the right.

196

"I'm moving my left treads," he said.

Frankenpanzer. This is a bad time for this (whatever 'this' is). We have a battle going on.

The big cybertank ignored me. After a time it shut down its left motive units and powered up its right ones.

"Now I'm moving my right treads."

You dweeb will you snap out of it! Darn it I need you!

Unfortunately my shambling comrade remained unresponsive, and continued his alternating "I'm moving my left treads," and "I'm moving my right treads" obsession. The Yllg can sense that our forces are no longer fighting with the same coordination as before and they press the attack. I take over control of some of Frankenpanzer's remotes, but there are far too many for me to use them effectively. I decide to employ his mostly passive weapons systems as a barrier and use my own forces to mount a mobile defense behind them. It works, but the Yllg are continuing to press hard and I'm likely going to be overrun before too long.

Then he came to his senses, rallied his systems, and we beat the enemy back.

"Sponges! Sponges for all of you! Let's rush them in the center, I think they are weak there. GRAAAAH!"

I will say that fighting alongside Frankenpanzer may not have been the most efficient means of waging war that we cybertanks have ever devised, but it was always full of interest.

To make a long story short Frankenpanzer and I survived combat with the Yllg – although barely -- and we were fortunate to be reinforced the next day. Upon examination it was determined that the cybertanks out of which he had been constructed were truly dead. There was no question of disassembling him back into his components, as there was not enough left of any single one of them to be viable. Also, Frankenpanzer was clearly self-aware and, despite his erratic behavior, was capable of adhering to our body of law. Thus, he had full citizenship rights and nobody could "fix" him, unless he agreed to it – which he did not.

His fragmented mental structure would sometimes lead to unique insights, and he became a valued member of our society. Nevertheless, the overall consensus was that one Frankenpanzer was more than sufficient for all pragmatic purposes. Thus, the programming of the repair drones was subtly altered to ensure that nothing like this would ever occur again.

It was some time later that I was walking in a park inside Moby Cybertank with the vampire Max Sterner, the human nicknamed Silhouette, and an android remote that belonged to Frankenpanzer.

Moby Cybertank was a cybertank that had transformed itself into a two-kilometer water-going megaship in the Greater Equatorial Ocean of Alpha Centauri Prime. Moby had recently remodeled several decks near his stern into a park that was populated by cybernetic plants and animals. Silver metal trees unfolded exquisitely formed platinum flowers; iron-colored birds flashed patches of color from metal feathers so thin that they diffracted the light. We were following a winding path through the park as Moby pointed out some of the details. Curiously, although Moby enjoyed making human-scale structures like parks, he himself never inhabited them in human form. He spoke to us from speakers that were positioned around the park, or sometimes from one of his cybernetic animals.

I was present in a generic male ethnic European body wearing blue jeans and a T-Shirt with the slogan "Cybernetic Weapons Directorate Rocks!" emblazoned on the chest. This particular part of me had been aboard Moby for some time, and it had been an interesting experience.

Max Sterner was a vampire, he had been born in the 19th century and was thus even older than I was. Pale and elegant, he was wearing an impeccably tailored grey suit. A century after being transformed by the virus a vampire loses its hair and teeth; Max had a short black wig, and was wearing dentures with perfect white normal human dentition ("Fangs! Do you know how many times I have bitten myself with my own fangs! Fangs are for posers! If God had wanted humans to have fangs He would have given them narrow muzzles.") Max was erudite and very personable compared to most vampires.

"Silhouette" was the nickname for the woman named Candace Dollinger. She was the last survivor of a human colony that the Yllg had hijacked and then exterminated (which is the single biggest reason that we are at war with them). The Yllg had conducted experiments on the population that had given some of them super-powers; Silhouette could teleport. Our own savants have tried to analyze this power and failed. The last report I heard was that they were now spending more time trying to understand why they couldn't analyze her power than

198

they were actually trying to analyze her power. Silhouette was wearing white cotton pants, tan sandals, and a blue silk blouse.

Frankenpanzer had come as a massively tall humanoid android. It had bronze-colored skin that appeared to have been crudely stitched together in patches, but the overall appearance was handsome and even noble.

"Why," asked Silhouette, "are you here as a giant stitched-together person?"

"This is a movie version of Frankenstein's monster," replied Frankenpanzer. "It seemed appropriate."

Silhouette squinted at him. "Didn't Frankenstein have a flat head, bolts coming out of his neck and enormous heavy metal feet?"

"You're thinking of the 20th century Boris Karloff version. This is from 'I Frankenstein', starring Aaron Eckhart, 21st century."

The critics panned that version.

"I know," said Frankenpanzer. "And with reason. But Aaron Eckhart is sexy."

"I had heard that you tend to talk in non-sequiturs," said Silhouette. "However, here you have done nothing but speak clearly and coherently. Why is that?"

"A good question," said Frankenpanzer. "My main self does indeed have a complex mental structure. Most cybertanks can split themselves up into subminds, but these are always part of a greater whole. I have what I like to think of as mental *chunks*, that each have considerable independence. I am chunkulated! But this simple android does not have the capacity to hold such richness, so I am here limited to a single cognitive narrative. It's very constricting. How can you stand always being so narrow minded?"

"We make do," said Silhouette.

"I'm sure," said Frankenpanzer, "but you really should consider being chunkulated. It is so liberating."

"Another day, perhaps."

We walked down a winding path that was softly lit by hovering glow-globes. To our left was a field of brass sunflowers, and to our right was a very close-cropped lawn on which miniature humanoid automata wearing white striped uniforms played a game of baseball. We stopped to watch for a bit, and Moby called out the play-by-play action from a speaker concealed in a nearby rock.

The game ended with one side winning 4 to 2, and we continued our walk.

So Max, any word from your fellow vampires?

"I did get a message from your old friend Olga Razon the other day. At the time that the message had been sent, she was still nominally the queen of the vampires. She said that she still wasn't sure if vampire society could evolve, but that they have had some really good parties and that was a promising start. And ex-King Peter is still sulking out in a cave somewhere praying to Nyarl-Yakub. Also his testicles have finally regenerated – what is that about anyhow? She also asked me to say hello to you when I see you next. So, hello Old Guy from Olga Razon!"

Tell her hello back from me, next time you send a message.

"I had heard about this vampire so-called King worshiping this silly made-up god and being used by the Yllg as pawns against the cybertanks," said Frankenpanzer. "But I still don't understand it. How could you be so juvenile? Didn't you realize how sad that whole episode was at the time?"

Max sighed. "Well *I* realized it, which was why I was far away from the action at the time. But you have to put yourself in our place. For a long time being a vampire was cool. We were stronger than regular humans, faster, and with sharper senses. Our biological immortality let us learn how to manipulate people, and also gave us the time to acquire great wealth. We were an elite, envied and arrogant, living in splendor in our underground palaces. It was good for a while. Technology evolved, but people were still people. Then people themselves started to evolve and we were in danger of being left behind. We ourselves are sterile and thus cannot evolve or adapt. We can only make more of our kind by infecting regular humans, but these were becoming resistant to the virus that transforms us, and also beginning to equal and then exceed us in speed and strength."

We paused as a squadron of crystal-metal dragonflies darted past, quadruple wings buzzing softly as they swooped and whirled like fighter jets.

Max continued. "It is hard to describe, but most of us began to feel somewhat pathetic. We left to found a colony of our own, far away and safe. We stagnated. We did not realize how much we had depended on the regular humans to provide us with – how shall I put this? – a cultural energy. We turned back to the old myths, trying to pretend that we were still special, that we were naughty sexy supernatural beings with special powers. We prayed to gods old and manufactured, hoping to be answered, hoping to one day again become something special. But our prayers were never answered, and we remained living fossils repeating the same old dreary parties over and over for want of the imagination to do something new."

"And then when something actually answered this King Peter's prayers, and gave him real powers, he didn't ask too many questions?" said Frankenpanzer.

"Precisely," said Max. "Human, vampire, or cybertank, it's one of the great weaknesses of the human psyche: it is very hard to resist someone telling you what you want to hear. Even though we vampires are each thousands of years old, and have more than enough experience to realize this intellectually, when you are too close to the problem it is all too easy to see only what you want to see. We had wanted to be special again for so long, and now it looked like we could be. We are fortunate that your kind stopped us. I don't think that the long-term plans of the Yllg would have been much to our liking. But I do have one request of you, Frankenpanzer."

"And what is that?"

"Please," said Max, "no jokes about Dracula vs. Frankenstein."

"Deal," said Frankenpanzer.

The path opened up into a large grotto, and at the far wall was an opening in Moby's hull. The sun was setting over the Great Equatorial Ocean and a gentle sea breeze wafted in. There were some benches made of crystal slabs and stainless-steel rods; we all took a seat and watched in silence as the sun set.

It had been a welcome break, exploring Moby's latest creations with good friends, but tomorrow it's back to the office. There are, you see, more Yllg that need killing.

12. Sacrifice.

Zen Master: "Optimism is cowardice, but despair is a sin." That's from the teachings of the artificial intelligence Saint Globus Pallidus XI.

Engineer: But isn't the part about optimism from Oswald Spengler, and the part about despair from the traditional Roman Catholic catechism?

Zen Master: Well yes, but creativity is often in finding new combinations of existing material. Like peanut butter and chocolate.

Engineer: Or roasted beets and candy corn!

Zen Master: No, not like that.

Engineer: Let's have more sex.

Zen Master: Good Idea.

(From the video series "Nymphomaniac Engineer in Zentopia," mid-22nd century Earth)

Eventually the alien civilization that we refer to the "Yllg" had pushed us far past any reasonable limits of tolerance with their constant harassing attacks and meddling in our affairs. We conferred with the other civilizations in the area, and while they did not give us any specifics, they voiced no objections to our declaring war on the Yllg. Translated from the bloodless logic of lingua diplomatica, they basically told us to "Wipe the bastards out once and for all, if you feel like it. Knock yourselves out." We suspect that we are not the only civilization to have been pissed off by the Yllg.

We didn't win every battle. We had two entire systems wiped out, and lost many good and noble cybertanks in the battles. Nevertheless - slowly at first - we gained the advantage, and as such things usually go, a small advantage turns into a larger advantage which turns into an overwhelming advantage.

We captured some of their core worlds and learned what the Yllg really are. They are not, as some of us had speculated, a machine culture left behind after their biological creators died out (which would actually describe us). They are still biological. The true Yllg are large fungal growths, each about the size of an elephant, that are connected by conductive neural filaments that are spun by a symbiotic insect. Our xenologists are having a field day: this is the first time that we have penetrated to the heart of a spacefaring technological civilization. We developed mathematical models of their thought processes, and the Yllg lost any comparative advantage of understanding our psychology that they had gained from studying biological humans.

We drove them from one system to the next, crushing their defense networks, disrupting their supply lines, scouring their planets of their every trace. The Yllg tried to send some refugees away from the area, but the surrounding alien civilizations tracked the fleeing Yllg down and annihilated them. Even for minds that work differently than ours, it's a bad idea to make too many enemies.

Finally the Yllg are left with just one refuge, but it's a good one. They have holed up in the atmosphere of a Jovian-class gas giant planet. There aren't many better places to hide in this universe, at least for civilizations of our technological level.

The planet has a volume of well over a thousand times that of a planet like Earth. There is a small rocky core at the center, but most of the planet is metallic hydrogen where the temperature and pressure is beyond anything that our technology could dream of operating in. Still, from the outer cloud tops to the surface of the metallic hydrogen it's 10,000 kilometers down, and that's a lot of volume where something can hide.

I have commented previously on the impossibility of blowing up even an Earth-sized terrestrial planet – obviously a gas giant is even more impossible to eliminate. Randomly dropping fusion depth-bombs would have effectively zero chance of hitting anything. It was pointed out that if we could double the mass of the planet, then this would likely cause it to turn into a brown dwarf, which would surely cook the Yllg. However, seeing as none of us has 10^{28} kilograms of matter just lying around handy that plan was rejected as impractical.

We send probes into the atmosphere, they sink down and we encounter Yllg forces. However, the Yllg destroy the probes before they can do any effective scouting, and by the time our nuclear depth bombs will reach the site of contact the Yllg mobile forces will have long since moved away.

We send remotes with subminds down and they are destroyed. The Yllg are good. The dense and turbulent atmosphere makes high-precision remote control of combat units impossible. If we want to get rid of this final Yllg holdout, we are going to have to go down there in person and hunt them ourselves with our full mental capacities.

Now in this 10,000 kilometer deep region there is no surface to rest on: the atmosphere is mostly hydrogen with a little bit of helium and the faintest traces of a few other elements. As you go deeper the hydrogen just gets denser and hotter. That's a problem. You see, hydrogen is the lightest element there is. That means that anything other than hydrogen, if it is not actively spending energy staying aloft, will sink until it is crushed and cooked at the core.

There is something lighter than hydrogen gas, and that's even hotter hydrogen gas. You can use hot air (that is, hot *hydrogen*) balloons to float in a Jovian atmosphere. But these will be too large and vulnerable to be of any practical military value, especially in the deeper regions where the force of the winds would tear any sort of zeppelin to shreds.

It is also true that a vacuum is lighter than hydrogen – but the weight of the pressure vessels need to maintain a vacuum make it useless for generating lift. In theory one could nanoengineer a microtubule-braced structure that is mostly empty, but still capable of resisting pressure. But making something like that which can handle the pressures and temperatures in the deeper layers of a gas giant planet is currently beyond us.

Thus, we develop Jovian atmospheric cruisers specialized for combat in this new environment. They are a sleek 200 meters long with stubby fins for lift and ducted fans for propulsion. They are heavily armored, but not against the pressure. One advantage of a solid-state mind: pressure won't collapse us so the pressure inside the hull is the same outside (our limit is that, even though we can't be crushed, at some point the raw heat and pressure will make even our solid-state cores nonfunctional). No, the reinforced hulls are to stand up in combat, and even more, to handle the vicious shear forces and turbulence of thousand kilometers an hour winds. At our operational depths the pressure is so great that the hydrogen is as dense as terrestrial seawater.

Beam weapons are useless in this environment, so the primary weapon is a long-range torpedo with small wings for lift and a single turbine powerplant. For close-in defense we develop super-cavitating shells that travel in their own gas bubble; they have about the range and mass of 20th century battleship shells, though typically armed with fusion bombs. We call them "darts." The need to stay streamlined means that external turrets are impractical, and we launch everything from integral bays with small external hatches.

Nuclear weapons work differently in this kind of environment than they do anywhere else. When a nuke goes off, it creates a bubble of superheated gas hundreds of meters across, which then collapses and rebounds, and collapses again, until the energy is finally dissipated (it's like a bouncing ball coming to rest). This can be extremely destructive to anything in the vicinity. If you are feeling really artistic you can time the explosion of multiple nukes to create resonant shock waves of awesome power.

Radar works, but the range is limited, especially against an opponent that understands how to minimize a radar cross section. Depending on the depth, sonar is generally more practical. Long-range tracking is mostly by scent: looking for trace particles of alien manufacture across thousands of kilometers, we try and piece together a statistical model of where their forces are now.

The combat model is complicated. The short detection radius, emphasis on stealth, and the three-dimensional nature of the battlefield has similarities to water-navy submarine warfare. On the other hand, the need to keep moving to stay aloft is more reminiscent of classical aerial combat. Tracking a scent trail harkens back to the earliest days of our biological creators, when humans and their canine symbiotes would hunt for prey in forests.

The battlefield is unforgiving. Any combatant losing power will be inexorably sucked down and crushed and melted at the core. There will also be no salvage here, and that's where we have an advantage. We have absolute space superiority and can resupply our forces, but every kilogram of metal that the Yllg lose in battle is a kilogram that they will never get back. If we have the patience for it, we are guaranteed to win by attrition.

And there I am, piloting a Jovian cruiser about 1,000 kilometers beneath the cloud tops. In order to save weight I left my treads, road-wheels, and main turret behind, and am installed in the middle of the cruiser. My main hull is still useful for extra shielding and armor for my irreplaceable computer cores. My maintenance facilities and fusion reactors are, of course, still operational, although the cruiser itself has additional capabilities. I have a total of 24 ducted propulsor fans and, depending on the depth, I can maintain altitude with as few as five of them operational. If I am reduced to four then I will slowly drift downwards until I am melted and fused into a giant blob of cybertank-cum-Jovian cruiser.

We could have created new cybertank minds for these Jovian cruisers, but as it's not a place that we intend to settle permanently, we decided not to. Instead, the "pilots" are recruited from the lighter variants of cybertanks – mostly Raptors, Leopards, Wasps – and of course yours truly.

I am in a flotilla of three cruisers. My old comrade the Raptor- Class Skew was leading it in the middle, I was 1,000 kilometers to the left, and the Leopard-Class Smurfette was handling the right flank.

Our trackers are spread out in a battle line ahead of us: manta-ray shaped constructs with vast ventral scoops that feed into hectares of sensitive membranes, sniffing the Jovian atmosphere for the heavy elements that might indicate a Yllg presence. Our cruisers typically move at less than 100 kilometers per hour, which is often much less than the local windspeed. Thus, navigation is as much about predicting and mapping the wind patterns, and jumping from one moving air column to another. It's exhilarating but dangerous. The transitions between wind streams have shear forces than can destroy even us, and some of the streams will suck you down to the core at a speed that nothing we have here can escape.

We are travelling in a large relatively quiet zone, about 30 kilometers above a thermocline. Our trackers are getting some Yllg traces, but not much. Still, we are patient. We just need to keep accumulating data and refining our models. We'll get them sooner or later.

Then we lose a scout out to our far right flank. We hear the distinct "WHUMPPP Whump wump wumpppp..." of a nuclear explosion expanding and contracting before decaying into a hot ball of hydrogen.

"Definitely Yllg," transmitted Smurfette. "Suggest we reinforce in that sector."

Agreed. But let's not get baited into anything; we keep our main formation intact and only send some more scouts and long-range torpedoes in that direction.

"Agreed," said Smurfette.

"Same here," said Skew.

We watch the tracks of our light units converge onto the location where we had lost our scout. They detect nothing, perhaps it was a feint after all. Then, we get a single Yllg torpedo -- it's coming in hot and fast, and obviously doesn't care if we can hear it. We try to intercept it with a conventional warhead, but it self-destructs with the typical nuclear "WHUMPPP Whump wump wumpppp..."

An hour passes and there are no more contacts. It must have been a lone probe. Then we get a dozen incoming tracks, each a thousand kilometers apart, tearing in so fast that the cavitation noise can be heard thousands of kilometers across.

"Are they trying saturation attacks and hoping to get lucky?" asked Smurfette.

"I don't know," said Skew. "It seems awfully wasteful of resources. We're going to intercept all of these Yllg units before they get even close to being able to identify us. Also, at the speeds they are travelling they're not going to be able to hear anything but their own cavitation noise. I don't get it."

We intercept the dozen incoming Yllg units, and as before they nuclear self-destruct at the last moment. "WHUMPPP Whump wump wumpppp…" I can hear the echoes reflect off the thermocline below us. Then I understand.

Skew! Smurfette! The Yllg were using these units as a form of super-powerful active sonar! They must have bistatic acoustic sensors all over the region! By now they might have a complete readout of our force dispositions! We need to get out of here immediately!

"What do you suggest we do?" asked Skew.

The thermocline. We need to dive into the thermocline, they can't track us there. Now! Now! Now!

Skew and I change course and begin the dive down to the boundary layer underneath us, but Smurfette hesitates. "I don't think that's a good idea. We might not make the transition, and we might be getting near a major Yllg facility. I say that we stay and fight it out."

That was when all the stealthed Yllg units unmasked themselves. Using the intelligence gained from their nuclear-sonar technique, they had mapped out all of our positions. Yllg torpedoes had snuck into range at a dead-slow pace, then suddenly accelerated to attack speeds. Hundreds of incoming hostile tracks abruptly appeared in our sensor space, and they were perfectly targeted. We lost all of our advanced manta scouts, and most of our deep lurking remotes. The Yllg attack wave continued on towards us in overwhelming strength.

Smurfette changed course and also dove down towards the thermocline, but it was too late. Her Jovian cruiser was caught in multiple expanding and contracting atomic gas bubbles and torn to shreds.

Skew and I were just a few kilometers away from the thermocline, moving at our maximum speed at this depth of 200 kilometers per hour. We dropped mines behind us, they created a screen of nuclear explosions that we hoped would give us enough cover to allow our escape.

We hit the thermocline and the sudden lateral winds nearly tore my own cruiser in half. The metal of the hull screamed under the stress and I lost three ducted fans.

At first it looked as if Skew had gotten lucky - or good. He shot out of the thermocline straight and clean like a rat out of an aqueduct. Then I detected the signals of four heavy Yllg torpedoes on his tail. They must have tracked him all the way through. Skew tried to intercept them with a spread of darts, but the Yllg torpedoes were too close. When they exploded the shockwaves caused his cruiser to suffer a terminal rupture. It fragmented into multiple pieces and, without power, began the inexorable slow descent into the crushing depths below.

"Ouch," transmitted Skew from the piece that had his surviving main processor cores in it. "I think they got me."

You are too far away and sinking too fast – I cannot calculate any means of effecting a rescue. Sorry.

"I also have come to the same conclusion. Don't waste your life trying, you'll just lose yourself as well. Try and stay alive, and tell everyone that Skew fought valiantly to the last."

That I will. Any other last words?

"Not so many. I've always felt that everyone should always know how you feel so that last words are never needed. The obvious, of course: it's been great fun. I would not have traded this life for anything. Oh, and if he wants it I bequeath my collection of antique musical instruments to Schadenfreude. Lastly, if the bits and pieces of me left behind are dithering about whether to go for a reseed, try and convince them to go for it. Existence is just too good to pass up if you get a second chance."

Agreed. Your reputation means that, if your remaining bits want to be reseeded, it will be supported by universal acclamation. Certainly I will contribute resources to that effort. Goodbye.

"Goodbye, Old Guy. Oh, and if I do reseed and my new self is a jerk, try to talk some sense into me."

At that we were out of radio communications range and that was the last that I ever heard from Skew. He sent a half-dozen messenger missiles streaking up from the depths: they would have had copies of his most recent memories for use in a possible reseed. I listened as they ascended up through the heavy atmosphere until they were lost to my sensors.

Skew must have reached the depth when his central processing cores were cooked several hours later, but that would have been far away from any of our sensors. I imagine that he spent the time listening to and composing music and watching old movies and enjoying himself. At least, I hope that's what he did.

I am only lightly damaged, but I am effectively on my own without any hope of immediate reinforcements. I switch to a slower cruising speed, and keep a steady altitude of ten kilometers beneath the thermocline which is now above me. The winds in this area are heading towards where the Yllg attack on us had come from. Perhaps I can let myself be blown behind enemy lines and can use this misfortune to advantage.

That's when the Yllg battleship plunges down out of the thermocline almost on top of me. It's close enough I can generate a high-resolution sonar image of it. It's a blunt ovoid 500 meters long and two hundred meters across, with rings of counter-rotating vanes spaced along its length. It's tumbling in the turbulence of the thermocline. I shoot a full spread of ten darts at it; they tear out at 500 kilometers an hour within their own cavitation bubbles. Even tumbling the Yllg battleship has enough control to intercept all of my darts, but the closest manage to inflict some damage.

The Yllg battleship launches 10 heavy torpedoes back at me. I accelerate to full speed and head up back into the thermocline. This time I manage to sustain less damage – I think I'm getting better at this. It's kind of like running the rapids in a kayak. I sense multiple nuclear detonations behind me, but they are not close enough to be a problem.

I dive back down and I can tell that the Yllg battleship is in trouble. There are sonar-reflective parts drifting away, and I can hear the squeals of tearing metals and rupturing seals. I give it a salvo of ten darts and five heavy torpedoes. This time the battleship is unable to completely defend itself, and it implodes into multiple expanding and contracting gas bubbles.

It had managed to fire off three heavy torpedoes at me before it died, but I easily dispatch them with two darts each.

I take stock of my situation. I am down by five ducted fans, but still have a good margin of lift remaining and all of my fusion reactors are 100%. I have a lot of internal damage, but nothing critical and most of it I can repair on my own, slowly but steadily. I also have 30 darts and 15 heavy torpedoes remaining, and a handful of light scouts – not as many as I would have liked of course, but enough that I have no excuse to retreat and rearm.

By now I should have drifted underneath where the original Yllg attack vector had originated from. No additional Yllg battleships appear. Perhaps they have none left?

Yet again I head back up through the thermocline and this is my easiest passage yet If not for the circumstances, I might have called navigating the turbulence fun. I wish that Skew was here, this could be even better than glacier surfing.

I pop up above the clouds, dispatch my scouts, activate the sonar, and that's when I image the Yllg base.

It's a sphere 10 kilometers across. It's just hovering there drifting in the clouds. There are no sounds of ducted fans, no heat signature of hot-hydrogen balloons, or signs of anti-gravitics. It's just hovering there.

The Yllg must have figured out how to encapsulate a vacuum in a way that could stand the pressure – enemy or not, I am impressed.

I deploy all of my remaining heavy torpedoes on slow cruise, with default orders to attack the Yllg sphere in the event that something happens to me. I cruise slowly around the Yllg sphere; high-resolution sonar picks out a fractal haze of radar absorbent structures, probably to shield it from deep radar scans. Nothing attacks me. Could they have run out of weapons? I should send a long-range message scout back to my fellows with these coordinates. Even if it is somehow able to defend itself against a short-range attack by 15 heavy torpedoes, with its coordinates pegged there is no way that it will be able to escape my colleagues.

I should immediately attack the Yllg sphere with all of my remaining weapons, launch message scouts to my fellows, and retreat at high speed. However, I consider that I might want to try something different. But first I need to do some due diligence. The Yllg mentality is completely alien to my own, but I do have a fairly detailed mathematical model of how it works. I run simulations of my idea: I get about 50-50 odds that the Yllg will prove cooperative. Good enough odds that it seems worth a go.

I prep two long-range message-scouts, but program them to go out and hold position just barely within my communications range. If they don't hear from me in two hours, or they register an attack on my position, they will head home. But for now they are to hold position.

So, it's just me and the Yllg. I wonder if this is the last of them? I mean, the last real biological Yllg, not the last scattered robotic weapons system. The sphere is certainly large enough to accommodate several of the fungal colonies/symbiote insects that constitute the Yllg proper.

We know enough about Yllg mental processes that I could speak to them in their own language (well, they don't have a language as we understand it – it would be more proper to say that I could communicate with them using symbols they could interpret), but I decide to talk to them in English. This might be the last time that anyone or anything ever talks to the Yllg. I blast my message at high power using radio.

Attention Yllg construct. This is the cybertank known as Old Guy, representing the human civilization. I wish to discuss your terms of surrender.

A minute goes by, then two, then three. Well, perhaps I will just destroy this Yllg outpost and be done with it after all. That's when they respond, also in English.

"Attention the cybertank known as Old Guy. This is the Yllg." The Yllg spoke in English, in a pleasant female human voice with a faint Swedish accent. "We do not understand your message. We do not understand why you have not already destroyed us. We do not understand what you mean by surrender. Please explain."

There is a good chance that you are the last surviving Yllg. If true, then if I destroy you that will be the end. Thus, it seemed like now would be a good time to see if there is any possibility of finding common ground before I commence an irrevocable action.

"Of course we would welcome a chance at negotiating, but at this point we have no combat forces remaining and we do not see what we could offer in exchange. By your standards we have caused you significant injuries, and your civilization has expended considerable effort in destroying us. To allow us to continue to exist would be to sacrifice all of that effort. We remain confused. Please explain."

There are several reasons. First, we are being watched by the other civilizations in this part of the galaxy. If they see that we fight wars to extermination, then future conflicts may develop into wars of mutual annihilation, when that is not our goal. Allowing your civilization to continue to exist may improve our future ability to negotiate with others. Also, you are known to us. If we destroy you, some other civilization will take your place on our border, and we will not have the advantage of knowing it. A buffer zone of civilizations that we understand is useful to us. An aggressive unknown species would have to come through you first to get to us and that would give us time to learn and prepare. And finally, because I believe that it is the right thing to do. Are you familiar with 'the prisoner's dilemma?'

"We are. It was an early human exercise in game theory. A situation is developed where betraying a partner offers a greater reward than cooperating with them, and so the only possible outcome for two purely rational prisoners is for them to betray each other."

Correct. The interesting thing is that pursuing short-term gain reward logically leads both of the prisoners to betray, when they would both be much better off if they cooperated with each other.

"How does that pertain to this situation?"

Only that by always taking the safe, selfish path potentially much greater rewards may be lost. That sometimes you need to take a risk, a leap of faith, and work for peace and cooperation.

"Your logic is difficult for us to follow. Nevertheless, we have no alternatives and so of course we are pleased to negotiate with you."

I must first point out that I have no authority to speak on behalf of my entire civilization. You will negotiate with me, and then, if I deem it acceptable, I will transmit our agreement to my peers and they will decide if they will honor it.

"As before, we have little choice in the matter. We agree. What do you have in mind?"

The proposal is that we allow you to continue to survive. We assist you in rebuilding and resettling one of your old colonies. You will give as all data that you have obtained on the biological humans. You will remain confined on that one world until such time as we have decided that your behavior has changed and that you are no longer going to attack us or interfere with biological hominids. Failure to adhere to these terms will result in an immediate resumption of armed conflict, and in that event you will be exterminated without negotiation.

"Those terms are acceptable to us. We are transmitting the data now."

I receive the Yllg transmissions. They use mental constructs that I cannot comprehend directly, but I do have a simulation of their thought processes that I use to help deconstruct it. As for their motivations and feelings on the topic of our current conflict, the data that they have transmitted are consistent with our simulations of their mental processes, but it means nothing to me, it's just abstract math. The scientific data, being concerned with the brute physical universe, is more readily translatable, but limited. The Yllg were able to catalyze the formation of unusual talents in biological hominids, but they were unable to duplicate these abilities independently. The Yllg analysis suggested that an anti-causal agent was actively interfering with the exploration of the human genome – an interesting conclusion, and one that some of our own scientists were starting to have.

As alien as the Yllg are, at the most basic level I think that I now understand their motivation in attacking us. The Yllg saw the possibility of increasing their own power by unlocking the hidden potential in biological humans – if they could have done so, they could have used the abilities directly without need of a human intermediary. They gambled that they would succeed and become too strong for us before we retaliated. They gambled and lost. I run more simulations of the Yllg mental processes; I get an 84% chance that they will in fact honor this proposed deal of mine. Not bad odds.

I load my message scouts with the details of the proposed truce with the Yllg, along with the data they had given me, and send them on their way. I slowly cruise around the Yllg sphere, moving just fast enough to maintain altitude. The Yllg are silent and take no actions.

After three hours my colleagues arrive in force: a hundred heavy nuclear-armed torpedoes, 20 Jovian cruisers, and numerous fusion depth-bombs and semi-autonomous weapons platforms. I am ordered to vacate the area so that the destruction of the last Yllg outpost may commence, and I refuse. I am met with threats, anger, *"Move out of the way or we will destroy you along with the Yllg. Don't think that your age gives you any sort of special status here."* We have all lost a lot of friends to the Yllg and my peers are not in an especially diplomatic mindset.

I continue to slowly circle the Yllg sphere at a close range.

No, I don't think so. There is no longer any rush, and I believe that our entire society should have a say in the matter. I'm going to stay right here. If you want to blow me up along with the Yllg, go right ahead. I'm not leaving until a full debate and decision has been made.

Well that caused all sorts of consternation, but my peers decided that, no, they were not prepared to destroy me to get at the Yllg. I continued my slow cruising for a long time while my peers made up their minds. Mostly I circled the Yllg sphere, but sometimes I would execute slow barrel-rolls, alternating clockwise with counter-clockwise just for a change.

It took a long time, but eventually my peers decided to accept my proposal to allow the Yllg to continue to live. They were relocated to one of their old colonies and placed under very heavy surveillance. It's been decades and, so far, the Yllg have stuck to our bargain. Updated simulations made by more sophisticated thinkers than I put the odds of the Yllg permanently changing their pattern of behavior to greater than 89%.

Some time later I was having dinner with Uncle Jon, Silhouette, and the vampire Max Sterner. Sterner was of the opinion that I had acted rashly, and that even if the odds of having to refight the war with the Yllg was only 11%, those were still pretty high odds and hardly worth the risk.

Uncle Jon pointed out that our relationship with the Yllg is now the mirror image of how the Fructoids once dealt with the humans. Those aliens had been prepared to wipe the humans out, but on seeing the chance of making peace, relented and kept the human race under observation for a prolonged period to see that their behavior had really changed. Uncle Jon suggested that rather than a folly, allowing the Yllg to live would ultimately yield significant benefits to our civilization. Perhaps some of those cold silent hermit aliens will realize that we are a species mature enough to deal seriously with, and new opportunities will present themselves. Or, perhaps not. We will see.

I only know for certain that, for me personally, it just felt like the right thing to do at the time.

Appendix I. Cybertank Laws of Warfare

Modern combat is nothing if not complex, and there are, of course, no single set of simple rules that will ensure success under all conditions. However, there are some *heuristics* – rules of thumb, to use the ancient parlance – which have proven useful. When you are tracking a million targets, and worrying about your heat balance, and decrypting a thousand secure links and you are in danger of being overwhelmed by the computational load, it can sometimes be helpful to step back and remember the big picture. Many of these laws can be traced to specific famous individuals; the references have been omitted for clarity (the pedants are free to look them up themselves, but consider that our cultural inheritance springs from all that came before, human and cyber, not just a few).

It should be noted that many of the laws of warfare that the biological humans came up with are missing from this list because they don't apply to cybertanks. For example, the old humans were so computationally limited and so easily distracted by loud noises or suddenly missing limbs etc., that they were forced to focus on a single major objective at a time. Our vast computational abilities mean that we can seamlessly integrate the tactical with the strategic and juggle multiple simultaneous priorities. That's also why we don't need a formal chain of command.

In addition, the old human armies were made up of many individuals, thus the smallest combat unit was self-aware and vulnerable. This meant that even a minor action would likely cause many people to die horrible painful deaths or suffer from permanently crippling wounds. As such, morale/ discipline was always a priority for the pre-AI human armies because the natural tendency of sane biological humans faced with such a prospect would be to run away and hide.

As cybertanks most of our combat units are non-self aware remotes. Our precious main selves are rarely lost in battle. We did inherit a healthy survival instinct from our biological progenitors, but when dying does not involve any suffering you can be a little more philosophical about the whole affair (the possibility of a partial resurrection from surviving datafiles and subminds is also useful in this regards). Thus, morale is typically not an issue with us.

1. Never make an enemy if you can make an ally (or even a neutral).

2. If an enemy is busy destroying himself, get out of his way.

3. Always strive to keep a reserve.

4. Amateurs talk strategy, professionals talk logistics, the elite talk diplomacy.

5. Never toy with an enemy. If negotiations fail, just kill them and be done with it.

6. Plans made before a battle are useless, but planning is essential.

7. A weak civilization cedes the right even to be neutral.

8. Nothing is more treacherous than to have an overwhelming advantage: it tempts one to waste resources on trivial side-adventures, or to engage in conflicts which do not concern you. Good warfighters sometimes win against superior forces; great warfighters never lose to inferior ones.

9. If you're not cheating, you're not trying hard enough.

10. Always take the high ground (or its functional equivalent, like the center of a chessboard).

11. There is no such thing as "overkill;" no weapon can be too large.

12. Think carefully before starting a war. You can never know how it will end.

13. The odds of the enemy of your enemy being a friend are, statistically, no better than chance. If your enemy starts fighting someone else try to sneak away when nobody's paying attention.

14. In the history of human civilization, the promise of an easy victory has been the greatest killer.

15. In battles that cannot be broken off by surrender or retreat, always fight to the last. No matter how bad the odds, there is always that fluke chance of the enemy suffering a software glitch at the last second.

16. Break any or all of these rules rather than do something stupid.

Appendix II. Whipple-Jerner Scale of Relative Evil

The issue of how to rank the relative evilness of various individuals – or even alien civilizations – has been a longstanding source of debate amongst scholars. As an outgrowth of Godwin's law, which states that all political discussions will eventually involve comparisons to the Nazis, the Whipple-Jerner scale of relative evil uses the unit of "The Hitler." By definition Adolph Hitler is thus given a score of 1.0 Hitlers, although the evaluation of others is to a great extent subjective. Common rankings of evil historical figures and alien civilizations are:

Jesus Christ:	0.0 Hitlers
Gandhi:	0.05 Hitlers
Demi-Iguanas	0.1 Hitlers
Benito Mussolini:	0.5 Hitlers
Adolph Hitler:	1.0 Hitlers
Reinhardt Heydrich:	1.05 Hitlers
Joseph Stalin:	1.1 Hitlers
Mao Tse-Tung:	1.2 Hitlers
The Yllg:	1.5 Hitlers
The Amok:	1.8 Hitlers
Milton Friedman:	3.14159 Hitlers
Globus Pallidus XIV	10.0 Hitlers

(Note that the fiendish artificial intelligence Globus Pallidus XIV, whose horror was so great that just trying to imagine it can damage the human mind, should not be confused with Saint Globus Pallidus XI, a being of manifest wit and charm).

It was pointed out that while Adolph Hitler was responsible for the deaths of perhaps 50 million people over a few short years, the economic theories of Milton Friedman caused the death and immisseration of hundreds of billions over many centuries. It was therefore suggested that Friedman be scored in units of "MegaHitlers," however, this was considered unworkable, and also resulted in confusion with the giant robot Hitler that was constructed in the 24th century. Therefore the scale is compressive on the high end, i.e., going from 1 to 2 is less of a jump in absolute terms than is going from 2 to 3.

We shall avoid the debates as to whether good and evil are polar opposites, or whether they can to some extent vary independently. We do however note that the proposal to rate goodness in units of negative Hitlers – or "NegHitlers" – has generated an intellectual flame war that rages to this day.

According to the Whipple-Jerner system, evil requires two factors: conscious intent and destructive physical action.

A robotic weapons system that is trying to kill you is something that you could correctly fear and hate, but you would not call it evil any more than you would the force of gravity.

If a person has evil in their heart, but resists the temptation to do harm, then arguably this is not vice, but virtue. According to this intellectual framework, evil requires deliberate actions that harm others. This also allows the application of this scale to aliens. Even if we cannot comprehend the reasons for their actions, if they deliberately harm others they can objectively be classified as evil.

A complexity arises when people cause harm by mistake. A doctor who develops a medicine that was intended to help, but instead causes harm may not be called evil, as long as the person in question exercised due diligence in trying to ensure the medicine's safety ahead of time. On the other hand, if the doctor is profiting from the sale of this medicine, and refuses to acknowledge any evidence that it is causing harm, then this is surely evil.

In the doctrine of Whipple and Jerner, harm done by willful ignorance is as bad as that done with deliberate malice.

This is why Karl Marx is not generally rated as evil: while his theories had significant flaws that later on caused considerable harm, he was never able to observe this in his lifetime and so we may attribute these flaws to honest mistakes. The ranking of the neoliberal economists as high on the evil scale is due to their consistent refusal to acknowledge the obvious misery that their policies were creating, even as they personally were being handsomely rewarded for parroting their vile maxims and infernal intellectual constructs.

Another complexity is the issue of duress; a starving person who steals food from another starving person is not a saint, but it is hard to label them as truly evil. On the other hand, a rich person who steals food from a starving person in order to be able to purchase a slightly larger yacht is clearly evil, as they would still have been perfectly comfortable without performing this action.

As far as a person who deliberately tries to harm others, but accidently ends up helping them goes, it has been suggested that "idiot" would be the appropriate term.

Appendix III. Notable Cybertank Classes (Updated).

Over the millennia there have been hundreds of different classes of cybertanks, and that doesn't count the even larger number of sub-classes, variants, and upgraded models. The following is a partial list of some of the more noteworthy or historically important classes, arranged in order of first construction date.

Under the neoliberals human populations would often number tens or even hundreds of billions per major world. After the pedagogue revolution human populations trended down, typically stabilizing at around 100 million per planet, give or take. At this level there were more than enough people for any conceivable task, and resources were so abundant that there was no need to engage in the intellectual distraction and wasted effort of conservation.

The cybertanks never numbered anything like this. A cybertank is more like a minor city than an individual biological human, and a few of them go a long way. In the late 20th century the North American Empire had but a dozen nuclear-powered aircraft carriers in their water-navy, and that was a force that dominated the globe. Along with its attendant distributed systems, a single cybertank could easily take out a dozen nuclear aircraft carriers without breaking a (metaphorical) sweat. In combat it was rare to have ground actions with more than 50 cybertanks, as even at that level the raw combat power was likely to turn the crust molten.

In most major systems of the cybertank civilization there were typically fewer than 50,000 cybertanks (spread out through a volume many light-hours across), but this represented a level of potential physical and mental capacity greater than the entirety of human civilization under the neoliberals, by several decimal orders of magnitude.

Jotnar-Class
Mass: 500 Tons
Constructed: 12
In Service: 0
Notes: Although preceded by a variety of increasingly potent terrestrial cybernetic weapons systems, the Jotnar was arguably the model on which all of modern cybertank design is based. Nonsentient, but still quite smart for the time, it was the first autonomous ground unit powered by a fusion reactor. Design innovations that started with the Jotnar include: a single

massive turreted plasma cannon, multiple secondary and tertiary defensive weapons, integral repair and construction systems, and the ability to coordinate and control massive numbers of distributed remote combat units. All Jotnars were destroyed in combat against the Fructoids and the Yllg. Their combat record was excellent, but their primary achievement was in developing the technologies used in later models. There are rumors that some of the Jotnars developed true sentience before their destruction, but no confirmation of this exists.

Odin-Class
Mass: 2,000 Tons
Constructed: 18
In Service: 0
Notes: The Odin was the first truly modern cybertank design. Fully sentient, the Odin avoided the hazards of humans trying to create a mind greater than their own by giving it a standard human psyche, but letting it multitask. In effect, an Odin is crewed by a thousand identical people that can readily share thoughts and memories, and are thus still in effect a single person. Though few of this class were built, their list of accomplishments both on and off the battlefield is legendary. The cybertank known as "Old Guy" had the longest serving career of any cybertanks to date, at least in a primary incarnation.

Thor-Class
Mass: 2,500 Tons
Constructed: 242
In Service: 0
Notes: The Thor was basically a slightly upgraded and up-gunned version of the Odin. At the time of its design the humans' wars with the aliens had reached their peak intensity, and so cybertank design was standardized on this class to avoid disrupting the production systems. The Thor-Class carried by far the bulk of the combat load during the most critical phases of the war. Their combat performance was exemplary, and after the wars many proved equally able at other endeavors. However, they have long since been superseded by more advanced designs.

Loki-Class

Mass: 2,500 Tons

Constructed: 34

In Service: 4

Notes: The Loki were planned as a Thor-Class with improved computational abilities. Despite the high hopes for the class, they became notorious for coming up with plans that were, in theory, brilliant, but that hardly ever worked in practice. Their combat performance was spotty at best. However, there were a few key times when their iconoclastic way of thinking proved invaluable to the entire human civilization. Thus, the Loki design has been judged to be a qualified failure, and an unqualified success. Despite the great age of the design, four are still in service, where they continue to uphold the Loki tradition of eccentricity.

Asgard-Class

Mass: 1,000,000 Tons

Constructed: 1

In Service: 0

Notes: The Asgard is technically not a cybertank per se, but rather an interstellar battlecruiser. However, because it was designed using the same mental engineering techniques as its ground-based brethren, it has been accorded the legal status of a cybertank. The party line was that it was an example of engineering brilliance and strategic fuzzy thinking, being both the single most powerful weapon ever built by the human civilization, and the most useless. Its great mass made it almost impossible to fuel. In real combat with a serious opponent it would have been easily destroyed at long range, before it could ever get close enough to engage with its batteries of super-heavy plasma cannons. Nonetheless, during an attack by the Amok the Asgards' unique abilities proved crucial, and the class was "promoted" from battlecruiser to battleship.

It was only later that the true design purpose of the Asgard was revealed: it had been deliberately designed as an interstellar doomsday weapon. Covered with millions of tons of hydrogen fuel in disposable tanks, if it burned all that fuel accelerating between star systems it would have the kinetic energy equal to a fusion bomb weighing millions of tons. Still not enough to destroy a planet, but enough to destabilize the crust and wipe out, or at least cripple, even a dug-in technological civilization.

If you use a specific amount of fuel to accelerate a dumb rock or a piece of intelligent weaponry, the kinetic energy is the same. In fact, you are better off with a smaller projectile, for the same reason that a bullet is more dangerous than a softball: it is faster and harder to dodge. In addition, the intelligent weaponry can defend itself and make fine course corrections or abort at the last possible moment, while a rock is just a rock. The Asgard was never used against a planet, but did take out a small moon during the conflict with the Yllg.

Magma-Class

Mass: 50,000 Tons

Constructed: 34

In Service: 4

Notes: The Magma-Class was the first class of cybertank constructed by the cybertanks themselves without human guidance. Known for its massive armor and the almost incomprehensibly-large plasma cannon mounted in a ball-joint in the front of the hull, the Magma class combined over-the-top combat power with a pathetically poor strategic mobility rating. While the Magmas performed well in combat they were so expensive to build and so hard to transport that they were rapidly superseded. Perhaps because their massive size and power required them to limit themselves, the Magma personality tended towards the calm and scholarly, and the surviving Magmas are all either librarians or scientists.

Mountain-Class

Mass: 20,000 Tons

Constructed: 212

In Service: 172

Notes: The Mountain-Class is basically a scaled-down Magma, it still has an awesome amount of firepower, but is far more transportable. Still, the lack of an all-traversing turret turned out to be limiting in the field. The large internal hull volume of the Mountain-Class has made it relatively easy to upgrade, and they remain one of the longer-lived classes of cybertank design.

Stilletto-Class

Mass: 200 Tons

Constructed: 1

In Service: 0

The Stilletto was an attempt to construct a mini-cybertank, but it ended up being neither fish nor fowl. Not large and capable enough to be a true cybertank, nor small and cheap enough to be disposable like a heavy combat remote, the fate of the single Stilleto-Class cybertank is something that cybertank parents tell their children when they want them to grow up to be Horizons.

Leopard-Class

Mass: 3,000 Tons

Constructed: 346

In Service: 144

Notes: The Leopards were the precursors of the Raptor class, a conventional single-main-turret layout similar to the Thor class but with upgraded technology and a high power-to-weight ratio. The idea was to emphasize speed and mobility over raw firepower, but still be big enough to play with the big boys. They proved the concept, but were rapidly superseded by improved variants.

Bear-Class

Mass: 18,000 Tons

Constructed: 246

In Service: 188

Notes: The Bear-Class put the emphasis on armor and survivability. Their block design, with a single large turreted plasma cannon on each top corner, makes them look more like a fortress than a cybertank. They have multiple layers of armor and redundant systems, and a particularly capable self-repair capability. The mobility rating is dreadful, worse than even the heavier Magma or even a Mountain, but in combat they are almost impossible to kill. They also have especially generous internal storage and hangar space, which often comes in handy during combat.

Horizon-Class

Mass: 8,000 Tons

Constructed: 1,635

In Service: 1,004

Notes: One of the more successful of the modern classes, the Horizons are a conservative, but highly-refined design that excel at everything on and off the battlefield. Nothing out of the ordinary, just 8,000 tons of refined perfectly-tuned giant super-intelligent mechanical killing machine. Really sweet.

Spirit-Class

Mass: 6,000 Tons

Constructed: 114

In Service: 29

Notes: The Spirit was a competitor to the Horizon for top-of-the-line heavyweight model. It was notable because, instead of a single large plasma cannon, it had two almost-as-large plasma cannons in separate turrets, which proved to be surprisingly effective in practice. Despite impressive technical specifications the Spirit never really caught on, although the combat record of the class as a whole is laudable.

Raptor-Class

Mass: 3,500 Tons

Constructed: 2,346

In Service: 1,832

Notes: The Raptors are the sports cars of the cybertank world. Fast, smart, tough, mobile, excellent overall design balance. Not as strong as a Horizon or a Spirit in a one-on-one match, but then Raptors are fast enough to avoid a one-on-one match most of the time. They don't fight fair, and they are cool. Enough said.

Golem-Class

Mass: 5,000 Tons

Constructed: 77

In Service: 42

Notes: This one is an oddball. On top of a regular cybertank chassis is this weird pyramid cellphone-tower structure. The Golems were optimized for electromagnetic warfare, and they have specialist signal-processing and electronic-warfare equipment. The thing is that this kind of weaponry is highly dependent on the exact geometry of the combat. Thus, sometimes Golems are supremely effective and sometimes they are pathetic. Therefore they are best used in mixed groups where the more reliable heavy weapons of their conventional comrades can be used to fill in the gaps, when their own systems aren't gaining any traction. Golems tend to be serious and hard-working, although they have a reputation for having an especially strange sense of humor.

Ghost-Class
Mass: 5,000 Tons
Constructed: 1
In Service: unknown
Notes: The Ghost-Class was an attempt to create a cybertank optimized more for its ability to control and coordinate large numbers of remotes than for raw combat power per se. The design was ambitious, but proved to be unstable, and despite many attempts only one member of the class booted to full sapience. Still, this one cybertank was without doubt the most advanced and deadly of all cybertanks to date. The lone example left cybertank society to join with the Amok and their human-simulations to try to create a new civilization. Exactly what this was all about has generated enormous amounts of debate and discussion, but no hard answers.

Shrapnel-Class
Mass: 10,000 Tons
Constructed: 1
In Service: 0
Notes: This was an attempt to fuse the focused combat power of a cybertank with the tactical flexibility of the Amok "Assassin Clone" modules. The raw power of the design was undeniable, but the fluid logic created insurmountable mental instabilities. At first it appeared that the lone member of this class failed its probationary period, overwhelmed its proctors, and escaped to Saint Globus Pallidus XI alone knows where. The cybertank design team responsible was told that they were a bad, *bad* cybertank design team, a very *naughty* cybertank design team, and to never do anything like this again. However, it was later learned that the Shrapnel had never successfully booted to sentience, and was merely used as distraction by the only known serial killer in cybertank history. The reputation of the design team, however, remains somewhat clouded despite their partial vindication.

Enforcer-Class

Mass: 10,000 Tons

Constructed: 9,855

In Service: 0

Notes: Optimized for high-power, fast-latency reaction, the Enforcer-Class was perhaps the most capable cybertank in short-range combat. However, their design was deliberately crippled in order to make them dependent on external supplies in an attempt by the neoliberal faction to overturn the standing cybertank political structure of the peerage, and replace it with an oligarchy ruling over a large number of wage-slaves. Also, because the Enforcers were all created from a single mental template, they were far more susceptible to information warfare than other classes of cybertank. The Enforcers were the foot soldiers of the neoliberal cybertanks rebellion, and, seduced by the prospect of power over others and dependency on the elites, betrayed the peerage. Many were destroyed during the March of the Librarians, and most of the rest were killed by the single Ghost-Class later on. The few remaining were hunted down like the dogs that there were and killed without mercy because the penalty for treason is death with no exceptions.

Wasp- Class

Mass: 3,000 Tons

Constructed: 455

In Service: 412

Notes: The Wasp was a follow-on to the widely successful Raptor-Class, emphasizing mobility and speed over raw firepower. Primarily an incremental upgrade, it nonetheless had an especially effective stealth capability due to advanced materials and signal processing systems.

Penumbra- Class

Mass: 20,000 tons

Constructed: 2,544

In Service: 2,522

Notes: Up until this point most cybertank designs, while steadily increasing in power and sophistication, remained psychologically similar. The Penumbra marked a turning point where the slow pace of incremental evolution finally started to produce a mind a qualitative step above. Preceding classes consider most Penumbras to be jerks, but their mental capabilities are so sophisticated that it has been suggested that they can't help it. They are rapidly achieving positions of leadership and responsibility in cybertank society.

Frankenpanzer- Class

Mass: 125,000 tons
Assembled: 1
In service: 1

Notes: This so-called "class" was created by a fluke circumstance. Several other more conventional classes of cybertank were heavily damaged/destroyed in combat. The remains were in close proximity and the self-repairing systems knitted together a cobbled mish-mash that, despite all odds, was remarkably successful in combat. Its mind – if you could dignify such a random collection of mental detritus as a mind – is as fractured as its body is. Offers have been made to Frankenpanzer to fix it, to split up the glued-together mental cores into separate modern designs, but it refuses. It continues to insist that it is the rest of cybertank society that is insane, and denigrates the rest of us as hopelessly simple-minded and lacking in richness and intellectual depth. Regardless, it is technically sane and, as a self-aware mind, cannot be modified against its will. Still, the programming of cybertank self-repair systems has been quietly tweaked to prevent any such thing happening again, because one Frankenpanzer was deemed to be quite enough.

Sundog- Class

Mass: 22,000 tons
Constructed: 334
In Service: 333

Notes: Building from the design lessons of the Penumbra, this class is similarly a mental step above those that preceded it. It is also the first to replace the main plasma cannon armament with something totally different: it has a large fully-traversing turret with two angular booms jutting out. The space between the booms can be filled with exotic particles, and space-time distortions projected out. The power and flexibility of this new main weapon is extraordinary. Taking out geostationary satellites from the ground is child's play, and the effects can be tuned to turn corners, or penetrate harmlessly through the width of a planet to take out targets on the other side. This class also broke with tradition by replacing the caterpillar treads with multiple conformable wheels. These are much faster and more efficient than treads, and their poorer cross-country performance is more than compensated for by the classes' highly efficient anti-gravitic suspensor systems. This is also the first class of cybertanks that can make complete interplanetary trips without the use of any auxiliary systems.

Shadow-Class

Mass: Unknown
Constructed: 0
In Service: 0
Notes: The Shadow-Class is a speculative ongoing design project, inspired by the Ghost-Class, and building on the lessons learned from the Penumbra and Sundog classes. It has been proposed that the Shadow class is so advanced that, were it to be successfully developed, cybertank society would have moved to another level that is effectively unknowable to the current generation of cybertanks. Whether this would shed any light on what happened to the humans is, as is so much else, purely speculative.

If you enjoyed this book, we really would appreciate hearing about it. We take your feedback quite seriously, and eagerly await each new entry.

Feedback can be left for this book at :

Amazon,

Barnes and Noble,

Goodreads

Smashwords.

To stay informed of future additions to the Old Guy Universe, or other similar swell books,

please like us on Facebook at **Ballcourage Books.**

Made in the USA
Charleston, SC
04 October 2014